FUCK NESS

ANDERSEN PRUNTY

ATLATL

DAYTON, OHIO

Fuckness

Also by Andersen Prunty

The Driver's Guide to Hitting Pedestrians
Hi I'm a Social Disease: Horror Stories
The Sorrow King
Slag Attack
My Fake War
Morning is Dead
The Beard
Jack and Mr. Grin
Zerostrata
The Overwhelming Urge

Introduction:
Fuckness and The Bad Time

My name is Wallace Black. Before I tell you anything about myself I should tell you about the Bad Time. And before I tell you about the Bad Time, I should tell you about my philosophy. Everyone, whether he knows it or not, lives his life by some type of philosophy. I'm not talking about the type of philosophy found in books, the shit nobody really understands. I'm talking about some innate code individuals are born with. The type of philosophy usually not thought about too much and often summed up in a few words. The kind of shit people wear on t-shirts and stick to their bumpers. And we see the proclamation of that philosophy on their t-shirt or bumper sticker and it, in turn, defines them.

There was this woman who lived down the street. She had a bumper sticker that read, "Life's a Bitch." I knew very little about this woman, but whenever I saw her emerge from her car—her dumpy frame crammed into a pair of stonewashed jeans, a pile of hair virtually scraping the sky—I knew that woman had it rough. Her life was, indeed, a bitch. As I watched her walk in that slouchingly comic way, knees seemingly before body, dragging heavy-assed into her house, I wondered how she could drive or walk at all. Life had undoubtedly beaten her down so much these tasks were something accomplished only through some masochistic necessity. And where did she drive, anyway? To a place filled with lots of other miserable people living out their grim, brief philosophies, too?

I called my philosophy the philosophy of fuckness. I first developed this philosophy when I realized I was the type of person who would go to just about any lengths necessary in order to avoid trouble and misery. That is, I just wanted to live life the way I wanted to live it without any interruptions or having to answer to anyone.

I quickly realized this was impossible.

No matter how actively I avoided just about every situation, trouble seemed to find me. This trouble is what I called fuckness.

All the world's absurdity quickly fell under the definition of fuckness. Loosely, the dictionary defines "absurd" as something so clearly untrue or unreasonable as to be laughable or ridiculous. When I was about twelve, when I first started thinking about this philosophy of fuckness, everything seemed ridiculous to me, only I wasn't laughing.

And I didn't even know the Bad Time was coming.

A man puts on a shirt and tie five or more mornings out of the week and no one finds this absurd. It is not the man putting on the shirt and tie I would define as fuckness, it is the fact no one else finds it ridiculous. And this man goes to work where he labors for someone else forty hours or more and at the end of the week he is given a paycheck. Does this man realize he is a rat? Does this man realize everything about him is ridiculous? If he realizes this then the situation surrounding him is not fuckness. "Carry on," I would tell him. However, if he is unaware of the heightened sense of absurdity surrounding him and the majority of his life, he is enveloped by fuckness. His whole situation reeks of fuckness. He might not have seen the Bad Time, but he's got plenty of fuckness.

There are, of course, various degrees of fuckness.

My troubles, my heavy fuckness, the Bad Time, happened about ten years back when I was sixteen and in my third year of eighth grade. That's when I really started thinking about divine punishment, redemption, my place in the world, and all that other coming of age bullshit.

I guess what it came down to was that I simply didn't fit in.

For starters, I was incredibly stupid. I mean, I didn't really consider *myself* stupid or anything. Actually, it was quite the opposite. I considered myself a genius. I considered myself to be one of the only alive and aware human beings on the planet, but I still knew I was somehow *less* than everybody else. It was seeing all those blobs so unaware their lives were nothing but big jokes that really bothered me. That they were so oblivious to the giant clouds of fuckness gathered around all their blobby heads and threatening to piss down some acidic rain that could tear away the fabric of their realities at any moment.

I figured it was all a game when you got right down to it. The blobs picked their games and played them, depending on which games were the easiest.

Everybody else seemed to know how to play this game. It was like they had their games all chosen for them. Those fucks seemed to have some cheat sheet built right into their brains that had all the rules and tips and clues to these games spelled out on them. They had control of the game. Maybe *that* was where my philosophy of fuckness came from. Maybe I never had control of the game. Like maybe I just wasn't made for it. If that was the case, if I were somehow chosen to do something other than play their ridiculous game, then their control of the game must have blossomed from their complete ignorance of it. Like they didn't even know somebody somewhere was laughing at them.

Regardless, whether I was born to play the game or not, I refused.

I knew I didn't have those rules built in. I didn't have any fucking cheat sheets and I figured, if I played one of their stupid little games, I'd be the one to end up dead last. There was one thing I was almost sure of—if I were meant to go out there in the world of fuckness, I would have had so much of it on me so quickly I would have crumbled under the pressure before I could wipe the mother's placenta from my eyes.

The only way to even half-cope with all the fuckness of the world was to say, "Fuck it." If I had to sum up my philosophy of fuckness in a few words so I could cram it on a bumper sticker or t-shirt, those were the words I would have chosen: "Fuck it." So, for brevity's sake, *that* was pretty much my philosophy at the time. And it was a real beautiful philosophy, too. I liked that philosophy so much because it could have a couple of meanings. One, of course, was kind of sexual. But it was sort of a mean kind of sexual. Kind of like rape. This sexual meaning implied some kind of force. "Fuck it"—like I was forcefully attacking the world, raping the hell out of it, actively eliminating the fuckness that filled it.

There was also something kind of pacifist about "Fuck it." Like just trying to avoid the fuckness altogether. Like not even taking part in the world, just sitting back and letting it all flame by, watching all the blobs trying to win the game and knowing there weren't any winners.

"Fuck it." Beautiful.

Of course, the fuckness always had a way of finding me. The harder I tried to avoid it, the harder it hit me.

Maybe from hearing that, you'll already understand I wasn't as bright as your average individual. I mean, most people wanted to say "fuck it," but they rarely did. Most people never truly fucked anything.

Most people had something to lose.

So maybe I wasn't a genius. But at least I was aware of the game and it bothered the hell out of me. Anybody who knew how to play the game without letting it bother them was a blob. A stinking, quivering blob.

So this isn't the story of a genius. It isn't even the story of a particularly intelligent person. But it is my story. My story of fuckness. Of how I let the fuckness bother me and how it found me, again and again.

Oh, and it's about the Bad Time. A swollen red image I'm trying to exorcise. Something I'll never forget because it sits on my bed when I go to sleep at night and sometimes I wake up with it sitting on my chest, breathing its hot stink in my face.

Maybe I could get rid of the fuckness, but I will never get rid of the Bad Time.

Chapter One
The Cloud Factory

Anyway, I was real dumb back then. Back then it felt like hate marrowed all my bones and the people around me were colorless, quivering masses, their shapeless mouths opening to coax my soul from my body. But I want you to know that I *knew* I was dumb. Or at least that I appeared dumb to most people. I wasn't so much head dumb as body dumb. I just wanted to be alone to twitch and wiggle and hum, the few things that made me happy, and it felt like everyone else wanted to stop me from doing those things. Like those things had any impact on how they lived their lives. The only thing I could figure was most people were so fucking self-righteous they liked to destroy others' wills so they felt like their own petty lives had some sense of purpose.

So the Bad Time began on the playground of Milltown Middle School.

No, that's not really true. All of the troubles I'd *been having* coalesced there on the playground. That playground was where I would eventually set myself free. Not an external, everlasting kind of freedom, but a freedom of the mind—a discovery of how it would feel to be free. I had a number of troubles at Milltown Middle School, most on account of my being sixteen and in the eighth grade, but this fuckness I'm getting ready to tell you about was what lead to my quest—except I think of it more as a stumbling than a quest. Milltown was like a fulcrum, there in the middle of a whole series of events that happened before and would happen after the Bad Time, an intricate web of fuckness that felt like it was intended to wipe me out completely. It probably had something to do with body chemicals.

Some people just seemed born to fail.

But, right now, I'll stick to telling you my story about Bucky Swarth and his gang. I'm still kind of dumb, my mind wanders.

Milltown Middle School was where the poor kids in Milltown went to school. Milltown was a large, industrialized city in south-western Ohio, somewhere between Dayton and Cincinnati, that had several elementary and middle schools. It was one of the larger towns in the area with some 40,000 residents. Because all these schools were located in neighborhoods and the kids living in those neighborhoods went to the closest schools, they were more or less divided by financial status. A lot of the poor parents complained because they had real smart kids but, because the rest of the poor parents couldn't afford Ritalin, they thought their children weren't getting as good of an education as the rich, heavily medicated kids.

The kids knew this wasn't true. Most of the rich little shits just took their Ritalin down to the park by Milltown Middle and sold it anyway. No, it was just part of the game. The poor were supposed to be stupid. The rich smart. But I didn't really care about any of that fuckness. I was dumb, poor, and completely unmedicated.

By the time these kids made it to high school, they were either all thrown together in Milltown High, which was in a little nicer, newer section of town, or they went to the Catholic high school, Saint Agnes. A lot of kids ended up going to St. Ag even if they weren't actually Catholic because it was in the absolute *nicest* section of town and was mostly white and more ordered and that kind of fuckall. Apparently the parents thought being lorded over by stiff-lipped sadistic nuns and boyflesh hungry priests would really do their kids some good. When the richer kids got to that high school, the public high school, was when *their* parents started griping. They said they were afraid that their weak- chinned little fucks were going to get hurt in that school because it was so *combined.* "The *guns!* What about the *guns!*" they'd whine in the papers. Did anyone ever tell them they were the reason their kids took guns to school in the first place? *Combined?* What the hell did that mean, anyway? I always took it to mean they didn't want their kids to go to school with the blacks and the poor kids.

Sometimes, if the parent of a poor kid could afford to send their child to St. Ag, they did. I guess they thought that once their kid was actually in that school, all decked out in that uniform, no one could actually tell how poor they were. Those poor kids' parents must have been really deluded blobs, thinking their kids weren't still going to smell poor and talk poor. You can never really hide poor. Like blood, it courses through the veins.

Anyway, like I was saying, Milltown Middle School was in a poor section of town. The only reason it had the honor of bearing Milltown's name, if that was in fact an honor, was because it was the first middle school built. It was back there with all the factories and fuckness. The factories were where all the poor people worked, if they actually had jobs. Apparently if the workers could keep their minds and bodies intact long enough, there was a good pension involved. After so many years and enough overtime, there was even the hope they could ingrain themselves firmly into the middle class.

Milltown Middle was small and dark and in a horrible state of disrepair. The outside of the school used to be red brick but had turned a dark brown from all the pollution. The playground was very small and dark, also. It was maybe about the size of one of the richer people's back yard. The school was up near the sidewalk, just off the road. There was a three-story parking garage to the right of the school, on the north side. The Korl Brothers factory butted up against the fence of the playground and sort of wrapped around the south side. It was a steel mill, so not only was there the distraction of those tweedling half-wits coming and going to work, there was also the clanging and clunking of giant sheets of metal being hurled around by even noisier machines. The main building of the factory had once been sort of a greenish-gray corrugated aluminum structure, the pride of Milltown's economy, but was all soot-covered and rusted when I went to Milltown. All those structures smothered the playground, burying it, looming ominously over top of it. On that day, the day I'm trying to tell you about, huge smoke-stacks rose into the cold gray March sky, pumping out their smoke and fire.

When I was a real young kid and a lot dumber than I am now, dumber even than when I went to Milltown, I used to think that factory was where clouds were made. Whenever the parents would drive me by Korl or one of Milltown's numerous other factories, I'd say, "Look at the pretty clouds!"

I thought the black smoke and flashing orange-white fire brought the thunderstorms and the white steam made the cottage cheese-looking clouds you see on somewhat pleasant days. My father, Racecar, would snarl, "Those ain't clouds, ass, that's a Death Factory."

Him saying that changed my whole cloud perspective and I began to think the smoke was caused by burning bodies, which was closer to the truth, I guess. The father blamed the Korl Brothers for taking his legs and making him an angry gimp. A hunk of compressed metal had fallen off a forklift and crushed the father's legs so badly they had to be removed. The factory paid for the operation but avoided a settlement for years, saying it was the father's fault. I guess they just figured Racecar was in the wrong place at the wrong time. When they finally decided to pay him it amounted to about what he would have made for working two years, which was inconsequential, considering he'd never be able to work again.

There really wasn't anything to play on in the playground at Milltown Middle. There was an old rusted swing set we were forbidden to play on and an extremely dangerous-looking contraption called the witch's hat that hardly anyone would *dare* to even go around, ever since Lenny Lester got gored a few years back. Still, if someone dared, like some new kid who hadn't heard about the goring, it was forbidden. Those objects sat there, temptation for the bored, a punishment waiting to happen. If the teachers didn't get you, the contraption would, sooner or later.

The majority of the children were left to run around somewhat aimlessly on the playground unless they wanted to engage in games like Tag or Ring-Around-the-Rosy or another game called Red

Fuckness

Rover. Red Rover involved two teams and each team was to send one of its members "over" to the other team when that member was called. All the kids had to know everybody else's name to play this because you had to say, "Red Rover, Red Rover, send *blah* over," or some fuckness. This game, on occasion, would turn violent and have to be stopped. The kids at Milltown managed to make just about everything violent. Even Tag usually ended in bruises and tears as though a more apt title would have been "Beat" or "Strike" or "Punish." It was rare for these games to actually be stopped, however. There usually weren't any teachers around to stop anything and if they were actually outside on the playground they had a convenient habit of looking away at the slightest hint of a disturbance.

Also, the grass in the playground was always covered in this soot so when the kids went in from recess their hands and clothes were always black and grimy. They wore that soot like a coat of poverty. If they rubbed their faces with their hands, they would leave giant smudge marks that looked like some form of tribal marking.

Anyway, what I'm trying to say is that there wasn't a whole helluva lot to do out there on the Milltown Middle School playground and that's maybe sort of the reason why Bucky Swarth was exactly the way he was, which was real violent-like. There seemed to be a lot of that type at Milltown. They either all banded together to form a massive, brow-ridged juggernaut, or they separated into various camps, destined to do battle for the rest of the school year.

Even though I was sixteen and most of the other kids were twelve or thirteen, I almost fit in; physically, anyway. That is, I think my proportions were about right. Even then, I was a little over six feet tall, but I'd been that tall since *I* was in the eighth grade for the first time. I was also rail thin and completely hairless, freckles all over my face.

If my proportions were about right for the eighth grade then my overall appearance wasn't right for any age. If I was going to be tall for my age and stick out like a sore thumb anyway, then the least I could have been blessed with was decent if not just plain looks. But this was not the case… I was ugly, almost freakishly so. An ugly person, a regular ugly person who isn't cursed with being terribly ugly, can go through life with virtually no problems at all. They may have issues with their self-esteem and all that fuckness, but there is absolutely no attention paid them and they're able to just muck around and pretty much do whatever the hell they want. The extremely good-looking can get through life fairly easily, but that's just because people will agree with what they say so they can fuck them or sometimes just be seen with them. And they're almost always attracting some sort of attention, but it's usually positive. The exceptionally ugly, like me, weren't going to be given any breaks in life. More than likely, we were the subjects of intense ridicule. Maybe some pity. What's worse is that I also, through the sheer uniqueness of my appearance, always had attention hoisted upon me. The attention was always negative, of course.

Because I'd grown so fast, I no longer had the ability to walk with a normal gait, so I lasciviously scuffled along, my feet rarely leaving the ground. It seemed like my eyeballs were made too big for their actual eyelids, creating the impression that my eyes were never fully opened but simply slits, like some big doped up snake. My mouth suffered some of the same circumstances. It was too small, the teeth shoved in there with demented abstract abandon— what the mother called a "crowded mouth." My canines hung down way past all the other teeth and if I tried to actually shut my mouth to where my lips met I looked like someone trying to form a horribly pompous face. Nevertheless, I kept my mouth fully closed most of the time and this may have generated more hostility toward me. My ears were like giant masts. If I slithered fast enough I could actually hear them slicing the wind.

Both years since I started failing, I had to go through a readjustment period and try not to let anyone in my class figure out that I was two or three years older than they were. It was hard enough to remain anonymous, being a hideous beast. And it never lasted very long. Inevitably, some other failure would point me out. "Well, *that* kid, he's failed *twice*."

After that happened, the stares and whispers would noticeably increase. I figured some of the parents told the kids to stay away from me. I guess they were afraid my ample helping of stupid would rub off on their children.

I always hated recess because I've never really liked having what the other kids considered fun. Playing stupid games and running around aimlessly and that kind of fuckall. So mostly I just wandered around the big rusty fence separating the playground from the factory and thought my own thoughts, which mostly involved ways of getting out of Milltown without much of an education and by doing as little work as possible. Recess was always a bad time anyway because it was one of the only times when being completely alone seemed abnormal. When it finally got out that I was Wallace Black, the dumb boy who couldn't pass the eighth grade, recess was when the bullies started laying into me.

That year, the Year of Bucky Swarth's Reign, I'd been pretty okay. That is, I'd avoided being beaten severely by him. I'd never been the subject of more than a few names, threats, or pushes. I think, initially, even though I wasn't particularly hard to notice, they were kind of intimidated by my age and I had to do something to really piss them off before they decided to let me have it. But on that chilly spring day, he finally came around and, looking back on it, it was probably my own damn stupid fault.

It was a Thursday morning, the year more than half gone, when he finally laid into me.

Chapter Two
Drifter Ken
and
The Sucker of Doom

That morning, on my walk to school, Drifter Ken had given me a big green sucker. Drifter Ken was this magnificent old guy who hung around the park between my house and the school. He was real suspicious but nobody ever caught him doing anything so they couldn't do much about it, like having him locked up or some fuckness like that. Besides, he never panhandled and he was never in the park at night. I just thought Drifter Ken liked kids or that being nice to the kids that came through the park gave him something to do with his day. The mother always said to stay away from Drifter Ken because he *really* liked kids, but she wore a wig and I found her hard to trust.

If I ever got home late from school, she would accuse me of hanging out with that "trashy, *trashy* man," her stroke-induced mumbling giving the words a lusty cant. The way she strumbled on about Drifter Ken made it sound like he was the type of man she'd like to bring home.

"You like what he does to you?" she asked me one time.

I had a pretty good idea of what she was talking about and knew

Fuckness

Drifter Ken sure didn't do that. I mean, it wouldn't really surprise me if he had managed to nail a couple of the high school girls but it wasn't abnormal to see the high schoolers dating 35 to 40-year- old men. So what if Drifter Ken was closer to 60? In a town like Mill-town, the general philosophy seemed to be that you had to snag them young, before pregnancy, drugs, alcoholism, and bad fashion used them up.

"You *like* the way that trashy, *trashy* man touches you?" It disgusted me, the throatiness of her voice.

"He's not like that."

"Not yet."

At that point, I grabbed a heavy glass and threw it across the room. The motion was strained and dramatic but I had trouble expressing myself vocally, so I had a tendency to throw and break things. Then I stormed into my room. It was pointless to argue with the mother.

It was the father's theory that Drifter Ken sold crack to the kids but, as I've already mentioned, the father was crippled and also untrustworthy. I'm guessing the father thought an adult would *have* to be high to get along with children.

Anyway, that morning I walked through the park as I always did. Some mornings Drifter Ken wasn't there. On the mornings he was in the park we always exchanged a few words, even if it was to just say "Hi." It was like we both understood each other. You can make contact with people all day but it only seems fulfilling when it's with someone you truly enjoy.

Drifter Ken was of near giant proportions. I was a little over six feet tall and had to look way up at Drifter Ken. His thick hands were the size of baseball mitts. He had flashy hair, all stiff and gray and piled up on top of his head in wild curls. That made him seem even taller. I thought about Racecar, pathetically sitting in his wheelchair and growling and I thought dads should always be taller than their children, if only by an inch or two. Drifter Ken would have been the perfect father for me. He always sucked on these unfiltered Camels that drew attention to his magnificent teeth. I say his teeth were magnificent because they had *character*. Teeth can really make or break a person. Drifter Ken's teeth were powerful, like giant evenly spaced blocks, the area between them defining them even further, making them blockier and more magnificent. I complimented him on his teeth one time, mainly so I could tell him about Mrs. Pearlbottom's, and he said hers probably got that way from chewing kids' asses. I laughed. I laughed at a lot of what Drifter Ken said. Drifter Ken was a funny man.

That morning, Drifter Ken had a surprise for me. I was passing through the park kind of quickly because I was already running a little late and I just raised my hand in a wave and nodded to him when he came rushing over to me.

"Hey there, Wally, whaddya say?" Most of our encounters were horribly repetitive but there was a deep sense of comfort to this repetition.

"Oh, not much, Drifter Ken." I used to call him "Mister," but he insisted I call him "Ken." It felt weird calling a grownup by his first name. And never mind that, at sixteen, I was almost a grownup myself. Since I was in the eighth grade, I still considered myself a child. And since I was well on my way to failing eighth grade again I considered myself even more of a child than the other eighth graders. I was downright feeble-minded. What the fuck did it matter what I called him, anyway? Names are ridiculous and the only thing more ridiculous than a name is a title.

"Hey Wally, I gotcha a little somethin."

"Oh yeah? Thanks." I didn't have any idea what it would be. I sure hoped it wasn't crack.

It wasn't. It was a giant green sucker.

It wasn't that I was ungrateful or anything. I guess I just expected something different. It seemed kind of hokey at first, like something you'd give to a baby. But a sucker was a sucker and I didn't really think you ever got too old for candy.

"Now you hide that from the teachers at that school. Tell you what to do… you save it til you go to recess, then you find some place nice and quiet and you enjoy that there lollipop."

I took the sucker and held it, feeling its heft. I nodded to Drifter Ken.

Fuckness

"Listen here now... you enjoy the *hell* out of that lollipop."

"I sure will," I said.

"Hey, say Wally, you got any good jokes for me?"

"I have to get to school."

"Run on then. A good joke gets better with time."

I usually tried to tell Drifter Ken all the jokes I'd heard. Sometimes they were horribly lame but it gave us something to talk about. I hated having to leave Drifter Ken's company so I could go to that miserable fuckhouse of a school.

So, anyway, I got to school that Thursday only a few minutes late. All I could think about was that big, bulgy green sucker in the right front pocket of my pants and I couldn't wait until recess. I didn't think I'd be able to eat all of it and I'd have to save the wrapper so I could store the rest of it until after school. That way I could enjoy the hell out of it on my way home, too. Drifter Ken, if he was still in the park, which he almost always was after school, would be happy to see me enjoying the hell out of that sucker. And the thing kind of kept me behaved, too. A lot of times I'd have to skip recess and stay inside with the surly Miss Pearlbottom, who was one of the *biggest* blobs I'd ever seen.

There was this one time when I had a fantastic vision about fat old Pearlbottom. In the vision, she wore one of those hideous floral-patterned dresses. It hung flappingly from her giant buttocks. Her ass was so huge it looked like she had children stuck in there. For no reason whatsoever, there was this cow in the hall of the school. Pearlbottom, with a grace I'd never seen her obtain before was on this creature in a heartbeat, driving it to the ground with her girth. After wrestling it down to the floor, she began to rapidly devour it, poking her fingers into its flesh, moving pieces of it around with her pudgy little fingers in search of the choicest bites. The entire cow was gone in minutes. In my dream, I looked on, horrified, like it had been a brash act of cannibalism or something. Finishing her meal she looked up at me, wiping the blood from her mouth with the back of her hand and picking some of the cow's coarse hide out of her teeth, looking as though nothing out of the ordinary had happened. Needless to say, I was shaken upon awakening.

Most days, I'd have to stay in from recess for doing something real stupid like sitting back in my little desk and flipping my head back and forth on my shoulders while singing some stupid shit like, "Da doo doo doo," or some fuckall like that.

Pearlbottom reminded me of someone who should be working at a truck stop, not in a school. She'd tell me to stop acting out. Sometimes she would tell me that I was way off task, like I was supposed to know what the hell that meant.

It didn't matter. I'd keep flicking my head and making the sounds. Mainly, I kept doing this because of the real soft but sort of mean way she had of telling me to stop, like I needed to be reminded of what I was doing. I knew exactly what I was doing and figured it was disruptive as hell, but I just didn't care. I was more entertained by the way my hair would briefly raise up off my scalp as I snapped my head and I would try to snap it quicker and quicker every time. I tried to make the sounds loud and clear, yet distinctly my own, by adding occasional flourishes to it. Like sometimes I'd see what it sounded like with a lot of spit in my throat or with a bunch of paper in my mouth. And Miss Pearlbottom, she just kept shoveling on the fuckness.

My desk was in the back of the classroom, which had two doors—one in front and one in back. I knew I was intentionally sat by the back door so that when I started in with something like the head snapping and sounds, Pearlbottom could open up that back door and pull my desk out so I was sitting real lonely and all in the hallway. She was a very burly woman and she didn't have to extend a lot of effort to do this.

Simplified, the breakdown went something like this: I would be immersed in my own little world, managing to have a decent time because I didn't want to be at school to begin with. She would yank me out into the hall for having a relatively good time when nobody else was. Then her brashness would make me cry. I'd felt like that for about the past three years, always on the verge of crying. I always felt so sad and sorry for myself that it didn't take much to send me on a crying jag. Then, Miss Pearlbottom would take away my recess for crying. Having my recess taken away wasn't even that much of a punishment. But when that happened I had to stay in the lunchroom with one of the monitors while they stared at me. There I would sit, pitifully looking down at my half-eaten tray of food.

"You've really done it now," Pearlbottom would say, leaning down so close to me I could see the pores on her face, close to gaping, cheap and shiny make-up slathered over top of them. And this snide blob had the worst breath I'd ever smelled. She chewed cinnamon-flavored gum and drank coffee all day and this combination created an amazingly shit-like type of halitosis. Her teeth were all decayed so they looked like little Tic Tacs, the green kind, hanging from her gums. "Some people just never learn. You see if you're still in here at the end of the year, Wally."

Sometimes it seemed like all people did was threaten me and that smegma drenched cunthole was probably right. I wouldn't be there at the end of the year. At least, I didn't *want* to be there at the end of the year. And, even more, I didn't want to have to come back to the middle school the next year, either.

That sucker of Drifter Ken's got me through the day. Or, at least, the first part of the day. When recess came, it was the sucker that finally got me into trouble. By the time recess did finally come, I was practically salivating over that damn thing. My hand rested on the bulge in my pants. With the sweaty tips of my twitching fingers, I could practically taste that sucker through the denim of my pants and its thin plastic wrapper. I had to be careful not to twitch too much though, so Blob Pearlbottom wouldn't think I was playing with myself, which is apparently a very serious offense in school. The last time it happened, I didn't even get the hallway. I was sent straight to the office where Mr. Rheingold, another blob, suspended me for the rest of the week.

I didn't see what the big fuss was. It wasn't like I had it out or anything. Wasn't school a place for exploration? No one even noticed except Pearlbottom. If it hadn't been for Becky Trawlers' ass crack hanging out the back of her pants, it wouldn't have happened anyway. To me, it seemed more indecent to have your ass exposed than it did to have your hand discreetly shoved down the front of your pants. The kids called me "Whack Off Wally" for the rest of that year, the Year of Lottie Simpson's Reign.

The bell finally rang for recess and I was the first one out of the classroom, one of the conveniences of being in my hall-yanking position. Then I burst through those double doors, their long horizontal steel levers and the wire in the glass of the windows the only thing separating me from outside. I beat hell out to the playground and the fence. It was raining a little bit. Nothing more than a mist really but, without a coat, I should have been freezing. It didn't really bother me though. My desire for that sucker kept me hot.

I pulled the green knob out of my pocket and unwrapped it with shaky, sugar-starved hands when I heard a soft voice behind me, freezing me.

"Whatcha got there?" At first I thought it might be Pearlbottom.

I turned around and saw that it was Mary Lou Dover, the hottest girl in my class. She was already fully developed and she had on a tight shirt that ended above her bellybutton, despite the cold. I guess that was so everyone could see how flat and tan her stomach was. A soot smear sat, birthmarkishly, beside her navel. I knew she was as vacant as the rest of the blobs but her beauty or, perhaps at that moment, her militantly erect nipples, kept me from really noticing this blobbishness. It would come out later, as soon as the beauty faded. I guessed that would be like in her mid-twenties, when those legs and that stomach started bulging, after she'd been fucked and beat senseless by every huge-dicked football player that looked at her. Maybe she would take another route and marry a cockwrinkle of a lawyer who would twist her words like soft metal until she was voiceless.

Mary Lou, the trophy wife.

Mary Lou, a big fuckable future blob.

What *did* I have there?

"Nothin." I answered her quickly, hiding the sucker behind my back. I thought she might tell on me. She was that type of person. Mary Lou was very mean. She had the two twins on either side of her, Cathy and Denise Something-or-the-other, looking as though they'd had their spirits stolen by Mary Lou.

"I know you got somethin. I seen it. It's a sucker, ain't it?"

"No."

"Yer lyin. Wallace Black is a *liar*."

"No I'm not."

"And a... mo*lest*er."

I don't know where she got that from. I'd never even kissed a girl, of any age. The only girls I'd even seen with their clothes off were on the television. I had a few fuzzy memories of seeing the mother naked as a small child but that seemed more appropriate for vomition rather than anything else, really.

"No I'm not."

"I bet you are."

"I bet I'm not."

"I want that sucker."

"You can't have it. It was a present."

"From who?"

"That's for me to know and you to find out."

"I want that sucker."

"No."

"I'll let you kiss me if you give me that sucker."

Then I lied. I suddenly realized what it was I might have. A bartering tool.

Everybody loves a lollipop.

"Aw, I kiss girls all the time. I'm sixteen. That's almost an adult. Kissing's what adults do."

"Yer a big fat liar is what you are, Wally Black. I know you want to kiss me. Everybody does."

It was true that I wanted to kiss her. I figured that would make me more like at least twenty-five other kids in the middle school. Hell, even the high school. Mary Lou was one of the girls that would hang out outside the middle school until the loser high schoolers drove by in their battered cars. Only, I guess I was a bigger loser than they were. At least they were *in* high school. But I felt like I needed more than a kiss from Mary Lou. I wanted to up the ante at least a notch.

"Can I use my tongue?" I figured that might be worth it and it seemed like something she would plausibly go for. I knew she wouldn't suck me or let me finger her like I'd heard she'd done with Johnny Listo.

"Only for a second? For the sucker?"

I nodded. I was starting to choke up. It felt like somebody had poured cement on the inside of my body and it was rapidly hardening. The only thing that wasn't hardening was Mr. Lawrence. Maybe if we hadn't been on the playground. I had ogled Mary Lou all year. I had never even touched a girl and, with the prospect of sticking my tongue in that mouth, I felt weak all over. I think hearing about Mary Lou's exploits made me even more excited. Like I thought that anything she could do would be really good.

"You ain't got AIDS or nothin, do ya? You look like somebody who's got AIDS."

"I don't have AIDS. I promise."

I guess that was good enough for her. She took a step toward me and closed her eyes. She was a lot shorter than me so I had to bend way down. I shook uncontrollably. As soon as I was close enough to smell her skin under her perfume I kind of lost it, I guess. Once our lips touched, it couldn't have been more than a few seconds before I tried to put my tongue in her mouth. I really wasn't sure how it should be done. I mean, I'd seen people do it on the television but you never really got to see how the tongue got there. I just stuck it out like an insult. I wanted to slip it halfway down her blobby throat. At that point, I thought sex must be more about destroying each other. Just touching her made me want to like step inside of her body. To somehow stretch it to the point of bursting.

But she kept her teeth clenched. That felt like an embarrassing eternity, standing there as my tongue moved wetly against the plaque on her teeth. So I got this other idea. Real quickly, I put my clammy palm against her tan stomach and ran my hand straight down until it was in her pants.

For the slightest fraction of a second, I realized what this was all about. Mr. Lawrence picked up, stiffening against my briefs. I realized I didn't give a fuck about Mary Lou. It was the senses I felt. Everything in that one breath. I tasted the inside of her mouth, smelled the oil on her skin, felt the thin cloth of her underwear on the back of my hand and that moist warmth on my palm. I wanted to do a lot more. I wanted to rip her pants off. I didn't care where the hell we were. She pulled away, jumping back, and I could tell by the way she was looking at me she was really mad.

Hell, I would've been mad too. How many times had Mary Lou felt that predatory stiffening? How many times had her essence completely ceased to exist leaving her to become nothing more than a body? How many more times would she feel it? And how did she feel being able to use that as her only tool, her only asset? Had she went down on Johnny Listo willingly or had his stiffness become so completely overpowering she didn't have a choice?

She reached out and snatched the sucker out of my hand. I was too nervous and shaky and full-feeling to tell her that a deal was a deal and she didn't let me use my tongue. If she'd just let me use my tongue then maybe it would've stopped there and I wouldn't be standing on the playground feeling so guilty.

She started yelling at me, bouncing that sucker toward me in the air, the way Pearlbottom sometimes did with the yardstick.

"You *are* a molester, Wally Black. Yer almost an adult, you said so yourself, and my momma says that older men ain't supposed to be touching me. Especially *there*. Yer not just a molester, yer a big fat rapist. I never asked you to touch me, you stupid freak. I could have you locked up for this, just like Mom did Stephen. And I *asked* him to touch me."

I got even more nervous and scared when she said that, but my guilt virtually vanished. "You got the sucker."

"Damn right I got the sucker. That's why I ain't gonna tell Miss Pearlbottom bout this but choo better watch out cause I'm tellin Bucky *all* about it."

That made me even *more* nervous and scared. My Swarth-free year was about ready to come to an end. Before trotting over to Swarth, Mary Lou leaned toward me and said, "If you'da played yer cards right, Wally Black, I woulda showed you my tits for this here sucker."

Now, whether the sucker was watermelon or lime or sour apple, I would never know. The only thing I'd got out of the deal was a cheap feel of a crotch that I'm certain was diseased, if only by a low-grade form of crabs. And, even worse, it was a feel I'd felt guilty about.

Chapter Three
The Year of Swarth

Mary Lou stalked up to Bucky Swarth. I stayed over by the fence, bracing myself. I could have run but the playground was very small, so there really wasn't any place to go, and I probably would have fallen down anyway. I had never really run away from the bullies. At first, I'd tried to fight back. Then I learned to just accept the beatings. Usually, if a teacher happened to come along while I was taking a good beating and not even fighting back, the bully would get in worse trouble than I would.

Bucky stood in the middle of the playground, his gang of five surrounding him. They stood there like they belonged, puffing away at their cigarettes. Some of them hadn't grown to their full height yet, but I was certain that they all weighed over 200 pounds. Bucky was the biggest, naturally—the leader. It looked like he wore a new pair of pants every day, they were so stiff and blue-looking. He always had the bottoms of them cuffed-up and I knew he probably shopped in the husky section, his mother telling him that he was just big for his age. But he was a fatass. Weren't *fat* people supposed to be made fun of? The bottom of his stomach stuck out of his striped shirt. I could tell he already shaved. Wiry, black hair covered his vast white stomach. He wore a big black leather jacket with lots of shiny silver buckles on it. The arms were too short and I questioned the physics required to zip it over his gut. He kept his black hair in a very retro crew cut.

I stood there, quivering with fear, watching Mary Lou talk to him, rubbing those breasts all over his arm. She was rather coy about it, throwing her arms into some sort of gesticulation, moving in to ever so slightly *swipe* Swarth with her chest. For treatment like that, I would have beat the hell out of me if I were Bucky Swarth. He tried to push her away, but she just kept rubbing herself all over him. I'm sure his leather-clad arm was numb to those stabbing, excited nipples. Boy, she was really mad. I heard her caterwauling from over where I was.

Apparently, she finally said something to catch his attention and shove his bloodlust into action. I was guessing she probably promised him anal sex without a condom or some fuckness like that. He leaned over to her and kissed her for a few seconds, massaging one of her breasts with a meaty hand. They broke up and he kind of pointed at me, mumbling something. Confirming her accusations, I guess. And then he was on his way over, throwing down his cigarette and aiming that big blobby head right at me. His gang followed him, their chests all pumped up. They all looked like they had tits and if they weren't capable of inflicting such physical harm, I would have found the situation too absurd to take seriously. I imagined Pearlbottom sending a note home stating that I'd been whapped to death by bosoms.

There I was, standing frozen by the fence, shaking even more violently by that point. Bucky came over and just stood there, staring at me. Hate boiled in those eyes, but it was real *unspecific* hate. Like he looked at everyone like that and I was no one special. That look was what made me most afraid. It was a zombiefied look that said there must be some form of altercation, some end, and there wasn't going to be a shred of mercy in that conclusion.

"You wanna start some shit?" he said and spit onto the ground.

I was going to tell him about the deal and how the fucking blob bag had copped out on everything and then figured, why bother? Fuck it.

"No," I said instead.

"My girl over there says you raped her good."

"That's not true."

I knew there was no way I could talk myself out of it. I had trouble talking anyway and, being nervous and all, I could just forget it. My throat felt constricted. If I started talking, I'd just end up twittering like a girl hopped up on diet pills.

"You callin er a liar?"

"No."

"Then you must be callin *me* a liar. You think I'm a liar, you fuckin molester piece of trash shit?" Whenever he said "liar" it sounded more like "lar."

I knew the beating was coming and I could tell it was going to be real good and humiliating so I did something I didn't expect. I spit in the fat blobfuck's face. I did. I hawked a real thick one that felt like it sucked everything out of my brain and I aimed right in the middle of his sizable head, rolling my tongue around the mucous like a fleshy gun barrel. The glob hit him with surprising accuracy and hung there on the end of his puggy, piggish nose.

His gang collectively winced, "Oooh."

Bucky tried to wipe the glob off real cool, but it hung there on the end of his fingers. He tried to flick it off with his thumb but the goober steadfastly latched onto that. He wildly flapped his arm but it just swung up and stuck onto the back of his hand. He bent down and wiped it on the damp grass, exposing an expansive backside the color of Swiss cheese. I was certain that he had a forest of ass hair.

"You're dead."

He stood up and shoved me back into the rusty fence.

I sprang forward and took a wild swing, completely missing him and throwing me off balance. One of his gang members stuck out his foot and tripped me up while Bucky pushed me forward onto the wet grass. I hit the ground and went skidding a couple of feet. Two gang members got each of my arms and lifted me up. My eyes were watering but I could see Bucky slip a set of brass knuckles onto his hand. He was out to do serious damage. He tried to hide his newly metallic right hand behind his left, so I wouldn't know what was coming. He took a huge, overhanded swing and his iron-covered fist smashed into my face. I felt my nose break. It made a loud pop inside my head and I felt the blood coming out of it in a warm rapid trickle like I had a runny nose all of a sudden. I tasted it on the back of my tongue. The gang members kept me upright. This time Bucky took a huge underhanded swing and rammed my jaws together. I felt my teeth click and grind. My lower jaw felt like it was broken. There was more blood. I think I swallowed a couple of my teeth. This time I blacked out for a couple of seconds. Bucky took some quick shots at my ribs and body and fuckall and the gang members let me fall to my knees. They actually kind of shoved me to my knees. Bucky got in front of me and bent over, sticking that big blob of an ass right in my face.

I could smell the newness of those pants. One of the gang members steadied my head there close to Bucky's ass.

I heard the fart before I smelled it.

Suddenly it was there, surrounding my head with a brown heat. The smell was the worst thing. Maybe even worse than the beating itself. Not only was it humiliating, it smelled worse than rotting fruit. It was worse than all the locked-up-in-a-hot-room shits I'd ever had in my life. It was like Bucky had at one time devoured an entire human and those were the gases released from that exploit, a sickening decay of flesh. I visualized that smell, a wet fume rolling out of that damp black forest. I felt my gorge rise and I vomited, the heaving action exuding an excruciating pain. My vomit smelled better than Swarth's flatulence. Bucky stood upright again and overhanded the back of my skull with those brass knucks, driving my face into the cool wet ground. This time I went out for I don't know how long. As I was going out, sort of a sickeningly uncontrolled spiral down into blackness, I heard his gang's laughter fading and somewhere beyond that, I heard the bell, felt the warmth of my bile on the side of my face.

I think I woke up because I was drowning. I'm not sure if it was because of the rain that was now beating down in steadily heavy sheets or all the blood that was congealing in my nose and running down the back of my throat. Nevertheless, I woke up because I couldn't breathe. I stood up as fast as I could. An intense feeling of vertigo surged up from inside, tilting me crazily back down to my knees. I stayed like that for a moment. At least until the initial pain and nausea passed. The only reason I tried to get up at all was because I knew Pearlbottom would have some sort of punishment waiting for me that would be more severe the later I was. Fuck it. What did it matter now? I'd already lost the sucker. That's what really started this whole thing anyway, wasn't it? Maybe now Bucky could shove the stick up his urethra and let Mary Lou lick the shiny green knob.

When I stood up the dizziness was still there but it wasn't nearly so overwhelming. My head whummed with pain. I tried to focus on the school but it kept darting out of my field of vision. It shot out the far corner of my left eye and then came back in the far corner of my right. I took a few more moments to gather my bearings and then skipped back to the school because skipping makes me happy and I thought it might make the whumming go away. The skipping didn't make me any happier, though. The only thing I could muster was a heavy-headed, broken kind of skip. I got to the classroom and accidentally went into the door at the front of the class because I still didn't quite know where I was. The whumming made it impossible to think. If I had went into the back door I maybe would have had a chance to sit down unnoticed. Or, if not completely unnoticed, then at least *less* noticed. Instead, I nearly ran Pearlbottom over.

She turned to face me, real shocked-looking, like I was going to attack her or something. Her lips worked dryly against those Tic Tac teeth.

"It looks like *some*body got into some trouble."

And I was going to tell her all about it, even if I had to stand up there and yammer like a little girl, but before I could, she reached out and plucked a blade of grass from just under my nose. She pulled a Kleenex from the floral box on her desk and wiped her finger distastefully. She reached out again, turning me around by the shoulders, touching me with only the very tips of her fingers.

"Why don't you just go on home before you can interrupt my class any more for the day." She gave me a gentle push toward the door.

My shoulders slumped. They slumped anyway, but this time it

felt like my whole damn spine hit the floor. I walked in the direction I was nudged. The whumming sound was huge.

"Oh, and Mr. Wallace?"

I turned back around to look at her and tried to say, "Yes, Miss Pearlbottom," but I couldn't move my mouth.

"Why don't you shower up when you get home? You smell like death." The class burst into laughter, peppered with random words like "molester," "freak," and "AIDS."

I was sure I smelled. It was at that point that I was fairly certain I'd defecated in my pants.

I went home the same way as always, passing by the park. I didn't have the energy to skip or whoop and I didn't even really feel like it at the moment. The blobs had won today, I thought. The blobs kicked the hell out of me.

Drifter Ken was in the park, lying down on one of those thickly green painted wooden benches, sound asleep. He lay there on his back with his gray raincoat pulled up over his head. I was kind of glad he was asleep. I was really embarrassed about how bad the blobs had got ahold of me. I didn't want him to see me like that. I also didn't want to tell him about the sucker and my moment of weakness that had caused me to lose it. Drifter Ken was definitely not a blob. He was one of the only adults I had met that wasn't. He said he'd never graduated school. I was pretty sure he didn't even have a job. From talking to Drifter Ken, I got the impression a job turns a lot of adults into blobs just like school does a lot of kids. He said a job would take a man's will to live more completely than anything else. I believed him. I believed just about everything Drifter Ken said, mainly because he wasn't a blob. I had made it a point to never believe anything a blob told me. I dreamed of a place that had absolutely no blobs in it. If I could have convinced myself a place like that existed, I could have had a little happier day.

Chapter Four
Racecar and The Wig

The parents had to be a couple of the biggest blobs I'd ever known. They weren't always that bad. I mean, I didn't always see them that way. Maybe I'm the reason they were the way they were. Maybe they were the reason I was who I was. Who knows? Fuck it.

To start with, there was the mother. Her name was Sadie. There's a song called "Sexy Sadie," I think it's by the Beatles, that couldn't come further from describing the mother. In fact, if you were to hear that song in your head while watching the mother in action, it would seem cruelly humorous. I'm sure most sons wouldn't consider their mother sexy even if she truly was but the mother, man. She was a stout woman—very large and broad-shouldered. Quite mannish, now that I think about it. Never leaving the house removed any impulse she may have had for ever getting out of her nightgown. She wore the same gown for days on end. It collected all kinds of stains and worked up an odor that could be called rank even by the gentlest of standards. Even though she never left the house or changed her gown she went through the trouble of putting on her wig every morning, a sloppy brown thing she never managed to put on straight.

She had a stroke a few years back. This was mostly because of me, she said. She said her stroke came the first time I failed. "It was God's way of striking me down. Of waking me up and telling me that I had to stop sparing the rod." I tried to tell her I had been failing since birth. This stroke that I or God or whoever gave her made her slur her words. She smoked constantly, her cigarette dangling out of her mouth. The cigarette coupled with the slur made it nearly impossible to understand a thing she said.

After my fist time failing, she also became a devoted follower of vodka and gin, which probably didn't help the slurring either. She only drank the bottom-shelf stuff, the kind that comes in plastic bottles. Invariably, these bottles could be found below the kitchen sink and, wherever the mother was, a snifter was always at arm's length. Her boozing usually knocked her out shortly after I got home, after her stories had gone off on the television.

She lived for those stories! Sometimes I think the people on the television had become more real to her than me and Racecar. I couldn't really blame her, though. I was a dumb boring shit, fun to laugh *at* but never *with*. Nothing but trouble. Virtually retarded. And the father, the father was something different altogether.

He was, as I said before, an angry gimp. He'd lost both of his legs in a work-related incident of dubious cause. I never talked to him much, anyway—especially about that. He had this old motorized wheelchair he zoomed around the house in and he was always knocking things over—ashtrays and glasses off the coffee table, the *TV Guide* off the mother's end table. All the lower cabinets in the kitchen had this horizontal strip of raw wood down close to the floor from him slamming into them with the unused metal footrests on that damn gimpy wheelchair. That's all he did with his day, zooming around the house like he was in some fucking marathon for cripples. The carpet, which wasn't in too good of shape anyway, was all worn bare from his continuous buzzing. He was trying to wean himself off the motor, though. He saw the motor, undoubtedly a modern convenience to most, as some sign of weakness. A classic case of overcompensation, he wanted to make his arms and torso huge to make up for not having any legs. He didn't talk much and when he did it was with his teeth clenched around this old yellowed-plastic cigarette filter. He had stopped smoking after he lost his legs. He said if he ever had to go on some sort of lung gadget, it would make the wheelchair too heavy to whir around the house like that. When he did talk it was usually a fervidly passionate and obsessive rant about getting the basement all cleared out so he would have a decent place to ride his chair around. I wasn't even sure the basement needed "all cleared out." Nobody had ever gone down there. It could have been used as a body farm for all we knew.

The mother described the father as a "bundle of nerves."

"Why don't you just *stop* for a minute," she would strumble. "Stop turning this place into the goddamned Grand Prix."

Even with the television turned to top volume, the mother still had to strain to hear her stories over the buzzing and clunking of the father. Sometimes he growled around that filter. This really drove the mother nuts. When he started with the growling she usually had to go into the bedroom and lie down. That's something else she was doing more of lately, just going into the bedroom and falling asleep. If I was ever too sick to go to school, she usually stayed in bed all day. Like a whole day with me was just too much for her. Needless to say, she was bedridden most of the weekend. She would make me move the television stand over to her doorway so she could still watch it. She never let me push it all the way into the room. She said it cluttered up her room to push it all the way in. Since she made me her personal servant when I was there all day, bringing her this and that, I had to go through the tedious process of moving the television out of the doorway to get to her bed.

So that's what the parents were like. That's not really fair. That's what the parents had *become*. I really hated them. I hadn't always hated them but, lately, I hated them an awful lot. I didn't really blame them for anything, like my failing and all that fuckness. Before I started failing, back when I actually tried to fit in, I blamed them for a lot because, even at an earlier age, I knew they had somehow created me. I never saw myself as something that came from God. I wasn't familiar with the eggs and the sperm and all that fuckness but I could tell I was like two puzzles that had the pieces all mixed up, making a third puzzle that didn't really look like anything. So when I was younger, I blamed them a lot because I didn't have my own personality so I was just a combination of them and they sure were terrifically blobby wastes. But I grew out of that and I just started wondering why I had to be born to *them*. That's really when I started hating them. I knew I still wouldn't have fit in, but at least I could have maybe had new clothes and good food and all that fuckness.

I was sure there were a lot of other people out there who would have made better parents. Maybe if I'd been born to one of those other countless parents I could have had some sort of plan or goal or fuckness like that. Mostly I just sat around wondering how I could have been born to such slothful and ridiculous blobs like the parents.

When Miss Pearlbottom sent me home that day, I knew I had it coming. Miss Pearlbottom liked to call the parents from school whenever she thought she didn't have an opportunity to punish me enough for one day. Like I could tell that some days she wanted to haul off and smack me, I could see it in her eyes. Those were the days she would call home so that the mother and father could properly lay into me. I hated them all. The mother, the father, and Pearlbottom combined formed some kind of fuckness triumvirate. A web of fuckness. Those three lead the fuck-Wallace-Black-in-the-ass parade.

That day, walking home through the rain, I hated them—especially the parents—with an even greater passion than usual. The only thing I could think about was getting the fuck out of Mill-town and never looking at any of those blobby faces with their seeping rectum mouths ever again. I walked down the sidewalk and remembered that old saying, "Step on a crack, break your mother's back," and I made sure to step on every fucking crack along my way. I briefly hoped the parents would be too tired to really punish me or maybe they would have a stroke of understanding or compassion but I guess, deep down, I knew that wouldn't happen. They always had their ways.

Sometimes, when they didn't jump my ass the second I walked through the door, they punished me in different ways. Like some-

Fuckness

times the mother wouldn't make dinner because demons didn't deserve dinner. That thing I said about wishing I hadn't been born to them, well, I knew they had the same feelings. Like they wished that *I* had never been born to *them*. The mother really did think I was a demon. I would catch her saying pitiful little prayers over my bed when I was asleep, trying to get the demon to fly out. Sometimes she would make me say prayers, too. They were stupid things I tried to forget right after saying them. They all sounded like something you'd find on a napkin or book of matches. I bet the father prayed he would've had a son like Bucky Swarth. A stout little shit who was smart enough to get away with everything he did. Making me skip dinner was actually one of the better punishments they had in store for me. That is, I didn't really mind it too much. The best punishment was when they flat out gave me a beating and sent me to my room. That was the best punishment because it was over so quickly. Any beating was better than thinking you're not going to get punished and then getting punished when you least expected it.

One time I got in trouble for some stupid fuckness or the other and they didn't say anything when I walked into the house. This was one of the first alternative punishments I can think of. So this one time there was no yelling or hitting and I didn't bring up anything that happened at school and a couple hours went by with me at home and nothing happening. I stood by the kitchen sink, drinking a glass of ice water, thinking everything was just fine, like I'd got away with something, when the father barreled out of the living room on that wheelchair and rammed it straight into me. The hard steel hit me at the same level it usually did the cabinets and I thought that leg he hit, the left one, was broken. But I couldn't say anything like, "What the fuck're you doing?" because I knew that was part of my punishment. There was something inside of me that said I deserved the punishments. That it was just something I had to put up with. And the crazy fuck kept doing that for the rest of the night. I'd have my back turned and right when I heard that whirring and growling I'd try to move but it got me anyway. And it hurt like hell every time. You'd think I would have wised up after the second or third time, but that's where my stupidity comes in. Was it stupidity or optimism? After every hit I told myself *that* had to be the last one. How could he think I could possibly take more than that?

There was this other time I got all the way to bed thinking I wasn't going to get punished and woke up the next morning with an incredibly bad haircut. It was that morning more than any other that I awoke wishing I wasn't such a sound sleeper. We lived right behind some train tracks and that loud sound kind of dulled me to noises and fuckall, I think. So, because I slept so fucking heavy, I woke up and had these wild tufts of hair sticking up all over my head. I looked like a crazed chemotherapy patient. I wasn't attracting anyone anyway, but that fucking ridiculous haircut made it even worse. Like I could give up all hope of *ever* attracting anyone, or even going unnoticed which, at that point, was the best thing I could really do. It worked too, the punishment that is. The kids at school taunted me for the next month, making all kinds of stupid remarks and jokes and fuckness. Like, "Hey, Wally had a fight with a lawnmower and the lawnmower won." I must have heard that a hundred times by the end of the month and I wanted to smash all those blobby people's teeth out. If you ever see someone who's had a really bad haircut, you should never start all that shit about the lawnmower because they've probably heard the same thing three times that day. Some of them just called me "Leukemia Boy," like leukemia's a disease you get from jerking off or something. I'd never hated those blobs at that fucking school more than that month I had the really bad haircut. Did they think I didn't know my hair was ridiculous?

I eventually found the clippers and evened it out myself. I got hit for that. The mother busted her drinking glass against my face and strumbled, "I didn't tell you you could do that yet." She acted like I was some kid who was put on the couch for quiet time and got up before my fifteen minutes were served. She was a really vacant mean sick piece of blobshit.

Anyway, what I'm trying to say is that I never really knew how things were going to be when I walked in the door of my house. I braced myself that day I got thumped by Swarth. It felt like I had already been through so much. I didn't really know how much more I'd be able to take.

I imagined that fatass Swarth going home to his family.

"Hello, son," his mom would say. "How was school?"

"School was *great*, Mom!"

"Oh yeah, what'd you guys *do*?"

"Well, I beat the absolute *shit* out of this kid named Wally Black."

"Hmmm... I don't know if that's so... Wait... Wally Black, he's that half-wit molester, isn't he?"

"Yeah, he's a real queer, too."

"Well, that's just *won*derful, Bucky. It's nice to see you're looking out for your fellow classmates like that. Looky what I bought you... A new pair of *pants*!"

I imagined things like that just to amuse myself. There were some days when I imagined things about everybody. It was like I lived this whole other world in my head, where the people I hated were truly despicable people. It depended on the person, I guess, and sometimes these things were quite mundane. That girl had a brother who was dying and she thought it was funny. That kid had sex with his mother. This other kid was a ravenous drug addict. This girl's parents sold her into white slavery and on the weekends she had to have sex with people of exotic origins, slimy men with huge mustaches. That boy made love to a sheep. That kid had prosthetic legs. His dad was a Nazi. This kid's gay. That one's a Satanist. Maybe it shouldn't have been a surprise no one liked me.

I got onto our street, Walnut, and my body didn't want to go any further. I wanted to be home as fast as possible if I had to be there at all, but my battered body forced me to walk kind of slowly. It was work just to focus on the sidewalk. I'd never felt so tired and sore in my life. I wanted to get the beating over with and go to my room. My room was the only place I felt even sort of comfortable in that house. Hell, it was the only place in the world I felt comfortable. That had to be my goal. That tiny room, as sad as it was, became my reason for going back to that house.

Andersen Prunty

Our street wasn't the absolute worst street to live on in Mill-town but it was definitely a lower rung on the social ladder. There were three houses on the street that were just burnt out shells. The mother said that was from the crackheads. I believed her when she had first told me that but since I had stopped believing anything blobs ever said, I wasn't so sure. The rest of the houses, like ours, looked like they were sinking into the ground or collapsing or some fuckness like that. Black soot had accumulated on all of the houses, quelling them into a monotonous gray color, the paint peeling away to reveal the weathered wood beneath. Some of the windows were boarded up. In other houses, odd things like shirts, quilts, and Con-federate flags were used as blinds. Some people didn't even have proper front doors. The whole road smelled like gasoline, oil, and sewage.

I reached our door and figured, what the hell, might as well get it over with. Had to get to my room, you know. And then I opened the door, hoping it wasn't one of those nights where they decided to fuck around.

It wasn't.

Chapter Five
The Horns

Fucking Racecar. He was waiting right there at the door for me. The combined smell of rotting wood and stale cigarette smoke greeted me as I stood there in front of the door, not having any idea of what was coming.

I opened the door, swinging it inside and to my left, thinking about how stiff I was from the Swarth beating. About the time I thought that thought, Racecar launched himself out of his wheelchair like a bizarre armed missile, barreling into me. The blow hurt like holy hell. I stayed upright, though, Racecar deflecting off me, thudding to the floor and rolling around. My first reaction was to tear his face off. I was so mad and sad anyway that it didn't really matter. I could have done it. I could have killed Racecar right then and there. Not only could I have killed him, I wanted to. I just wanted it to be over. I wanted to snuff the life right out of the nightmare. But nothing wanted to move. I had those dreams sometimes where somebody was trying to fight me and when I went to fight back my punches were slow and leaden and if I tried to run away then it felt like I was trying to pull myself through water. This felt just like those dreams. By the time I had gained some sense of what was going on, Racecar wrapped a muscular hand around my ankle and yanked it out from under me. I went down hard.

"Fuck it," I said, mumbling it through swollen jaws and a

whumming head. It was almost like I was proving a point, lying there and taking Racecar's blows like that.

Even though he had no legs to speak of, his arms were like tree trunks from pulling himself around in that wheelchair so much. Why couldn't he just use the motor?

I hated that fucking wheelchair.

I was face down on the carpet and those heavy hands kept hitting the back of my head. One of them was wrapped around one of my arms. I couldn't tell which arm it was. I wasn't sure which side of my body was which. I felt his huge eagle-shaped belt buckle digging into my back and I'm pretty sure he was trying to jab that plastic cigarette filter into one of my ears. Worst of all, I could picture him rubbing those hideous stumps all over me. I could *feel* them. The pain became a giant blur, like a huge red-black womb I tried to viciously tear myself out of. I could hear him grunting and growling, "You little shit. You little piece of shit. Fuckin lowlife trash. Never even *offered* to help me clean the goddamn basement."

Once it felt like I slid out of that womb, everything was kind of dark and foggy and numb. It made me think of being wrapped in cotton. The impact of the blows resonated through my body but the sharp, stinging pain was gone. The mother's voice came down all around me like a big brassy bullhorn, amplified strumbling, a needle through the cotton.

"We've had it! We've *had* it! You're gonna get it this time you little shit. You've ruined our lives. Do you *hear* me? Ruined them! We're nothing because of you. You and your stupid failing and your shitty rotten brain. What *are* you?!" Seeing that I was a bit lost for words, she graciously strumbled the answer to her own question. "Demonshit! Demonshit! That's what you are! Jesus *Christ*, we're gonna mess you up this time. You're getting the fucking demon horns you deserve and I hope you wear em til you die!"

Then I felt her wrestling with my head, pulling it up off the floor, sending snapping red shivers of pain shooting down my spine. I could smell that horrible smoke and liquor stink hanging around her in an acrid cloud. I found it in me to thrash.

The horns.

Fuckness

I'd seen the horns.

The Wig had threatened me with those horns before. Mostly she started using them as a way to keep me in my room at night. She told me that if I took a notion to wander, I'd wake up with those giant grotesque things on my head. I squirmed and bucked her off, managing to stand.

Racecar quickly yanked my legs out from under me, being expertly positioned to do so. I flew backward and bashed my head on the door, legs sprawled out in front of me. The mother knelt on my legs, facing me, smothering me with her mannish girth. With each breath I took, consciousness slowly slipped away.

That was the first time I felt the red crawlies and I thought maybe the mother was right.

I *did* have some kind of demon in me.

I could feel it come through my skin when the mother put those huge reddish-brown things on my head. It swirled around inside my skull, ricocheting back and forth before shooting down my spine, exploding through my heart, stomach, and groin.

In an instant, I was fully conscious. It was almost like some kind of hyper-consciousness. I could taste and sense everything in the small house. I could see everything not only as it was but also how it would look a hundred years from now.

The mother sensed it, this thing that had entered me, the red crawlies feverishly pushing against the underside of my skin, forcing me into action.

And I could smell her fear, thick and sweaty like an old dirty blanket.

She was immediately on me again, trying to undo the straps, sensing she had done something terribly wrong. With newfound strength I shoved her off. She went careering dramatically into the back of the TV, knocking it onto the flimsy coffee table before landing on the whole heap. She looked at me from below her lopsided wig and mumbled words I couldn't hear. Words I didn't want to hear. Words I only wanted to end.

I hoisted the TV up above my head, imagining how much pleasure she had derived from it. How many hours she had spent catatonically staring into it and then I brought it down on her head. There was a brittle, shattering sound followed by something meatier, pulpier. I picked up the TV again. Her head was a mess. The wig was split and tattered. The face beneath was unrecognizable. Her legs kicked out in the twitches of early death. I let the TV drop again and her movements ceased.

In the time it took me to do that, Racecar had managed to reach the end table and was trying to pull himself up on it. I didn't imagine that would really do him a whole lot of good.

He pulled himself up on the ends of his stubs, his arms vibrating with anger. The end table rocked and threw him off, a lamp tumbling to the floor with him. The light bulb threw crazy shadows across the room.

Grabbing the cord from the television, I wrapped it around my hand and gave it a great yank. It came out with a stretching pop. I took the frayed end in my hand and walked over to Racecar. Yielding the cord like a whip, I lashed the father with the plug-in. He yelped in pain as the copper bit into his skin. I got down on top of him and wrapped the cord around his arms, cinching it up tight. Then I rolled him over onto his arms, his back, where he rocked and rolled like an overturned beetle.

I grabbed the base of the lamp and knocked the shade off. Racecar stared at me and I realized, I think for the first time, that his eyes were blue.

He shouted words but, to me, they were just the facial contortions of the mute.

I stood overtop of him, that feeling dancing around inside me, and I slowly moved the lamp toward his eye socket. I pressed the hot bulb further and further into his eye, watching his screams.

Then I did the other eye.

I got down on my knees beside Racecar and wrapped the lamp cord around his neck, squeezing it tighter and tighter until it started to bite into the flesh and Racecar stopped moving.

I stood, surveying the room and, with a silent whoosh, the red crawlies crawled out. The feeling was gone, leaving me to swoon there in the middle of the living room. Everything became black

Fuckness

and blurry. My body felt like a piece of lead.

This isn't what I wanted, I thought. And with that thought, I passed out.

Chapter Six
The Room of Idols

I woke up in my bed. The bed was really an old army cot with some blankets thrown over it. The cot. That was another punishment. The more I thought about it, the more I realized the punishments were just some form of vicious cycle. The parents would punish me and I would fail or, more often, get sent home from school or suspended, the small failures I imagined culminating into a life of failure. The night of the particular failure, they would punish me. I, in turn, probably wouldn't do my homework, creating another failure. The cot was what I got for burning my bed. I can't even remember what the punishment that brought that on was.

I waited for the day they both left the house, which was a very rare occurrence. I yanked the mattress and box spring out into the backyard, went back in for the wooden bed frame, doused them all in gasoline, choked down one of the mother's Basic Menthol Lights and threw the butt onto the heap. The rancid fire warmed my soul. I even burned my blankets on the fire. I presently used whatever dirty clothes I could as covers. I wanted the mother to come into my room each morning and see what a pathetic heap she'd turned me into.

That happened a lot, me waking up in my bed without actually falling asleep in it. I knew the mother put me there. Either that or she lifted me up and slung me over Racecar's wheelchair and had him roll me in there. This latter technique resulted in minimal work for the both of them so it was rapidly becoming the preferred method. I usually stayed in my room but a lot of nights, the folks would both be asleep before eight o'clock. That's when I came out of my room to do the wandering. Racecar often exhausted himself from rolling around the house continuously. Even when he kept the motor on, it was still a lot of work to navigate that machine at the high speeds he chose to travel. The mother's drinks made her doze. If I knew they were both asleep, it felt like I had the whole house to myself. Some nights I would stay up late watching cable television. Mostly I waited for them to show something with naked women in it. Sometimes I watched music videos. For whatever reason, I never masturbated unless there was a woman on the television in front of me. I always imagined it was me who was sticking Mr. Lawrence inside of the girl on the television even though they rarely showed the thing Mr. Lawrence was entering and they never showed the guys' dicks. Because the women on the television were never naked for very long, I usually had to be pretty fastidious about my beating off. Many nights I stood there behind the couch, the remote control in one hand, the other hand shoved down my pants and vigorously stroking Mr. Lawrence, trying to come before the mother moved and busted up the erection or, even worse, woke up. If she happened to come out of her mini-coma, I quickly changed the channel back to whatever she had been watching and scurried back to my room, my underwear wet against Mr. Lawrence and that whole area down there. It's a wonder no one at school ever accused me of smelling like semen.

Whenever I couldn't find an appropriate amount of nudity on the television or if I just didn't feel like playing with Mr. Lawrence, I'd see what I could find to eat. It usually wasn't much. Sometimes it would just be some mustard on a piece of bread. There was usually cheese or potato chips. Most of the food was something you had to cook and I never really knew how to use the stove. This was a process I refused to learn. I guess I was so happy some nights just to have the house almost to myself that I didn't want to go to bed and I would end up just staying awake until I collapsed somewhere, usually on the couch or the floor in front of the couch. No doubt, sitting on the floor, the fresh linen-scented disinfectant that was sprayed there daily contributed to my drowsiness.

Usually, as soon as I woke up, I jumped out of the cot. This was for the same reason as staying up late. Waking up early was, many times, better than staying up late because by then the mother had usually woken up and got in bed with Racecar. Those were the mornings I could sprawl out on the couch and masturbate with wild abandon if they were still actually showing the dirty stuff on TV. Sometimes, on less lusty mornings, I would simply stroll around the house and enjoy the blue dawn. But that morning I couldn't move. Getting out of the cot was like a physical reaction—wake up, jump out of the cot. Not being able to do that was something like not being able to breathe. My attempt to move felt like rolling into a wall of spikes. My whole body hurt. It throbbed and somewhere, beneath the swollen throbbing, a sharper pain twinged steadily along. I imagined my bones were grinding together, that's what it felt like.

Gradually, I remembered what had happened when I blacked out, the pain serving as a hyperbolic reminder. I remembered the horns. I tried to lift my arms to the top of my head to see if they were actually there, but my arms wouldn't move. It wasn't like the numb type of motionlessness I imagined paralytics enjoyed. To try and move was to be punished by the grinding, scraping bonefeel. Damn it, this pain was worse than the two beatings that had caused it.

I remembered something else, too. What was it, though?

Managing to tilt my head back, I heard the hard tapping on the wall behind me. The Wig had done it. She had strapped on the horns—giant, reddish-brown things sticking up nearly a foot in their arcing length. And I had one of them on each side of my head. Now that I knew I had the horns strapped on, I felt the thick hot leather straps running down both sides of my face in front of my ears and joining in a heavy itchy buckle that dug in under my chin. I don't know how long I let that itchy buckle drive me insane. I couldn't move my jaws around against the strap and itch it that way. The jaws had stopped working, too. And, of course, to raise my arms and attempt to scratch it would bring that grinding bonefeel on again, with its hot swarm.

Fuckness

"Fuck it," I said, the dawn's blue fingers filling my room.

I just lay there and imagined that Racecar and the Wig were roaming around the house so I wouldn't feel like I was missing out on any time to be out there alone. But that thought, for whatever reason, didn't feel right. Maybe my brain was as fucked up and out of joint as my body.

I had a sinking feeling in my stomach of a missed opportunity that was almost worse than the bonefeel. I had kind of a love-hate relationship with my room. When I was there by choice, hiding out from the parents or napping, I loved it. But whenever I felt like a prisoner in there, like when I was being punished or if the mother stayed up much later than she normally did, it seemed like the most boring place in the world.

My room was completely bare except for a poster beside my bed and a book that always changed positions around my room. The mother sold all of my toys a couple years back. She told me stupid demonshits like me didn't need to waste their time playing with toys. I cried a lot at the time but lying there at age sixteen, I was kind of glad she'd sold my toys. There probably weren't any sixteen-year-olds who still played with toys and I was sure I wouldn't have been able to get rid of them on my own.

The book was called *The Jackthief* and, at the time, it was one of the few books I'd ever read and enjoyed. Every time I'd had to do a book report, since the fifth grade, I'd done it on *The Jackthief*. Since I was in my third year of eighth grade and had had old Pearl-bottom twice, all I did was change the title. We didn't have to bring the books in or anything and I knew if she remembered the title she wouldn't remember what it was about. They just assigned book reports to make the kids be doing something, anyway. She probably just blobbed around back there and fantasized about eating kids or some fuckness like that. Maybe she fondled the dildo I was certain she kept in her desk drawer. It wasn't like they were that interested in what eighth graders were reading.

Most of the kids just picked the shortest book off of a big list anyway. But that was stupid because it was something everybody and their pedophile uncle had read so, even if they got the reading done quickly, they had to put more work into the actual report. *The Jackthief* wasn't on any kind of list so, if I'd wanted to, I could have just made something up. But I didn't do that. I read it every time I had to do a report, which made it kind of honest, I guess. Besides, it was no easy chore to read every time since it was well over 500 pages. That was one of the reasons I bought it. The drugstore had other things by Holger Blackwell, but *The Jackthief* was the longest and it made me feel like I was getting my money's worth. The mother had rolled her eyes and said it was a sick piece of trash, but she thought it was good for me to read.

The first time I read the book I was about twelve and I read it just for fun. It made me feel really smart to read a book that thick. I enjoyed the sex and violence in it, too. I must have read that book something like ten times. I had whole passages memorized but there was still something new that kind of jumped out at me when I read it.

I won't attempt to tell you the whole thing but it was sort of about this guy who marries this really pretty woman and them trying to start a new life out in a country house somewhere in New England. But it's really about the Jackthief. The Jackthief is something that is totally beyond human understanding. He's kind of like a vampire but he doesn't drink blood or any stupid fuckness like that. What he does is destroy everything else like the important shit *around* a human and, eventually, their very soul. That's how they always say it in the book. They never just say "soul." It's always their "very soul." He takes it, their very soul, away from whoever he's decided to haunt. And this main character guy, the one who's just married the pretty blond girl from New York, has been haunted by the Jackthief since he was a real little kid only it has to make some sort of bargain with people before it can take all these important things away from them. So, even though the Jackthief haunted this guy when he was a child, he couldn't do anything about it because the bargain has to be meaningful. A kid would sell his soul for a can of pop, but a grownup has to think more about it.

So the Jackthief waits until this poor guy's been married for a few years. And this guy, he's a real big blob. I think that's one of

Fuckness

the reasons I liked that book so much. It's like Blackwell knows what blobs are like and he makes this main character a classic blob and has the Jackthief be really cruel to him. Anyway, this blob is married for a few years and he starts to get bored of his pretty wife who hasn't done anything to really make him bored—"variety's the spice of life" and all that shit was this blob's philosophy, I guess. So the Jackthief creates this other woman who isn't real—she's like a ghost or something—but she's so beautiful that no man, let alone a blob, could possibly resist her. And this man's been looking for another pretty woman to put his dick into, anyway. So when the man's pretty wife is away at work, the man fucks this other woman. From the first time he sees her, he can't think of doing anything else. He goes around for a while feeling really sorry about what he did. Afterwards, though, Blackwell makes the blob feel really guilty but mainly because the fuck wasn't anything too special. The guy realizes he just needed to get it out of his system. A couple months later his wife tells him she's pregnant and he's overjoyed because he thinks the baby will bring them closer together and they live like this for a few months, blissfully happy, until his wife tells him that she doesn't think the baby is his. When he finds out that his wife might have fucked someone else, too, he gets worked up into a psychotic rage and kills his wife by throwing a blender at her head. At the pinnacle of his rage he cuts her open and drags the baby out, dancing around the house with it, "wearing the umbilical cord like a necklace." By morning, he's cleaned himself up and decides to go to work. As soon as he walks in, the boss is standing there telling him he's no longer needed, he's fired. Then the guy says, "But we're expecting a baby."

The whole book builds to this great climax when the Jackthief sends this other ghost woman back to the blob and the blob follows her out into the woods because she's told him that if he follows her then everything will be as it was before. Instead, he's dragged into the heart of the Jackthief who ends up being this ancient spirit that forms itself from the black twisted trees and the moon above, with red dripping fangs and crazy angry eyes. The Jackthief forces the man to watch his house imploding and disappearing into the ground, his wife fucking another man, images of him dancing around the house with the fetus. Then the Jackthief takes the man's soul and Blackwell has this really great description that goes on for a few pages about what it feels like when the man's soul is being ripped from his body. It ends with the man waking up on the subway in New York and all the faces in the windows streaming by look like his wife's. He wants to scream but he can't. He doesn't even remember much about who he used to be. It's almost like he's only a body, which I think is the best metaphor for somebody being a blob.

Lying there, cotridden, I didn't feel like screaming. I was starting to feel comfortable. I wondered what it would be like if I could never move again. I could lie there and try to be a blob, without the twitching or fidgeting to separate me from the rest of the blobs. I wouldn't have to go to school. The mother would bring me food because she'd feel sorry for me. I would read *The Jackthief* over and over and maybe try and get the mother to bring me more books by Blackwell. I didn't think anyone could write books like him. Maybe he had a short story collection because really, short stories were much easier. To be honest, I thought there was a lot of stuff in the big books that didn't really need to be there. Maybe I could even get a more comfortable bed to read those books in. Something adjustable.

Who was I kidding? Actually, this is probably what would happen: the parents would forget I was in the room at all, they'd think I had run away or something. I imagined lying there, getting thinner and thinner, too weak to yell. The parents would find me a few months later, one arm totally devoured, my mouth pulled back in a horrible bloodstained rictus. Or would the parents look for me at all? For some reason, I didn't sense their presence in the house. Even though they wouldn't have been awake yet. I found it odd that I couldn't even hear Racecar snoring. I got that sinking feeling in my stomach again, except this time it didn't seem so much like it was for a missed opportunity. No, it was for some other reason. But I couldn't tell what. My brain still popped and sizzled.

The only other thing in my room was a giant poster of Bobby

Fuckness

DeHaven that hung on the wall beside my cot. While reading *The Jackthief* showed me how horrible life could be, looking at the Bobby DeHaven poster made me think of how glamorous life could be. Bobby DeHaven was a true inspiration for me. Until I got that poster, he was a complete mystery to me. I'd heard his songs on the radio, when I still had one, and I loved his music. They played two or three of his songs all the time. There was something about it that really made it stick in my head. It got to where I'd be sitting in my room, all alone, and one of his songs would come on the radio and I would get up and start doing this elaborate dance routine.

One time, I was dancing to one of his songs, the one called "Little Heartmaker," when the mother opened my door and caught me at it. I think she'd been standing there a little while before I finally noticed her. I immediately stopped, waiting for some punishment to follow. She just laughed and strumbled, "What the fuck kind of fit was that?"

She called it a fit because I did that sometimes, rapidly jerking my body back and forth. Only, most of the time, there wasn't any music. My natural movements were more impulsive. Stare at someone too long and I had to whip my head to one side so I didn't go on staring. When I heard DeHaven though, I wanted to move. It was great to be able to move to his music like that. To feel something so deep inside it forces you to move. To move in response to something that came from outside of my rotten body.

"I was just dancing," I said.

"Well it looked like nothin but a buncha arms n legs."

"I don't know. It's just what I felt like doing."

"A good way to hurt yourself."

I was happy she left quickly so I could get back to the song and working out my routine. During my DeHaven phase, I entertained dreamy thoughts about being some kind of backup dancer for him but it was like I had to get that poster to find out he was real. It became nearly an obsession to find out how real he was. What did he look like? What did he sound like when he talked? What did he do when he wasn't on tour? Getting the poster was like a small window into Bobby DeHaven's world. Scoring the poster turned out to be a real hassle too.

Luckily, almost right after I heard the guy on the radio say Bobby DeHaven had a totally free fan club and then give the address, we got this assignment in school where we were supposed to write a business-type letter to some important person like a congressman or the President or some King Blob like that. And they gave us stamps and envelopes and all kinds of ideas of who to write to. I, of course, took that opportunity to write a gushing letter to Bobby DeHaven, telling him about what a big fan I was and how I was really glad he had a club and all. The letter was something like five pages long but my writing was pretty big. I hoped he had time to read it. I'm pretty sure I put something in there about my routine. About how, if he was ever in the area, I could show him. I was a little more naïve at the time. I figured he would at least sign the poster or something.

A few weeks later I got the poster in the mail. I unrolled it and was a little bit disappointed to find out that Bobby DeHaven didn't look exactly the way I expected him to, but I grew to like the way he looked. And I started imagining that person on the poster singing all those songs on the radio. There was something kind of disappointing about it, though. Like now, when I heard the music I just thought of the picture.

In the picture he was at the microphone, singing. A number of band members stood behind him but they were just a blur. I couldn't make out if he had any dancers back there or not. He had his eyes closed and looked soulful as shit. I could tell he wore some make-up on his eyelids. The way he kept his hair reminded me of some of the haircuts the kids at school were getting. Except Bobby DeHaven's looked so much better. It looked like the real thing and all those haircuts on all those blobs at school were just imitations. Bobby DeHaven probably didn't even have to get his hair styled like that. It was blond and flowed down to his shoulders in the back but the sides and top were cut short and feathered. He looked like an exotic bird. His voice was really deep so I was surprised to see how thin he was. It was like his voice came from that huge

Fuckness

Adam's apple. He was almost as thin as me and he wasn't wearing a shirt. He didn't have any of the coarse chest hair like Racecar, or like the hair that covered Bucky Swarth's stomach under that assortment of striped shirts. In the picture, he had on a pair of tight black pants that I almost didn't even notice because the background was almost completely black too, but I could see enough to tell his hips were almost womanly. He looked just like this pale floating head and body.

That Bobby DeHaven had it made, I thought. He could write his songs and sing them for a million people. I was sure he had all the girls he ever wanted and I pictured him just going down into the crowd and saying, "Yeah, that one looks good," and the girl would just go with him because he was gorgeous and they could tell by his songs what a sensitive person he was. The other person they played on the radio all the time was a woman named Pinky Lopez and I imagined Bobby DeHaven fucking her all the time, like whenever they played the same city or some fuckness like that. But I knew Bobby DeHaven probably didn't fuck people, he probably made love to them. Making love sounds like two people are creating something and I knew DeHaven probably wouldn't do anything that wasn't creative.

Bobby DeHaven made a lot of my evenings go by real quickly when I would lie there on my bed and wait and wait for them to play something by him. I didn't really care when the mother threw my radio away though because, for some reason, they stopped playing Bobby DeHaven. But I still had the poster and I would look at the poster and all those songs would come back and make me happy for as long as I could lie there. I even made a few up myself.

And that was what kept me content lying there in the dawn that morning, looking at that poster and telling myself that when I could finally get the hell out of Milltown I would run off and go on tour with Bobby DeHaven. I was pretty deluded at the time I had that thought, retarded with pain, swimming in and out of the morning blue.

I heard trundling in the hallway before the mother barged into my room and strumbled, "You have to get up for school!"

I had sort of drifted off into a slumber, like where the mind is still working but your eyes are closed. The first thing I said was, "But... the horns." And I clicked them ominously against the wall. There was no way she could expect me to go to school with those things.

"I've already wrote a note to your teacher about that." And she slapped the note down hard onto my chest, sending out those waves of pain. As she got closer to me I saw that some drool had worked its way out of her mouth, racing down one of her frownlines. That was her Drool of Fury. You know someone is mad when they cease caring about the retention of their bodily fluids.

The drool wasn't the only body fluid she was leaking. As my eyes focused, I noticed the ratty, blood-matted wig, how she seemed to be missing half her head or how it was sort of caved in or something. Last night came back to me in bright, flashbulb images that made me think of an autopsy.

"Get up! Get up!" she shouted a couple more times. Then, just as quickly as she had come, she turned to leave, her trundling dwindling toward the front of the house.

I looked at the note and this is what it said:
WALLACE HAS TOO WARE THESE HORNS FORE THE RETS OF HIS LIFE

And it was signed: "Msr. Black."

I crumpled it up and put it in the pocket of my pants.

I laughed nervously and decided to get out of the cot.

I wondered if I should move real slowly so it wouldn't hurt so much. Finally, I decided to just face the pain and do it as fast as possible and hope I got used to it. Like jumping into a pool or ripping a Band-Aid off. So I did this thing where I kind of threw myself up in the air and in the direction of the floor. It was sort of what I normally did, but this version was a little more intense. I knew I had to really put my all into it. By the time I realized what a horrible idea it was, it was way too late. My legs would barely move so I couldn't bring them up in time to get the necessary lift that I needed. I collapsed onto the carpet with a loud thump. That jolt made that horrible grinding bonefeel shoot all the way through my body and I think I screamed then. No. I *know* I screamed because it brought Racecar rolling into my room, angry as ever.

"Come on, you fuckin pansy shit. I can't eat breakfast around all that screamin. The sooner I eat my breakfast, the sooner I can get down in that basement. In here screamin like a fuckin little girl. You think I screamed when I got my legs lopped off? Huh! Do ya! You think I'd let those fuckin whiteshirts hear me screamin? Huh!"

"I don'…" I started, managing to get up on my hands and knees. My skin felt prickly, like it wanted to get up and move but my skeleton desperately wanted to slouch to the floor.

"Answer me, ass! *Answer me!*"

Then I screamed again, but not out of any sort of bodily pain this time. I was mad and the anger sort of made all the other pain go away. The anger was hot and electric, surging through my skin and veins, grabbing my bones and lifting them up.

I screamed, "Leave me alone! You're dead! Both of you! I killed you! You can't do this!"

I charged at him. Only it wasn't just him I charged at. It was everything. The hopelessness I felt inside. All the punishments of the past. Everything.

He sat blobbishly in his wheelchair, shooting an angry glance at me, wheeling the chair sideways so it blocked the door. I hit him in his giant head with my sharp, girlish elbow. The force of the blow sent the chair spinning. Racecar flew right out of it, sliding down the wall beside the door. He thrashed around on the floor, grunting and growling. I swear, at one point, I heard him growl, "Basement." That single burst of energy took it out of me. I bounced off the wall, coincidentally collapsing into his wheelchair. Before I knew it, my hands were working the levers Racecar, more and more, refused to use. I had to move the little joystick quickly back and forth to get the chair straightened. I threw it in reverse and backed it into my room a little, so I could get through the door. As I did that, I accidentally rolled over one of Racecar's stumps. Then, as I shot forward, I ran over one of his stumps again. That time it almost toppled the chair. He screamed like someone was murdering him. But he didn't really scream at all. I only imagined him screaming. He was still in the living room, exactly as I had left him. Both of them were.

And I was in the wheelchair, breathing hard, confused.

I buzzed for the front door, leaving those screams behind. If someone could have seen the look on my face, they would have thought I was the happiest crippled alive.

"Nobody's going to treat a Bobby DeHaven dancer like this. *Nobody*!"

I don't know why I said that or even, really, who I was talking to. Maybe I wanted their ghosts to know they were going to blob-bishly rot away in this house and I was heading into a world filled with money and girls and fame. I struggled for a few minutes, banging the door open against the wheelchair. But I got it open and I was outside and sure I wasn't ever stepping foot in that house again.

Chapter Seven
What Do You Want To Be When You Grow Up?

Rolling out of the house, the morning was surprisingly bright and sunny for Milltown. Even on most clear days, a dingy brown cloud usually extended its dusky wings over the horizon. I had no idea what I was going to do. I certainly wasn't in any sort of shape to go to school. I got out to the sidewalk, as though some direction I might choose would provide me with an idea. I rolled the chair down the sidewalk and over to the little alley beside our garage. I decided to just putter around the town for awhile, trying to avoid everyone.

Going one way would lead me to the southwest part of the town. The Saints River made up the town's southwestern border. That was one filthy river. Most days it was a grayish black and carried a scent of rotten decayed fish with it. These fish could be seen, white and bloated on the steep banks of the river. On its cleanest days, it was a sort of brownish green, swirls of oily color twisting on its surface.

For as many people who lived in Milltown, the town itself was surprisingly small. It didn't take up a lot of space. No matter where I decided to go, I wouldn't be far from any other area. Therefore, it didn't really matter where the hell I went.

The Historic District was located about five miles east of the river. For all the pollution and dirtiness and other fuckness, the

Historic District looked pretty nice. The few times my family had ever taken me out of town I remember liking this part of Milltown the best, when we were just driving through. If I ever had to stay there, in that shitty little town, I guess the Historic District was where I would have liked to end up. It was quiet and all the houses were brick. Although, I didn't know how valid the title of Historic District was. The houses were built just after World War I. They weren't even the oldest buildings in Milltown. It was like the founders botched their first attempt, trashing it up, and just decided to start over.

As the town sloped southwest toward the river, it got even dirtier and smelled like all hell. The area closest to the river was called the Tar District. Those were the earliest buildings. My Uncle Skad lived in the Tar District. Uncle Skad was the mother's brother and I only knew about him through stories. There were a few foggy memories the name conjured up from childhood but I didn't think I'd be able to pick him out of a crowd. The parents apparently wanted nothing to do with Uncle Skad. Racecar told me while other boys were off fighting for their country and freedom and all that fuckness, Uncle Skad sat in a cozy institution, faking a disability. The mother didn't talk to Uncle Skad because Racecar's reasons were good enough for her. The parents always said Uncle Skad lived in the "flat out most disgusting house in the Tar District." The Tar District was typically seen as the home of the lowest common denominator. The only people lower than the people who lived in the houses in the Tar District were those who couldn't even find a house, the homeless. They lived around the Tar District, waiting for a house to open up. In other words, they were waiting for someone to die. The Tar District was kind of a mythical area. It was blamed for most of the town's problems. Some said it claimed souls and when people talked about it, it was like none of the individual places had names, or the people either, for that matter. The places were referred to as "that place in the Tar District" or, sometimes, simply the Tar District, as though it were all one sprawling complex of sin and crime. The people were simply called the dregs or the bums or the hobos.

Fuckness

I really didn't know where the fuckall I was going. I think there was a part of me that knew I would eventually try to find Uncle Skad's house in the Tar District, but that seemed too depressing at the moment. So, keeping the wheelchair and, mainly, my giant horned head off the more heavily traveled roads, I stayed around the outside of the Historic District, in between that and the new large homes. The people who ran the mills and factories in Milltown built most of the new large homes. I always thought of them as "The Clean People." They were the people who could make money without getting shit on their hands. They were the people Racecar called the whiteshirts. The Clean People really knew how to play the game. If the game had a power structure, like the food chain, these were the people at the top. The only thing separating them from blobs was their overzealous obsession with cleanliness and order. In a way though, they *were* blobs. They were like superblobs, an entirely different class. They were what most lower blobs aspired to be.

By going by that area, brimming with those blobs in suits and their blobbish families, I figured I would be able to really get in touch with my anger. And I was starting to feel like I should be really angry, like back there at the house, but I didn't really feel that way at all. A sort of serenity enshrouded itself around me. I just rolled along and looked up at the sky that was actually blue and at all those huge houses with happy people living in them.

Why couldn't I have been born to one of them?

It was a tired, resigned thought, not full of any sort of anger. Only I knew it wouldn't really have done me any good to be born there. I wouldn't belong there any more than anywhere else and I knew they probably weren't happier than anybody else. They were rich people with problems of their own, even if their problems were just blobbish inventions.

Suddenly, overwhelmingly, a feeling swept over me. It was the feeling that I should, at that point, decide who I wanted to be. I fought to resist the temptation. I knew there were several types of person to become. There were those who had material wealth. Those people living in the houses up on the hills in the near distance. But what did those people really have? They were the people who made their living by controlling other people's lives. They made the rules, the policies—they hired and fired people. They decided whether or not the people below them would be eating in weeks to come. I didn't think I could ever become like that. They were the human gods, the new breed of gods who built the new nature, the machines, something for the mere mortals to spend their days toiling with. No, I could never be a god.

Then there were others, people like Drifter Ken, who seemed perfectly content to live with nothing. Like all of their happiness came from the inside and how they treated people and all that Biblical kind of fuckness. I could kind of see myself being one of those people, if I could ever get rid of the giant waves of fuckness that seemed to wash over me on a daily basis. If the fuckness would just let me be, maybe I could be a little nicer to people. If I could exterminate the red crawlies. Nearly everyone has a desire to be successful and make money but, for people like me, I knew it didn't happen that way.

There was, of course, a third class of people. The types of people that if I could have been I wouldn't have chosen. This type of person never gives up. They're not *allowed* to give up. They never rest to develop any kind of happiness on the inside because they are too busy trying to make money, trying to be one of the Clean People. So, not only do they not get to lead the life of expensive distraction, they also didn't get to rest and enjoy life.

Most of all, I didn't want to be one of those people who had no idea who they were. The type of person who would whither up and die if you gave them an empty room. Those malleable, blobbish souls who were so busy presenting the world with an image they thought the world wanted to see, that they forgot who they started out as. This type of person can be found in each of the above classes, no doubt.

After thinking that, I guess I really started wallowing in self-pity because I started thinking of all the mean things the parents had done to me and wondering if all that meant I *had* to be who I was. Like maybe I didn't have to choose what type of person I should become because it was already chosen for me. For starters, the mother gave birth to me. And I was pretty sure my genes were somehow faulty because nobody acted like I did. Even the LD kids could go to their special classes and manage to go up to the next grade. I couldn't get into those classes, though. All the tests said I was at least of average intelligence. That is, they said all of my problems were physical. Or that I chose to act the way I did. I was sure the parents had taken some pieces of the puzzle out of their respective boxes. Giving birth to me also meant I had to see them on a day to day basis.

And then there were the horrible punishments.

At first, they started out kind of subtle. I was certain, however much the parents denied it, that other kids' parents bought clothes and all kinds of stuff for them. After I started failing, the parents didn't even buy Christmas presents. They said presents cheapened the spirituality of Christmas. The parents had never struck me as very spiritual people and their lies blew up when I, on Christmas Eve one year, watched wide-eyed as they exchanged presents. Birthdays also went uncelebrated, one age sliding smoothly into the next. I doubted the parents even remembered when my birthday was. The punishments roughened in texture, growing more brutal and physical. But I kept focusing on this one thing. This one thing was what had made me finally decide Racecar was one of the blob-biest people in the world. In other words, if I hated Racecar, if that was what I was feeling, then this was the reason why.

Ever since I turned ten, it had been my job to mow the lawn. The yard was easy to mow, being equal parts grass and dirt, but the family had had the same lawnmower for as long as I could remember and something new would go wrong with this lawnmower every year. Racecar obviously couldn't mow the grass unless he could find a way to strap a blade under that chair and when the lawnmower developed all those special tricks you had to know to operate it the mother decided it just wasn't ladies' work and that I was plenty old enough to start mowing it myself.

The only thing Racecar had to do was show me how to start it and turn it off. The pull cord that had come connected to it had been ripped off, so the father improvised with a piece of thick yellow rope that was knotted at both ends. To start it, he had to wrap this rope around some cylindrical thing at the top of the engine and pull. It took him about ten more pulls than it had before the pull cord was dislocated. To turn it off, you had to take hold of these two naked wires and touch them to this hot part of the engine and keep them held there until the damn thing sputtered to a stop. This seemed kind of dangerous because the lawnmower didn't have a gas cap and the strenuously bucking exercise of starting it caused gas to slosh everywhere and, when you touched those wires to that metal, there were usually some sparks. I waited for that lawnmower to turn me into an instant burn victim. Then I would creep people out even more with my baby pink, eyebrowless face.

I stood beside him, both of us looking down at the gimpish lawnmower, a grime-covered gas can sitting beside it. Racecar made me bend down and wrap the rope around the top of the engine and hand the end of the rope to him.

"Now all you gotta do is give it a yank." He pulled violently up on the rope, his wheelchair shifting a little in the grass.

He pulled on the rope a few more times, getting more and more frustrated with each pull.

"Now you try it, you little ass. A growing boy should be able to do more than an old cripple."

I always hated it when he called himself a cripple. It made him sound so much more innocent than he really was.

I wrapped the rope around the top of the engine and gave it a yank, my hands slick with sweat. My right hand slipped off the rope, the back of my hand smacking Racecar in the forehead. I burst out laughing. I'm not sure whether it was the accidental cuffing or the laughter, but Racecar was furious. He snatched the rope off the lawnmower, grunted, and smacked me on the arm with the knot at the end of the rope.

I accidentally shouted, "Fuck," and he belted me again on the other arm. That was the worst pain I'd ever felt at that time in my life. The pain was red hot and lingering. I imagined it felt like being hit by a bullet. Racecar rolled back to the house. I silently wished

Fuckness

the uneven yard would pitch him out of his wheelchair. I told myself if that happened I would hover over him, sadistically belting him with that rope until he was a giant welt. Then I would dance around him singing a song I'd invented for just an occasion called, "I Got Legs and You Don't."

"You're on your own, you little shit, and you better have the whole fucking thing mowed before dark," he called over his shoulder. To my disappointment, he made it to the house unpitched.

I managed to get the job done and, by the time I was finished, there was a giant purple knot painted on each of my arms. If it wasn't for being able to rest them on the lawnmower's handle, I don't think I could've even kept them held up.

I didn't know why that, of all things, had come to me on my day of escape and then I had an even crazier thought. I thought about that piece of shit lawnmower I'd never have to use again and that piece of rope, now blackened, that I always tied around the handle when I was finished and then I thought about that gas can and how the garage always smelled full of gas. I thought about what a dry day it was.

Then I had a truly awful idea. Sometimes thinking too much led me to those truly awful, ugly ideas.

The parents were already dead. I was already a murderer. Why should I give them the satisfaction of a decent burial? Why should any other blob think I was a murderer, that I hadn't died right alongside them?

I was wrong when I thought I would never be going back to that house. I would go back this one last time, I told myself, and I wouldn't even have to go inside.

I turned the wheelchair around and headed back home.

Chapter Eight
The Confession

Starting back home, and knowing full well what I planned to do, I decided I didn't have the proper resources. I briefly thought about trying to use the sparks from the lawnmower but that would be noisy and there was the whole creepy burn victim thing. I would need matches or a lighter, any incendiary device would do, and I knew exactly where to go. I turned the wheelchair around. I started back the way I came, figuring that would kill more time. Right after I'd had the first ugly thought, another one blossomed, almost as bad as the first. Timing figured in heavily with the second idea. The parents would always be there but, after the second idea was fulfilled, I knew I would have to leave town. My work would be done. I'd only been out of the house for a couple hours and I was already starting to feel like a different person. My thoughts seemed clearer. From the usual low-grade whumming I never really noticed, another voice was making itself heard. Only it didn't seem like a voice as much as it did a feeling, a tug, some form of direction.

I would start back the way I came, branching off near the house so I could go by the park and see Drifter Ken. I felt like I *had* to say bye to him. It seemed like he was one of the only people who'd ever been nice to me and I figured he was sure to have matches or a lighter. Something for the job.

On the way there, I thoroughly enjoyed the wheelchair. For a relatively lazy person like myself, it sure beat the hell out of walking. I just rolled right along in the crisp air and looked up at that

Fuckness

blue sky and those nice old houses and if my head and neck weren't so sore I could have thrashed around and had a great time thinking my thoughts. When you're tall and gangly, sometimes you have to concentrate on walking. The wheelchair allowed me to listen to that new feeling, going where it told me to go. Until the discovery of the wheelchair, skipping had been my favorite mode of transportation because, when I skipped, I didn't have time to think any thoughts at all and, most of the time, that was best. And, realistically, that would have been impossibly far to skip.

A few cars rolled past real slow. I could tell the people inside were staring at me. Hell, I would have stared too. It's not every day you see someone, hideous under regular circumstances, with horns on his head. Like the horns drew attention to all the rotten fuckness below. I imagined them edging their holy cars over to the other side of the road because the horns said I was evil and they didn't want anything to do with evil and rottenness. I was probably lucky it wasn't the time of day when the cruel high schoolers were out cruising around. I don't know why it didn't occur to me to just go ahead and take the stupid things off. It was like there was something inside of me that wanted to be punished. I just kept my head down, trying not to make any eye contact.

When I first got to the park, I stayed behind the hedges. A cop was talking to Drifter Ken. Even though Drifter Ken didn't normally talk about his problems, I'd heard him complain about the cops on a few occasions.

"The cops in this here town. *Shit*. I'm just an ol man who likes to sit down on this here ol bench with compulsive regguhlarity and they always wanna give me shit about it."

Drifter Ken was amazing. If it weren't for that something inside of me, that feeling or calling or whatever, that thing that yelled at me and told me I had to get out of Milltown, I could have seen myself living with Drifter Ken. Well, the *living* part was kind of in question, since I wasn't sure if he had a house or not. There was just something so unblobbish about him I knew we'd get along fine. Of course, there was always the possibility he would think I was a blob.

As I sat in my chair watching him talk to that cop, I could tell he was making the cop break up. I heard the cop laughing all the way over there in the bushes and, before walking away, he gave Drifter Ken a pat on the arm as if to say, "You keep em laughing, Drifter Ken."

The cop got in his car and started up toward the school. I was far enough off the road to where he wouldn't notice me. I didn't even really stop to think I could be the person the cop was looking for. That would be one of the worst things in the world, a major setback, that cop dragging me back into the school. He would smile at Pearlbottom. A secret smile that said they were both members in the society of keeping kids' lives joyless and free of fun. "I found a little piece of trash for yuh," he'd say. "Didn't know whether to take him here or straight back to hell." No, I figured I was pretty safe. Who was going to harass a crippled boy, anyway?

I waited for him to vanish out of sight and pulled around the hedgerow, wheeling toward Drifter Ken. I could tell he didn't know who the hell I was when he first saw me coming. He looked hard and squinted those huge eyes. His top lip raised up and I could see those teeth getting bigger and bigger as I pulled closer to him. I was sure Drifter Ken dreaded new kids coming around the park. That was just someone else to go home and tell warped malicious lies about him.

Finally he recognized me.

"Hey hey, Wally Black! How's my favorite eighth grader?"

"I'm okay. How are you?"

"Oh, I'm doin all right, I guess. If the fuckin cops'd get off my back I'd be doin a helluva lot better. Why don't you tell me somethin to brighten up my day. School done started. You got time today, ain't ya?"

"A little, yeah," I said.

"Well, shoot then."

I did have the time, sure, but I didn't really have a joke in my head. I improvised with the first thing I could think of.

"Knock knock."

"Who's there?"

Fuckness

"Beats."

"Beats who?"

"Beats just forgot his name."

Drifter Ken cracked up. "Now," he said, "that was pretty good, a real classic, but the next time you say it, I think it's s'posed to be, 'Beats *me*, I just forgot *my* name.'"

"How could someone forget their own name?"

"Beats me."

We both laughed at that, Drifter Ken reaching down and poking me on the shoulder. That's what he always did when he got to laughing—reached right down and gave me a good jab. For some reason, that always made me laugh harder. This time it kind of hurt.

"Say, you gotta setta wheels."

"Yeah."

"You get paralyzed or somethin."

"No, just a little sore."

"Oh yeah, what happened?"

I really hadn't expected to have to explain what happened to anybody. I kind of fell silent for a while, searching for the answers to that question. I wanted to just give him a summary, tell him a few things. He probably wasn't interested in hearing all of it. But the more I tried to assemble a few logical events, the more they came apart, making little sense.

I broke down and told him everything. I realized I'd been dying to tell somebody, probably because I didn't think anybody would actually ask. I broke down a lot, like when I had the crying jags at school sometimes and Pearlbottom would drag me out into the hall. But usually when I broke down, I never *told* anybody anything. I could never find the right words. This time felt a lot different. I found myself becoming fluid, I wanted to make him *see* everything that happened and then I thought that wouldn't make a lot of sense either if I couldn't also make him *feel* what I was feeling at the time. Sometimes it felt like I carried this giant weight around. Sometimes I visualized like a giant rock or cement block. Other times, it felt like a huge sad wave of melancholy. Whatever it was, it inevitably came down on me, crushing me into innumerable pieces, that feeling of yellow-purple soulhurt emerging from the rubble. That feeling had loosed itself on me as I stood there talking away.

Drifter Ken listened to everything, towering above me and sucking away on those Camels. Throughout me telling him this, he became my audience. I realized a little bit of what Bobby DeHaven must have felt, except mine was just an audience of one. I guess, in a way, Drifter Ken had always been my audience but, before, with the jokes, I always felt like I was trying to entertain him. Not only that, but the jokes were always something somebody else had made up or some fuckness like that.

When I got finished, I stopped and waited for what Drifter Ken would say.

He was silent for a moment and then he said, "Well, that Mary Lou's a real cocktease. And that Bucky Swarth, well, he sounds like he's got some real weight problems. And sometimes people with weight problems get real mean and hateful. You know what to say to him if he gives you any more shit? You say, 'I bet your tits is bigger'n Mary Lou's.' That oughtta make him real mad. Someone's gonna beat the shit outta you like that, you gotta get smart and fight back with your tongue. If they're gonna do it anyway, you might as well give em a reason to do it."

Drifter Ken always gave me the best advice. When most people gave me advice, it was just a polite way of telling me what to do. I always got mad when someone tried to tell me what to do and then I'd make damn sure not to do what they asked me. This usually, in turn, made them mad for not listening to them. People only told me what to do so their lives would be easier, anyway. It never made me mad when Drifter Ken gave me advice.

"I'm real sorry about tradin that sucker for nothin."

"Aw, that's okay, I can get you another sucker. Besides, it doesn't sound like it weren't for nothin. You gotta quick feel of that snatch didn't ya?"

I didn't know what he meant. Given a few moments, I'm sure I could have figured it out. I'd just never heard it called that before.

"Her privates, boy. You gotta quick feela them didn't ya?"

In my crying jag I must have told him *every* little detail. I thought

Fuckness

I'd left that part out. I nodded.

"Then it weren't for nothin. You remember what that felt like and I'll tell you this now: the woman's snatch is a powerful thing. You'll feel its power for the rest of your life. Shit, a *sucker*. You should be lucky *all* you lost was a sucker. I've lost a house and two kids to the power of that fuckin thing."

I imagined one of those women on the television spreading her legs and sucking objects into that patch of hair. Only, it hadn't felt like there was much hair on Mary Lou's.

"You say those horns is some kind of punishment?"

I nodded.

"You think your mom'd get mad if I take em off?" Then he paused, chuckled, and said, "I guess that doesn't matter much now, does it?"

"Guess not," I said.

"Well, where ya goin?"

"I don't know. I have to leave Milltown. I think I'm gonna try and go see my Uncle Skad over in the Tar District. After that, I'm not really sure. I gotta get out of Milltown."

Drifter Ken smiled. "Ah, the Tar District." Then he became serious. "You be careful in those parts. We'll be sorry to see ya go round here. But a man's gotta do whatta man's gotta do."

Yeah, fuck it, I thought.

"So why don't you let me take those foolish things off?"

He reached under my chin and I could smell his hands. They smelled like one of the mother's ashtrays. Smelling ashtrays had been a hobby of mine a few years before. Like a lot of other things about myself it was something I couldn't really explain. It was merely another frivolous desire in a life of necessity.

The skin got pinched up in the buckle as his giant fingers unfastened it.

"Here we go," he said and pulled the strap through the buckle. Then, "Holy shit."

"What?"

He reached out and slapped at the left horn. His hand made a dull sound like *whap* and I felt my scalp twitch, the horn tugging against it.

"What?" I repeated, fearing the worst.

"Hate to tell you this, but it looks like them horns might just be stayin on a little longer."

I broke down and started crying again. At that moment, I really did feel like a demon. A giant horned demon. If it wasn't the strap holding those things on, then I figured it must be some other force. I reached up and felt the sides of my head. My worst fear had come true. The straps were nowhere to be felt. They had vanished. Simply disintegrated. I was sure that had to mean I was evil. It had to be some kind of punishment from God or something. That made the evil a little more meaningful. I mean, I'd been called evil by all sorts of people but I just kind of dismissed it. This felt like God had finally ordained me as a certifiable demon.

I was able to compose myself and ask Drifter Ken, "Do you think I'm a demon?"

"Naw, you're a real sweet kid. There *are* demons out in that world though, and I think one of em mighta put his horns on you." I hadn't really thought of it like that. Weren't there saints who got struck with stigmata?

There were a few moments of silence, Drifter Ken taking deep drags off his cigarette, staring off at the horizon. "Hey," he said, "they look fine. They give you a sort of... *ostentatious flair* you ain't never had before. Not that you wasn't fine before but they add..." he groped for the right phrase. "Shit, they're like a new pair of shoes or a fancy shirt of somethin. Maybe a pair of tight pants. They're just... unconventional, that's all."

I liked the sound of "ostentatious flair."

"Really?" I asked.

"Yeah. They're kinda neat. Make you look tough."

That made me feel a little better, seeing them in this new light. After all, if some magic or force had made those straps disappear, didn't that mean there was also some kind of *good* magic out there?

"You know," Drifter Ken said, "one time I had a melanoma— it's like a huge moley growth of some kind—growin on my forehead right between my eyes. When I had that thing I always walked aroun feelin embarrassed as shit so I finally saved up enough money to go have that motherfucker lanced. They did it and I looked perfectly normal afterwards but I kind of missed the growth. I kind of missed the people lookin at me, you know. At least I was known for somethin."

I figured he probably made that up just to make me feel better. I couldn't see Drifter Ken with a giant thing growing off his head. That just wasn't him. Besides, I didn't really want to be known for anything unless it was going to be something glamorous like dancing for Bobby DeHaven or some fuckness like that. I appreciated his attempt to cheer me up, anyway.

Suddenly, I was overcome with the feeling that I was running out of time. The doomwave unexpectedly surged over me and I remembered one of the reasons I had come by the park in the first place.

"I've gotta be gettin outta here," I said. "Say, uh, do you happen to have some matches I could have." I hated asking for things. I never minded people giving me things, but I absolutely hated having to ask for them. I'd go around for the rest of my life feeling like I owed that person something. But I was running out of time and I knew I might never see Drifter Ken again and what I needed *was* an absolute necessity.

"All I got's this one lighter. I tell you what, you let me light one cigarette with it and I'll just keep on lightin the next one from the one before. That way you can take the lighter."

"What if one of your cigarettes goes out?"

"I'll be fine. You consider that a goin away present."

He lit his Camel, bent down, and gave me a hug. I was glad he gave me a going away present. Now it felt like I *had* to get out of Milltown.

Chapter Nine
Burning Down The House

I got back to Walnut in no time at all. I stayed on the opposite side of the street from the house. If an outsider paid any attention to the cars lining the street, they might think they were living twenty years ago. An abnormal amount of the cars had the cardboard temporary tags taped to them. Most of the cars would expire before the thirty-day tags. I guess I kept to the other side of the road to further dismiss myself from the house. I didn't have to worry about the parents catching me.

I still had this paranoid feeling like maybe *somebody* was looking for me. Like the school or the police or something. It was ridiculous, of course. The parents rarely left the house so they didn't really have anywhere to be missing from and I knew the school would probably rather not have me there. I knew for a fact, when I was absent, Pearlbottom never reported it.

My mind started playing tricks on me again. I didn't know why it wouldn't just leave me the fuck alone. I began to think maybe the parents weren't really dead. After all, how much faith could I actually place in my mind? Wasn't it just that morning that I had imagined them alive?

I remembered the note the mother had slapped onto my chest.

I stuck my hand in my pocket and pulled out the crumpled piece of paper.

Something had been written on it, but I couldn't tell what it was.

Fuckness

Not that I really had anything to worry about, anyway. They kept all the blinds drawn and usually only came outside to get the mail in the evening. Even to do that, all the mother had to do was open the door and stick a meaty hand outside. Racecar couldn't get the mail, of course. He couldn't reach it. And I knew they wouldn't be on the lookout for me. At least not very actively, anyway. Racecar would say something like, "The little shit gets what he deserves." And the mother would strumble, "If he thinks I'm gonna quit my stories to look for his sorry demon ass, he's got another thing comin."

I waited for a few minutes there on the other side of the street, hidden behind a battered black Buick nearly the size of a schoolbus. The house looked quiet. I was struck with the feeling that, through all the fuckness that had happened in the house, it probably looked quiet from the outside, the blinds shut against the world, the steam from the furnace serenely drifting at an unchanging pace toward the sky. If alive, I wondered what Racecar was doing without his wheelchair. Did he have a spare? Did he just roll around on the floor? That was something I could picture him doing. Rolling around on the floor, grunting and drooling. Who cared? Fuck it. Let them rot.

I made a break for the garage, going as fast as the wheelchair allowed, its hum heightening my sense of paranoia. The garage was in even worse shape than the house. There wasn't a fleck of paint left on it, just gray rotting wood, gaping with neglect. Racecar always insisted I lock everything inside with a padlock when I put the lawnmower away but I never could understand why. With those huge holes all over it, anyone could probably pull down an entire wall with just their bare hands. Those holes used to bother me when I was a kid because Racecar always acted like all of our really important stuff was in that garage and it bothered me that someone could just walk in and steal it. It took me a while to realize we didn't have any important stuff, that's why we lived where we did. Racecar was just pretending to have important stuff, which was what most people did.

At first I thought I'd have to get at the inside barehanded, maybe yank the lock right out of the soft wood, and I kind of panicked because I thought that would take more time and might cause enough of a commotion to bring Racecar or the Wig outside. Then I remembered he always kept those keys on a little ring in a pouch on the side of his wheelchair. I reached down to reassure myself they were still there.

I edged up to the garage and grabbed the cold steel lock in my hand. Even standing out there in the cool fresh air I could smell that gasoline smell from inside. Years of it being splashed upon the cement floor, sinking in, greasing it up. The smell had nauseated me before, but now it filled me with a sense of purpose. Hopefully, the little gas can would be full. Before then, I hadn't even thought about whether or not it would have any gas in it. I hadn't had to mow the grass yet that year. It most probably wouldn't, I assumed. I took the keyring out of the pouch and started trying the keys. There were about fifteen keys on the ring and I tried to go as fast as I could, wondering why in the hell we had all of those fucking keys. Had they saved the keys from every place they'd ever lived, every car they'd ever driven? The seventh key fit and I struggled to twist the barrel around in the lock, my hands shaking. All the while I could hear Racecar's voice in my head, "It's not that hard, ass." The barrel caught, turned, and I pulled the lock apart with ease.

The garage door wasn't one of the modern types most people would think about when they thought about a garage. Not that I thought anyone did much of that, thinking about garage doors. No, ours was just two standard doors, joining in the middle. One of them swung to the left, the other to the right. None of that sliding up and back into the garage bullshit. I opened the door on the right just enough to reach in and grab the can. I didn't bother shutting it. After the horrible thing I was about to do, I didn't figure it would make a whole lot of difference.

Wild, unkempt hedges grew all across the front of the house, thick and bushy. I rolled over to the hedges in front of the kitchen. That way they wouldn't be able to see my now incriminating silhouette from the living room where they spent most of their time. I didn't think they'd mistake me for the mailman or the meter read-er with those horns on my head. There was a moment when I wanted to open the door. To just peek inside and make sure they were really dead. But it would be like sticking my hand in a bear trap. I poured the gasoline all over the hedges, scattering the gallon-can around as much as I could. It didn't go very far.

I'd kept the lighter sitting in my lap. I grabbed it up and gave it a few flicks. It occurred to me I had never even held a lighter in my hands before. The mother always used matches to light her cigarettes. I flicked it and flicked it, my thumb slipping off. I'd developed a nervous sweat. After it felt like a blister was forming on my thumb, the damn thing started. I held it out to the hedges as slowly as possible so its small flame wouldn't go out. Once I got the flame to the bush I had to keep holding it there and it started to get really hot but I didn't want to let go of it again. Plus I was starting to get even more nervous. A few moments had determined the difference between someone merely catching me skulking around outside the house and them catching me skulking around outside the house while holding a lighter to the precariously gasoline-drenched hedges. It was the difference between truancy and arson. I kept imagining I could hear the mother walking toward the door, strumbling to herself. I even imagined I heard Racecar in there, growling and rolling around on a new wheelchair. A fast one, I told myself, picturing a maliciously modern contraption with machine-gun turrets on the handles.

No ,no, I told myself. *They're dead. Dead. Dead!*

And just as I imagined having some sort of wheelchair race with Racecar rapidly gaining and firing away, when I didn't think I'd be able to hold the hot lighter any longer, the shrubs went up— *whoosh!*—and scared the shit out of me.

I crammed the lighter into the wheelchair's little side pocket and headed back out to the road as fast as the motor allowed, which was about as fast as someone with polio could jog. I would have abandoned the wheelchair and ran, I was so scared, but my body still had that grinding bonefeel. Blood pounded in my ears, a horrible whumming ricocheting around. Now, not only was I just afraid of the parents catching me, I was also afraid of someone else seeing me. I could see the headline in some low rent tabloid: "Boy Demon Tries to Catch Neighborhood on Fire and Make the World His Personal Hell... *After* Murdering Parents!"

When I finally got to the end of Walnut and looked back, the fire was burning pretty nicely. The flames licked up against the window, spreading over toward the other side of the house. I thought maybe I should have set the fire around back where they wouldn't notice it so quickly. So they'd have less time to put it out. But I knew there wouldn't be any putting it out. The parents were dead as dead could be and the neighbors surely realized it was more economically feasible to let the shithouse burn.

Looking at the other three blackened shells on the street, I wondered if the same thing had happened to them. Was it bumbling crackheads or disgruntled youth?

I figured it was probably somewhere in between.

I took a deep breath, smelling the sweet smoke of the rancid house, and headed for Milltown Middle School.

Chapter Ten
Let Revenge Set You Free

By the time I got to the school, the eighth graders were out for their recess, trudging along on that sad playground. I turned toward the playground, going right by the school and hoping none of the teachers saw me. Most of the kids were too busy with their running and their games to notice.

I spotted Bucky Swarth, his gang thuggishly gathered there around him, smoking. I could tell by the way they vampirishly leaned in toward him that they were really interested in something he was saying. I pulled onto the playground. I rolled right up there to their circle just like I wasn't afraid of anything at all. Only I *was* afraid. I was terrified as all hell. And I sat there in that wheelchair, twitching and squirming, trying not to hoot or call out. I wondered what it was about that school that made me more retarded than anywhere else.

This is what Swarth was saying:

"Shit, man, I had er all leaned up against a fuckin tree n shit n got er pants down an er shirt up n shit an this fuckin train starts comin n she gets real nervous. I tole the bitch to fuckin shut the fuck up n shit cause that fuckin train weren't stoppin fer nothin so there weren't no fuckin way we was gonna get in trouble n shit. So she starts sayin stupid fuckin shit like they's gonna see her tits n pussy n shit n I just tole her to shut the fuck up. I took her fuckin unnerwear off 'n pushed er fuckin bra all up n shit. Man, them tits was fuckin huge. You think them look big now, you shoulda fuckin seen em thout a shirt..."

And I wheeled my wheelchair further up in there, just like I was a member of their gang or something and, instead of hooting some tune that was in my head, I blurted out: "I bet you have bigger tits than Mary Lou."

"Shit, man, this weren't fuckin Mary Do-You Lou. It was an *older* fuckin chick." He said that just like he didn't know who said what I said.

"I bet your tits were bigger than *hers*, then. Did the guys on the train see *your* tits?" It was like I wanted the beating. Like one of my main goals in life was hospitalization.

This last thing I said stopped him cold. He turned and fixed those boiling hate eyes on me. I didn't know why I said it. I'd never said anything like that to any of the bullies. I knew I was going to get the shit beat out of me but I had a bigger plan and that was all I could think about. The fear was there, black and intense, but it didn't matter.

"Wally Black," he said. "You look like a fuckin retard ith them horns. And what's ith the wheelchair?" He turned to his friends and said, "I beat the walk right out of him." Then he turned back to me. "Didn't you learn yer lesson yesterday, you piece uh shit?"

One of his friends tipped the wheelchair over and I fell out onto the grass. As soon as I went down, Swarth was right on top of me, working me over with those brass knuckles. I heard them slapping the skin and felt reverberations of pain all over my body. This pain wasn't quite as bad as the day before because I knew what kind of pain to expect. What I did to the parents last night told me I could do just about anything if I got mad enough and I wasn't mad yet. I didn't really have a reason to be mad. The red crawlies hadn't come yet. What I had said to Swarth was mean and completely unprovoked. I deserved the beating I got. I almost wanted it to stop so I wouldn't have to follow through with my plan. I almost wanted one of the teachers to come out and say, "Oh my Lord, you stop beating on that cripple. He's just a... a *cripple*."

But it didn't stop. Swarth kept beating down. And then the anger was back, the red crawlies, entering my veins with a liquid electric rush. The beating wasn't really what caused the anger. It was what the rest of his gang was doing. They were all kicking at the wheelchair and pulling it apart. One of the larger ones kept picking it up over his head and slamming it back down on the ground. And they laughed ridiculous animal sounds while they did it. All I could think about was Racecar. And that was the only time I think I ever felt sorry for him. That wheelchair was the only thing he ever did. I had stolen it, but at least it was intact, a sort of memorial. But it didn't matter to them. They just smashed and smashed and smashed like it didn't have any meaning or use or value at all.

I rolled out from under Swarth's thundering fists. I didn't know if I'd be able to stand up or not so I just kept rolling.

Mary Lou noticed what was happening and came over to watch. I heard her yelling, "Kick the shit out of him, Bucky!" And then, taunting, "Mo*lest*er! Mo*lest*er!"

A couple of his gang members grabbed me under the arms and pulled me up. The wheelchair was totally demolished, silver pieces scattered all over the playground. Swarth was bent over, his ass stretched tight in those dark blue jeans, his bowels roiling. A gang member grabbed each horn and shoved my nose right up against that fat ass. Everything was familiar. The new smell of the denim. The sounds of the fart starting. This one sounded strained. It was going to be a long one. I knew I couldn't take it. That smell would have killed me. I stumbled back and thrashed my head from side to side, shaking the gang members off. Then I crouched down and sprang forward, driving my right horn toward that deadly squeaking sound. The sound stopped. It was like a balloon suddenly running out of air, twisted shut at the opening.

Bucky Swarth screamed. It was a horrible sound, high- pitched and girlish.

I had gone face first into the ground when Bucky went down and I couldn't see anything. My head hit something small and hard. All I could smell was grass, dirt, and the metallic tang of pollution and blood. I got ahold of everything I could and stood up, twisting my head as I did so, remaining bent over at the waist, still attached to Swarth. I looked down and saw the lighter Drifter Ken had given me. Blood trickled down onto it. I had a feeling Swarth was bleeding a lot more than I was. He kept screaming as the tip of my horn scraped around on his insides. I stepped back, yanking the horn out with a sickening suction sound, grabbed that assblood-stained lighter, and took off running for the road. That anger made me numb to all the pain and soreness. That feeling inside me told me it was time to get out of there.

Swarth screamed: "My asshole! My asshole!"

I imagined the other kids on the playground were cheering me on as I ran faster than I ever had. In actuality, they had all gathered into a mob and taken up the chant, "Molester." I imagined Swarth's hand clasped around his sizable buttocks, blood seeping between the fingers. I ran as fast as I could. It felt like I was running toward some unknown freedom. Into the blueness of the day. Before, it wasn't like it mattered how hard I ran from all the bullies because I would still end up in that house with the family every night, only to be bullied some more.

But that day, I ran toward the river, toward the Tar District, toward anything at all and all I could imagine was the parents' diseased house burning down to the ground and Bucky Swarth's asshole, impaled on my horn like a trophy.

Chapter Eleven
Attack of the Clean People

It didn't feel like there was anything I could do but run. I slowed down once to look back over my shoulder. Black clouds gathered up over the Korl Brothers factory. The March weather was about ready to turn from pleasant and warm to downright violent and cold. I didn't care. It didn't matter. I wasn't afraid of the stormsmoke of the dead, coming to take me with them.

I felt weightless!

I waited for the coming storm, longed for it to come and crackle electricity into my steps. I longed for its freezing rain to beat down and further numb my sore skin, to calm the raging red anger that made me go go go.

I didn't know what waited for me at Uncle Skad's house. Whatever it was it had to be better than the house I'd just left. I wasn't even really sure if I could find Uncle Skad's, exactly. I left it up to that inner feeling to guide me. There was no way Uncle Skad and his house could live up to the expectations I had already set for them. In my mind, Uncle Skad's had become some sort of way station, a middle point, somewhere between here and there—but also a beginning. I thought maybe once I got to Uncle Skad's, I could take some time to rest and cleanse my mind, so I could focus on what lay ahead. It was still in Milltown, true, but it was the Tar District, at the very fringes of not only the physical town but so-called "decent society," also.

The horns were heavy on my head but I imagined them slicing

out the direction I was going like the rudders of a boat. My lungs burned. My shoes were splitting, the Velcro barely holding, and I knew there was no turning back. I felt great.

Once the school and the factory were out of sight, I stopped to catch my breath. I felt like I *could* stop. When the wind blew real hard around the factories and all that fuckness, it had a way of dragging the pollution and the foul smells away and I smelled the air the way it was supposed to smell, the way some other town smelled it. It was nice, trotting along there on the side of the road. Beneath the wind, the air was almost balmy, hinting of the summer to come. Then the wind would kick up, reminding me of the winter left behind and bringing with it those deep black, ominous storm clouds. I knew there was no hope of making it to the Tar District before the storm hit. I doubted I'd even be there before dark. And I didn't feel like rushing. In one fell swoop, I had rid myself of the restrictions of the parents and the school. Maybe it was just giddiness but it was a feeling I'd only felt once before when I was seven or eight.

It was a little while after the father lost his legs. We had had to move from our much nicer house in Farmertown to that dump on Walnut. Shortly after moving there, the mother said someone would be visiting and I'd have to be on my best behavior. It took me a while to realize the someone was a social worker. It was the mother's theory that some do-good, wealthy housefrau had reported them. Later, there were investigations into that. The logic was that this rich family of mill owners wanted that land for another mill or, their newest endeavor, low income apartments, and they figured if they could get all of those houses condemned, they could buy the land good and cheap. And if they built low income apartments there, it was guaranteed the rent would be on the government's tab. The social services were obligated to investigate every claim and they had called the parents to tell them they would like to arrange a meeting.

At the time, I didn't know if the mother was being honest or if she was just trying to scare the hell out of me. She told me they might try and take me away from them. I'd never been more terrified in my life. Sure, I had my moments of wishing I lived with a different family, but what kid didn't. More than anything, I was comfortable with the parents. As a child, there was no feeling better than love and comfort. I imagined myself living with another family. I would be like a pet, exciting and new for a few months, little more than a burden after a year. The thought of being taken away from my parents occupied my every thought. Every night, it felt like my insides were scoured by horrible nightmares that, upon waking, I could never remember.

I know from what I've told you so far, you probably think that house was a terrible place to live but it didn't really get like that until after I started failing and the mother had her stroke. I didn't just feel bad for myself, either. I felt bad for my parents. Now I get the impression that having the social services called on them was one of the things that really broke the parents down. Like after that they felt like nothing they ever did would be good enough. From my room, I heard the mother asking the father what they were going to do if the services took me. I heard the sobs from my bedroom. Those were the only times I could remember her crying when it wasn't out of anger.

I'm sure she was overwhelmed. The house was truly a shambles but it was the only thing they could afford and it had come that way. The shambles wasn't something they created. Since the father was pretty much completely incapable of doing anything physical they had planned to put back a little bit of money and have it fixed piece by piece. Once they knew they had to get it fixed quickly, they sold everything worth anything. It wasn't long before we were living in a house devoid of records, stereo, or television. The mother also sold the few pieces of jewelry she had. "Well," she said, "we'll just tell them we're religious." The mother ended up buying the cheapest supplies and doing the labor by herself.

The whole house was in a state of extreme tension. The father was essentially resigned. First he'd lost his legs and now he was threatened with losing his child and he didn't really have any control over either event. The mother spent her days smoking furiously, running around the house and painting, stuffing the holes in the drywall, and cleaning years' worth of grime off the windows. I mostly stayed in my room, too anxious to do much of anything but scurry around and make sure my bed was made and all of my toys were in the *exact* correct location.

It was around that time, in the scared loneliness of night, that I started thinking of the social services as the Clean People. They were the first Clean People, the enforcers amidst the superblobs. I imagined them pulling up in a white, windowless van, a cage separating the cargo area from the cab so the feral children they dragged from these filthy homes couldn't attack the driver. They would get out of the van, a whole herd of them dressed in sparkling white jumpsuits, white gloves on their hands. They would undoubtedly hook me up to some form of lie detector.

I wasn't exactly right but I was on the right track. Two of them showed up, both women. They drove a clean, new white car and they were outrageously overdressed. I guess that was so they could feel slightly better than the people they were investigating. Laughing, they knocked on the door.

When the mother opened the door, their smiles were gone completely. The Clean People exchanged a volley of pleasantries with the mother and she invited them in. When it was just us, home alone, the mother was a very powerful woman, never failing to speak her mind. It was horrible to see her like this, wringing her hands and stumbling to get out of those other women's way.

"Well, I guess you're here to have a look around," she said.

"We received a complaint," the younger woman said. "We have to follow up on every complaint made." The older woman was letting the younger woman do the talking.

"I'm Mrs. Jones," the older woman said, holding out her hand. The mother wiped her hands off on her dress and shook hands with the woman. "And this is Mrs. Johnson. I'm training her, so she'll be conducting the session."

"Of course," the mother said. "I'm Sadie, that's my husband Carl over there in the wheelchair and this is Wallace."

"Hello, Wallace," the women said simultaneously and I was certain those smiles they flashed were nearly predatory. "Hello, Clean

Fuckness

People. Goodbye, Mom and Dad," I thought.

I sat there on the couch while the Clean People searched the house. Every muscle was drawn tight. It took a lot of effort to breathe and I felt like I was going to throw up. I yearned for a drink of water.

It seemed like they looked around for hours. I imagined them turning over every object in the house, looking for traces of drugs or blood or, hell, I didn't know, whatever it was that made people bad. But my parents weren't bad. Not yet, anyway. I wanted to tell the Clean People this. I felt like my tight little nerves could snap at any moment and I would have to run up to the Clean People, letting their shampoo and perfume smell they dragged with them envelop me, and tell them the parents weren't bad people and even if they were a little bit bad that was okay because I liked it there and didn't want to go anywhere in that little white car.

I had been digging my nails into my thighs so hard both my fingers and my legs were hurting. I looked over at the father, when he was just a gimp and not so angry. He stared straight ahead, his strong arms digging into the armrests of his wheelchair. I smelled the nervous sweat shooting out of his skin.

Eventually, the threesome emerged from the back of the house. I tried to gain some clue as to how things were going by looking at the mother's eyes, but she was playing it off pretty good. They were talking rather loudly, laughing it up, but I really couldn't make out anything they were saying. The whumming sound in my head was huge. Then I noticed their voices were lowered.

My heart pounded. This *had* to be it, I thought. Maybe they had just tried to make the mother feel comfortable before dropping the bomb. Now was the time they'd lean in and say, "Oh yeah, by the way, we gotta take the kid."

They broke up their little huddle and the mother walked over to where the father sat. I think she must have told him to act retarded or mute or something, the way he just sat there like that. The mother dropped her head to the floor, focusing very intently on moving the father into the kitchen. She refused to look at me.

Then the Clean People came over. Mrs. Johnson, the Clean

Person-in-Training, sat closest to me, her knees nearly touching mine. Mrs. Jones sat behind her, leaning back on the couch and crossing her arms over her girth.

The mother came back into the living room. She lifted me up off the couch and sat down, pulling me back onto her lap. I wanted to thrash. I wanted to throw myself off the mother and run outside, run away from those first horrifying glimpses of fuckness. At least that way I'd get to decide where it was I went. Knowing my instincts, I guess, the mother put her arms around me.

I don't remember all of the questions they asked. Mrs. Johnson read them off a piece of typing paper, jotting down comments while me or the mother talked. I remember the first question though and, now that I think about it, Mrs. Johnson must have been nervous too.

Her face was very composed as she looked at the mother. Then she asked, "Do you, uh, shit on the floor?"

Mrs. Johnson's face cracked like something whooshed out of her. Mrs. Jones immediately stepped up. "I'm *sorry*. What she meant to say was, 'Do you and your family ever, uh, *defecate* on the floor... rather than in the toilet?"

"Well, no," the mother said, slightly confused. "I mean, there has been a couple of times when Carl, if he was sick or something... You know he used to not be able to do that by himself. Wallace went through a phase a few years ago, but I always cleaned it up."

"I see," Mrs. Johnson said. She'd gained a little of her composure back.

All the questions they asked me were "yes"- or "no"-type things. My mouth was completely dry. I think if I'd actually tried to talk I would have vomited so I just shook or nodded my head. They were all stupid questions like: Does your mother cook dinner? Have you ever went to bed hungry? When you get in trouble, are you spanked? Have you ever been spanked so hard it's left a bruise? Do you go to school?

The more questions they asked, the more nervous I became. I still thought the hammer was going to fall, this was just some sick and twisted way to make all of this my fault. I was wiggling so much by the time Mrs. Johnson finally asked the last question that I had almost flopped off the mother entirely.

"It was nice meeting you, Wallace," Mrs. Johnson said, holding out her hand, again with that predatory stare. It made me think I'd be seeing her again, in the soft moonglow of my room, waiting to snatch me away.

At this point my mother followed them outside. I flopped down on the couch, grabbing a pillow and wrapping my arms tightly around it. I stared up at the light yellow water stains on the ceiling, wondering if the mother had successfully scrubbed out the poor. It was another eternity they were outside.

"You okay in there?" the father called, on his way into the living room.

I gave a response that the dry mouth and nausea turned into something like, "Yeeung."

"Hang in there."

"Tell me what they're doing out there."

He wheeled himself over to the window, pulling back the clean white curtains the mother had bought at the Dollar General.

"The cunts are leaving," he said.

I sat up.

"Really?"

"S'what it looks like."

"They gone yet?"

"Getting in the car."

The mother came in and shut the door. She leaned against it, throwing her weight against the world that could so easily penetrate it. A huge smile spread across her face.

"They're closing the case," she said.

The father hung his head. He was crying, his muscled arms trembling as he clutched the wheels of his chair.

"Does that mean I won't be going anywhere?"

"You're staying right here, baby."

That was the feeling. It flooded me. Over the past few weeks everything had seemed dark and depressing. Everywhere I looked, something else was flawed. My behavior wasn't right, despite the straight 'A's. But, in that moment, everything became bright. Everything became right. Energy rushed through my body. I couldn't help smiling. If I smiled like that now, I'd think I was an idiot, but then it was just the smile of a child. The smile of a creature who didn't have a care in the world, a creature who *shouldn't* have a care in the world.

The next few days I had walked around suppressing my laughter. I wanted to laugh at everyone and everything. I felt giddy.

Someone, if not those Clean People that came to the house, then the Clean People who called them, had figured the parents weren't doing a good enough job of turning me into a blob and they wanted to take me away from the parents, reckoning they could do it right. I wanted them to see me after they left, not the idiot sad child who refused to speak but the smiling, confident, fully-hydrated child who was willing to ramble endlessly about the talents of any major league baseball team or the Top 40 charts.

That's the way I felt as I left that school. I wanted to laugh at everything, even my own condition, trudging down the road with those ridiculous horns on top of my head. I wanted them to see me, all those faceless blobs that had made the last few years of my life a living hell. No, I didn't want them to see me at all. I wanted them to go away and that's what I imagined. I imagined all those shapeless, colorless masses melting into the ground, into the rotten soot and shit-covered earth that created them.

Feeling a second wind, I picked my speed up again and started back into a slow trot. Fuck it, fuck it, fuck them all—the thought meshed with my footsteps as I struggled not to fall down.

Chapter Twelve
Elf

I continued to trudge along by the side of the road, careful not to twist my ankle where the asphalt disintegrated into the grass. The landscape of Ohio is as erratic and temperamental as the weather. One mile, I was back there near all the factories and fuckness, miles of dingy brick and rusted iron, all coughing up into the sky. Now I was in relative countryside. The only houses were way back off the road. Soon I would be in relative filth again, in the Tar District. The Tar District's factories were much smaller and older than the ones in Milltown proper. They made things like paper and rubber and didn't have contracts with places like General Motors. Milltown kind of slouches down toward the Saints River, the Tar District, and I could see all that smoke against the deepening blue of the spring sky.

Behind me, the dark clouds were still rumbling and rolling, threatening to consume me. I slowed down and started thinking about a place to hide from the inevitable driving rains. There's a popular saying in Ohio that goes: "If you don't like the weather, stick around for about ten minutes and it'll change." If this storm had come a day earlier, it would have been snow. Today, it was nearly sixty before the clouds rolled over and the rain and wind would drop it to nearly freezing.

There weren't a lot of places to hide out there. I was kind of looking for a barn or something, but there weren't any in sight. I didn't think it would be such a good idea to run into the woods if there was going to be lightning. I still had that weightless feeling and I wasn't quite ready for God to strike me down just yet.

Fuck it, I thought. I didn't care about the storm a half an hour ago, so why the hell should I care now.

The fuckness was going to come. No matter how I combated it, the fuckness would come. The harder I fought, the worse it would be. Hadn't I battled fuckness enough for the day? Why not just let it land right on top of me?

I went over to the yellow grass beside the road and threw myself on the ground. I rolled over on my back and looked up at the sky. I liked the way the sky looked before a storm as much as I did at dawn or sunset. The colors were just as vibrant but they were darker—blue, gray, black. It was the type of thing I imagined bumpkins doing, lying there musing up at the sky except, in the classical image of this, it was usually a clear blue day, possibly sparkling, huge fluffy white clouds floating slowly across the sky. How many times was that said in the country, I wondered? "Look at the fluffy white clouds. Look at heaven floating by in the sky." I wondered what life would have been like if we'd never left Farmertown. We didn't have a farm or any fuckness like that but our house was a lot nicer and the school seemed a lot less violent and everything else didn't seem so threatening either.

I was sure of one thing—if the Clean People had taken me that day, things wouldn't have turned out any better. When I was in the sixth grade at Clinton Elementary, there was a new kid there. The elementary was small enough so whenever there was a new kid who showed up, everyone knew right away who they were. Everyone called this kid Elf because he was so much smaller than the other kids were and his ears were sort of abnormally pointed. Like a lot of losers did, we started talking to each other because no one else would give us the time of day.

The family had lived in Milltown since I was in the second grade and I had yet to meet a big enough loser to call a friend. I was in sixth grade before Elf came along. And I couldn't really say that Elf was a friend. Losers always have kind of shaky relationships, especially when they're adolescents, which pretty much puts them in the same category as a sociopath. Like they just spend time together until something better comes along, avoiding any real emotional attachments. For instance, I can't remember Elf's real name. He probably wouldn't remember my name at all.

Anyway, Elf had been through one of those blobbification programs. He was actually taken out of his home. The people who took him away from his folks though, he didn't call them the Clean People. He said his father called them the Ringmasters. Elf really didn't find out why he was taken out of the house until he went to live with the new people. They had told Elf how glad he should be to be living with them.

Apparently, his real parents didn't send him to school. I always thought that was weird because Elf was probably the smartest kid in the sixth grade. It sounded like Elf's real parents were fantastic. He couldn't stand the new parents. They already had three kids of their own and didn't really pay any attention to Elf. He said they only took him in so they could get paid for it. They left most of the discipline up to their oldest son, who would lock Elf in a closet just for the hell of it. Just like I had imagined, Elf was their pet, something cute and new for the family to fawn over for a few weeks until they realized he had needs like every other living thing.

Elf's real mother stayed home all day with Elf and they had their own school, without the distractions of the other kids. The most fantastic thing was that Elf's dad was a professional clown. Elf said his dad thoroughly enjoyed being a clown. Sometimes he wouldn't change his clothes when he came home from clowning. In fact, sometimes when his dad came home, Elf and his mother would dress like clowns before they all sat down to dinner. Elf's dad told him the only thing funnier than watching a clown was actually being a clown. Elf enjoyed dressing like a clown but he still had more fun watching his dad. Elf said dressing like a clown made him feel like he had to perform, like he was somehow obligated to entertain his parents. Like I said, Elf was the smartest kid I knew. These were the things Elf talked about. It wasn't until years later that I realized he could have been lying to me. Not about his being taken from his parents, I'm pretty sure he was telling the truth about that, but what his parents were actually like before he was taken away.

The new parents had also told Elf that his old house was a complete and total wreck. Elf said he was upset when he had to leave the house because, ever since he was able to pick up a crayon, the parents had let him draw on the walls. Just before he was taken away, Elf was heavy into magazines and was working on a giant collage in his bedroom. Even in the sixth grade, Elf could see that the walls of his house were going to be his life's work. Until being yanked out, he said he felt like that was what he was chosen to do.

About the other messes, Elf said his dad couldn't understand the point of putting anything back when you were just going to be getting it right back out. Shelving merely eliminated the wall space, which was invaluable for Elf's artistic endeavors. If they decided they didn't want something anymore, they would set it out on the curb for someone else to take. Also, through the week, they just threw all their trash out the backdoor and made this big pile. At the end of the week they would rake it all up and burn it. Elf's dad told him if they put all their stuff in the trashcan it would eventually just be buried into the earth. Elf's dad also had a hatred of trashbags. He said if humans weren't careful, they would find themselves living on a giant trashbag.

If there was one thing I didn't like about Elf, it was that he talked about himself too much. I would rather have *known* he was making everything up. While he knew virtually nothing about me, I had a firm handle on his life history. But I liked Elf. It's always seemed like everyone has annoyed me in some way or the other.

One day at school, Elf talked about running away. I think Elf had seen too many movies. He seemed to think he would be able to go to some large city and be taken in by some fabulously rich family who had always wanted a child. He said he wanted to go to New York. He'd heard that was where you could paint and get paid for it. Also, a lot of the trains that came through Milltown had elaborate spraypainted designs on them. He said if no one would *buy* his paintings then he would be perfectly happy spraypainting those trains and maybe walls and subways also. He said it would be like starting his life's work over again except, this way, the whole country would be able to see it. It always amazed me how serious Elf was. Lying there beside the road and waiting for those black clouds to break over my body, I didn't have any more plans or ideas than I did on that sixth grade playground talking to Elf. The next day, after telling me about running away, he wasn't at school. I never saw him again. I hoped he made it to New York. I hoped he was able to make it. I hoped he was able to make himself weightless enough to do whatever it was he wanted to do.

I never told anyone he had mentioned running away, not even the mother and father. When I thought about that, I wondered if Elf wasn't a rent-a-kid. That's what happens to the children the social services take. They don't always put them up for adoption into good homes. That usually only happened to babies. An older child was usually put into foster care, rented out. And maybe Elf *knew* he was like a book that had lain around the house too long. Maybe he knew he was going back to the library and decided to make it sound romantic and grand. No doubt the orphanages were just like a library. When a book first comes out, there is a waiting list for it. Two years later, people will deny they'd ever read the thing in the first place.

Even though that was most probably the truth, Elf's present parents simply returning him after they'd paid off the mortgage on the house or something, I didn't want to believe it. I realized that, more than anything, more than the fuckness or the parents or miserable little Milltown Middle, I was tired of reality. Maybe everything outside of reality was a lie but, lying there on the ground, I realized I needed all those fantasies. I needed Santa Claus and the Easter Bunny. I needed to believe the movies were just like real life. I needed to believe people weren't judged by how much money they made or how much schooling they'd had. I needed to believe the moon was made of cheese. Maybe I even needed to believe the parents were always right and maybe I even needed a God to pray to.

Maybe I needed it or maybe I needed to deny it all. There was a rip somewhere in the middle of my body or my brain—half of it said I needed to believe everything and the other half said I shouldn't believe any of it. Was it a breakdown? That's what it felt like except I thought of it as more of a meltdown. Like everything that had ever been said to me, everything I'd ever done, every feeling I'd ever felt—all pressed down on me. I felt it enter my skin and crawl around in my veins. I felt all the fuckness beating a tattoo against my bones.

The whumming clanged along in my skull, a black death train. Nausea wrestled with my stomach and fought its way up to the back of my throat.

What came out was a shriek.

I raised myself up to my knees, holding my whumming head with both hands. The storm broke, the rain a distant whisper over the hills before drumming down on my face. Wicked lightning snapped, a jagged blue across the black of the sky.

"Why the hell is this happening to me!" I shouted at the clouds.

I grabbed the horns and wrestled with them. Were they fate, handed down to me? If so, maybe this would be my last tangle with it, the last chance to change it. Violently, I tugged and pulled at them with every ounce of strength I had. I flopped all around on the wet ground, splashing around on the grass as I tried to brace myself against the ground, pulling and pulling to get them off.

It was hopeless. Exhausted, I sprawled back down on the grass, opening my eyes wide and letting the cold rain cleanse them, wash the burning away.

A car sped by and a McDonald's sack hit me in the face.

I stood up on trembling legs. My skin felt hot against the rain.

Maybe it *was* fate, I thought. Maybe I didn't have any will of my own. But there were directions. Above all the contradictory voices there was that singular feeling I felt, more and more, like I *had* to listen to. I knew I still had to get to the Tar District and, amazingly, I still felt weightless.

Chapter Thirteen
Johnny Metal

Maybe it was just the storm but it seemed like it was getting dark incredibly early. Of course, I had no real idea of what time it actually was. For all I knew, I could have lain down by the road for a half an hour or three hours. I didn't know and I didn't really care. Maybe I cared too much. I don't know. It seemed like as the sky got darker, my mood darkened also. The weightlessness was replaced with some sort of grim determination. The rain had tapered off a little. The lightning and thunder had rolled on. In the distance I could see the depressing yellow glow of the Tar District, the drizzle and mist creating tainted haloes around the street lamps.

Pretty much what I did was just stay on the state route. Honestly, I don't really know if it was Milltown that was curved or if it was the state route. One time, when we were still living in Farmertown, Racecar drove us out for a vacation on the East Coast. I remember we took all state routes because the mother wanted to see all the historical small towns of Eastern America for some reason I now found vaguely obscene. I remember it so well because Racecar was mad that he couldn't drive on the highway.

"If we'd taken the highway we coulda been there by now on half the gas."

He decided to elaborate on this theory when we were stuck at a traffic light at the end of a long line. "You wanted your chance to see the small towns, well, here you go. If you want to, you could probably get out and catch some local color before we ever get movin again. Damned state routes."

"Oh, Carl, relax," the mother said.

Perhaps from that experience, I should have known that all state routes were, in some form or the other, damned. I could still hear the click of the father's cigarette lighter, becoming more incessant as we got closer to Maine. Eventually he just lit one right off the other. He certainly didn't do a very good job of relaxing.

I felt kind of like the mother and the father as I slurped along the side of that road. All those conflicts that had first started a while ago were still raging along inside of me—half of them driving me onward, telling me I had to get to the Tar District and whatever wild bleak yonder lay after that and the other half telling me I should just *relax*, soak it all up.

"These are the best days of your life," I laughed to myself.

I still wondered if I cared about what was happening to me at all or if I cared too much. Maybe it was better not to care. None of the fucking blobs cared—they didn't care about anything. And there was something about their not caring that made them perfectly happy.

That kind of brought me back to the question of what the hell I was really doing. Was it some sort of moral dilemma or some sort of quest for freedom? I thought I was really too young to be having a moral dilemma and I guess it could have been both but those sets of voices in my head or body wanted things to be one way or another and they wanted those things to be in direct opposition to each other. A moral dilemma became a moral crisis. A quest for freedom became a violent and binding struggle.

Did Pearlbottom ever have a moral dilemma? I doubted it. I mean, the fucking blob devoured livestock in the hallway, for fucking Chrissake. And that fatass Swarth and his merry gang of Marlboro men. The only moral dilemma they had was when they raped someone, if they should do it single-handedly or if they should have their friends help. I was certain the only dilemma Mary Lou ever had was whether she should wear red or hot pink. I'm pretty sure there was a time when the parents had had moral dilemmas, but the mother had since used alcohol and a vigorous zest for cleaning to take her mind off any questions of morality. The father channeled all of it into hate—pure, unadulterated, stumpy hate.

Whatever it was I was feeling, it certainly wasn't weightlessness. Not anymore. It was now like some kind of heavy soulhurt.

I was in a daze, just about ready to enter the Tar District. I stood hypnotized by the closeness of the dingy brown buildings. The storefronts were all adorned with outdated neon signs. I was sure all of these places were still open. Unlike the Historic District of Milltown, there weren't 9-5 businesses like insurance agencies and banks. The Tar District was bars and tattoo parlors and bars and pool halls and triple- X video places and bars and pawnshops and bars and check cashing places and 24-hour diners for people to sober up in after the bars closed. I stood just outside that sickly yellow glow, watching the distant images of people shuffling around. According to the mother, these people were all either drunk or high on crack. A giant wave of depression washed over me. So this was where I wanted to come. This is where the inner feeling brought me. I felt both afraid and pathetic. Was I going to be one of them? Relax, I told myself, you're just here to meet your Uncle Skad.

But what if he's one of them?

And then I was lost, frozen. I stood there staring into the Tar District, nearly legendary for its seductive cruelty, and was completely unable to move.

I don't know how much time passed before I was finally jolted alive by an excruciatingly loud train horn. I realized that I was standing maybe five feet away from the tracks.

For those who haven't lived right next to train tracks, as I had for the past several years, a train's sound seems to be made only of the whistle, somewhere far off in the distance, dragging its mysterious freight through the thick night air. During the day, some other distraction could keep you from noticing the sound at all. But a train's sounds are really deafening. There's the whistle, sure, but it is augmented, as though it's funneled through a bullhorn. And there are other sounds, almost as deafening. There's the rumblesqueak of the train itself, shooting along those steel rails, coupled with a nearly constant bell that tingalings throughout the train's entire passing. Standing there, so close to the train, I was still overwhelmed by how loud it was. This one wasn't going very fast. I figured it must have been dragging something away from one of those factories.

I looked to my right, down the train's length. It was a long one. Something else caught my eye. Some dark object, not large enough to be a person, flew off the train, landed in the grass, and kind of skipped down the small incline there. I took a few steps toward the object, whatever the fuck it was, before the man flew out nearly right in front of me. He hit the ground with a bit of a grunt and went rolling down the hill, a few feet from the object he'd just hurled out.

I was excited to think this might be my first meeting with an honest-to-God hobo. Drifter Ken was adamant about being a drifter. According to him, a hobo was more clearly defined as someone who was constantly moving, often traveling in a pack, and usually by train. Sometimes they conjured up lovingly outdated images of a folksy person, a guitar slung over one shoulder, a knapsack tied around a stick slung over the other. Drifter Ken stayed some place until the law ran him out of town and then he want to the next place by foot. I think he liked the outlaw spin placed on drifters.

The man stood up, brushing wet grass off of his skintight pants. He looked dizzy and confused.

"Are you okay?" I asked.

He picked a couple pieces of grass out of his curly blond hair. Even in the darkness, there was nothing natural-looking about that hair. It looked like it had been bleached a while ago, hanging to his shoulders in curls. Bangs had been cut straight across his forehead.

"I've died and gone straight to hell." Then I guess he noticed I was trying to help and he smiled a little, his teeth gross within his mottled flesh. "What the hell's them things on your head?"

"They're horns."

"Well I can see they're horns, but why the hell're they there? On your head. What are you tryin to pull? You're not a Satan worshipper are you?"

Fuckness

"No."

"You gotta be careful. I hear the Satan worshippers are fairly prevalent around here. I'm from back East. Back there you got your occasional psycho or mass murderer, whatever the hell, some office worker snaps and fires off a few rounds in a mall somewhere but the cult stuff's spooky shit. I had a friend who's a cop over in Illinois. He says they pulled some dead sacka shit outta some ditch and the poor bastard didn't have any ears. Now whatta you reckon some sickos gonna do with this guy's *ears*?" I briefly imagined someone holding this pair of severed ears up to their head, having a joyous time at the thrill of having a new set of ears.

He looked around him on the ground. "By the way, you see somethin flyin out the train? Two something's maybe." He held his arms out from his body. "Bout this size?"

"Over there," I pointed into the darkness behind him.

Slowly, he backed up, not taking his eyes from me.

"So what is it, with them horns?"

"I was just born this way."

"And your folks? They ain't tried to sell you to some kind of freak show yet?"

"They tried to keep it under wraps."

"What are you doin around here after dark? This ain't the best place to be, you know."

It suddenly got quiet and I realized the train had fully passed, dragging its noise into the dark distance.

I didn't feel like telling this guy the whole story. I'd already told Drifter Ken and I imagined I'd be telling Uncle Skad if I ever found him. Twice was enough. I counted myself lucky if I could make it through something the first time.

"A freak show," I said. "I figured I'd run off and join a freak show. Make some money on my own." I was quickly learning that people desperately wanted *reasons* for just about everything.

The man bent down to pick up what I now realized was a guitar case and, a few feet away, an amp.

"Show business is rough," he held up the guitar case. "You got a few minutes, I can tell you a little bit about it. My name's Johnny

Metal." He said "Metal" in a low growly voice. He held out his lea-thery hand. Over the course of the evening, I would learn that he liked to say his name a lot, out of the blue. Sometimes in that low, growly voice, and other times in a high nasally whine.

"My name's Wallace Black."

"You a Wally?" he asked as he pumped my hand with a com-fortable and surprising strength.

"Whatever you wanna call me is fine."

"Wally, you happen to see a bandanna layin around anywhere. I coulda swore I was wearin a badanna."

I didn't remember seeing a bandanna fly off his head as he jumped out. I supposed it could have been tossed off before the guitar case and the amp. He looked around for a few minutes and then threw up his hands and rolled his eyes.

"Oh well," he said. "Guess I can always find another bandana. I liked that one. It smelled like pussy. Johnny *Meeetal*. A drink, though, I need a drink right now. Come on, Wally, come with me. Only alcoholics drink alone. You drink?"

"I'm only sixteen."

"Bah, had my first drink at twelve. Pussy at eleven, whiskey at twelve. Sixteen? Pot and maybe some coke. You got any pussy yet?"

"Uh, no. I guess I haven't."

We started walking toward the Tar District. "It's takin kids longer and longer to grow up."

"Nah, eleven or twelve still seems about the right age. I'm just incredibly ugly. Nobody would want much to do with me."

"You'll grow into them features. One day, if you're lucky, if take good care of yourself, you could look like me." He growled his name and began walking. I followed him. It looked like he had vents cut into the back of his sleeveless t-shirt. I thought that was kind of cool.

Chapter Fourteen
The Tar District

We slowly made our way into the Tar District, maintaining a shroud of relative silence. I really did get the palpable feeling I was walking *into* something. And it was like something that was felt without a sign to remind you. It got a lot brighter and those three and four-story buildings, most of them on the verge of dilapidation, had a way of leaning over me. Johnny Metal said he was looking for a place called Toady's because they had the cheapest whiskey. It was obvious he'd been here before. I wondered if he really came all this way just for a shot of whiskey. I've never been very good at small talk so I just stayed quiet, weaving the shroud a little tighter. I felt comfortable around this man and that was enough for now. I stayed as close to him as possible. There was something about this section of the Tar District that I found creepily terrifying.

We walked for a couple blocks. I could feel my muscles beginning to stiffen again. I'd woken up that morning feeling like total hell and had been moving ever since, the friction burning away some of the soreness. Metal, even though it looked like he was pretty old, still had a real fluid and cool way of walking. I was the one walking like an old man and he was the one who assumed the smooth gait of a seventeen or eighteen-year-old—someone who's too young to have let the world beat them down and old enough to know the adults couldn't *make* you do anything you didn't really want to. All you had to do was put up a fight. I was sure Johnny

Metal had put up a lot of fights in his time. His face kind of looked like it had been beaten with a mace.

Eventually, he turned right into a dark alleyway between two sagging glazed brick two-stories. A yellow light drifted out from a door open into the alley. The opening illuminated the wall opposite it, revealing an ancient faded mural for Bull Durham rolling tobacco.

"This's the place," Metal said over his shoulder before warbling out his name.

I wondered what kind of bar had a door that opened into an alley until I noticed the front of it was all boarded up—door and windows.

"You ever been in a bar, Wally?"

"No, sir," I said

"Goddammit, don't call me sir. That's a good way to make me feel old."

"Sorry."

"*Johnny Metal!*" He sang his name loudly, nearly shouting it. "It's a great name! Momma should not be ashamed for namin me that!"

I doubted he was born with that name.

"Well, if you ain't never been to a bar, this here's as good a place to start as any."

He walked into the yellow light and I followed him, innately sensing I wasn't going to be thrown out for being too young. I was pretty sure this place didn't even have a liquor license, therefore they didn't really have anything to lose if they sold to minors. But I had no urge for a drink of the alcoholic kind. I'd tried the mother's on a few occasions and they made me feel like throwing up and made my throat burn. Not only that, it seemed to make people talk and act dumber than they already did. I usually felt stupid enough.

"We'll get us a dark corner so no one notices them things on your head." Once inside, he lowered his voice to nearly a whisper. "If anybody happens to start givin you any funny looks, you just look away. Unless you think you can handle em, then you just stare em down." He showed me how to stare somebody down.

I didn't think I could handle a toddler whacked on heroin at that point having, as I was, a certain level of difficulty handling the fine art of standing while not allowing a sour grimace to grind its way over my face.

Metal motioned to a dark, smoky back corner with his guitar case. "You can take a seat right over there. I gotta go say 'hi' to Toady."

I shuffled over to the corner and sat down. The seat was old and musty. A sticky sheen coated the small table, swirls of dust and long strands of hair poking up in sporadic bursts. Looking around at the patrons in the bar, I became horribly depressed. That yellowish light glowed throughout the whole bar, emanating from no specific source. I imagined it coming from their nicotine-stained souls, shooting right up out of those bags bulging beneath their bloodshot, watery eyes. This wasn't at all what I expected from a bar. No TV. No pool table. No women. Just the bar, sitting warped beneath a mirror so filthy it had stopped reflecting. It turned all the faces it could manage to catch into faded, ghostlike images.

This was one of the first places I'd been to in a long time where I didn't know everyone else's name. This bothered me for some reason so I came up with my own names for them. One of the guys up by the bar I decided to call Wooden Leg because of the stiff way he stood there, one hip jutting out. Another guy who sat with his back facing the bar, I decided to call Meat Sandwich—his face had an oddly textured roll to it. In the opposite corner from our booth, slumped an exceptionally drunk man who I decided to call Death Swamp. Others were scattered around. Their names, for various reasons, were Slow Willy, Ol Round Paul Willard, Mr. Cindy Beckman, and Gout.

No one spoke. For the most part, it felt like they didn't even want to look at another human being. There was one sad looking guy, Gout, sitting under a patch of exposed insulation, who glanced up at me while I studied him. He quickly looked back into his beer. When I decided to look away, I felt his eyes boring into me, not necessarily hateful, just a perplexed stare at the horns on my head. I wondered if he thought they were caused by too much drink. Maybe he assumed they weren't really there at all. Except I knew that wasn't true. An alcoholic took whatever happened when they were drunk as reality. It dawned on me at that point that that was what the mother had become the last few years—a drunk. And she was hellbent on seeing that everyone felt her reality.

Metal came walking back with two paper cups in one large hand. Coming through the bar, he could have been virtually indistinguishable from all the other guys in the bar if it wasn't for his weird hair and skintight, neon-striped pants. Their skin all seemed to be a sickly gray-green color rather than the flesh tones usually found on healthy humans. Perhaps they formed a new race. Their hair was a uniform dark steel gray. Even Metal's, in this light, looked more gray than blond. Clothingwise, everyone except for Metal seemed to wearing brown.

Metal reached the corner, clunking the guitar case down on the floor. He pulled a rickety wooden chair across the floor with his foot and sat down in it, crossing his legs in an almost prissy manner.

"Gotcha a Coke," he said, proffering one of the paper cups to me. "Toady says he don't want you drunk and charging through this place. Stuff's too sweet for me."

Metal's voice sounded like he was about two months away from a stoma, but it had a quality that made me want to keep listening to him.

"Thanks," I said.

He took a gulp from his cup and fished in his breast pocket. He pulled out a pack of unfiltered Kools and threw them down on the table. Picking the pack up with a trembling hand, he pulled a cigarette out and lit it with a match, shaking out the flame and flicking it to the floor, his head enveloped in a web of smoke.

"Ah, these addictions," he said. "Crutches for an old battered soul. *Buy me a closet fulla new souls, cause this one's tattered and worn,*" he half-sang. It sounded more like a lullabye than a power ballad.

All Metal's companionable qualities aside, I was still depressed as all hell. I sipped the lukewarm Coke, unable to get comfortable because I had to keep my arms off that sticky table. I leaned my head back against the wall, the horns clunking. They chipped away a little bit of the old drywall and a small chunk of plaster tumbled down onto my shoulder.

Metal took another swig of his whiskey and there was a little more life in his eyes.

"What's got ya so sad?"

A grit had formed over my eyes. I wiped at them with the back of my hands.

"You do look really sad, ya know?"

"I don't know. I guess I don't really wanna talk about it." It was true. I had no idea what made me so sad. I wasn't thinking about the parents or any of the heavy fuckness that had happened earlier that day. If I'd been thinking about that, I would probably have been happier. Triumphant and weightless. That was how I'd felt earlier. I figured it must have been something in my head, chemicals or some fuckness like that, or I would have been sad all the time—which I wasn't. Miserable and angry, maybe I felt those feelings most of the time, but the sadness and the feeling of overwhelming doom only came in occasional waves. I knew after I started feeling the soulhurt, the tears weren't very far away, but I knew I couldn't cry in this place.

"I just... don't know," I nervously clunked my head against the wall for emphasis.

"Ya dohn know? Now, what kinda answer's that?"

"It's a damn good one," I said, trying to smile.

"Yer right about that, I guess." I noticed that, as Metal got drunker (and he seemed to become drunk with the first introduction of alcohol into his system), he made these weird arm gestures, throwing them out from his body like a man imitating a chicken. "Id is indeed a good answer. Yer right. A *damn* good answer. But I think you might juss know a little bit bout why yer so sad. Hell, we all got problems, I guess. I'm gonna go freshen the cup."

He stood up, staggered backward a little, catching himself and turning toward the bar. He walked up there with those wild chicken motions. Metal got to the bar and the bartender already had a paper cup waiting for him. I watched Metal pull the money out of the waistband of his pants and hand it over. Part of me wanted to stand up and leave, but I really didn't think I'd be able to. That old worn booth seemed extremely comfortable. I could have probably fallen asleep there and kept sleeping all night. I hoped he wasn't going to try and get me to talk. I thought it would physically hurt to open my mouth.

Metal came back and sat down in the chair. He quickly looked up at me. I really thought Metal was a good guy and all but, for some reason, I got the feeling it didn't really matter who he was sitting there with. Like he could strike up a conversation with just about anybody.

"So, uh, where yuh headin?"

"The big freak show."

"Oh, yeah, thass right. Say, uh, didn't I say I was gonna tell ya bout the show business."

"Yeah."

"You, uh, listen to much music?"

"Not a lot. I like Bobby DeHaven."

"Bobby DeHaven..." Metal tilted his head, trying to drag the name from memory.

"He sang that song that was really big last year."

"Oh, yeah. *That* song. I play some music."

I figured he did, what with the guitar case and amp and all.

"You know, I almost got real big and popular, too." I found myself a litte more interested at that point, thinking maybe I'd heard of him. "That was a long time ago, though. Prob'ly before you was born, even. You ever listen to metal?"

I didn't guess I had. I said, "No."

"Yeah, well, you ain't missin much. Now, when I was a helluva lot younger than I am now, metal was the shit. It was pure. It was out of control. It was fun." He rocked back in his chair and did some air guitar and throw his hair around. Then he polished off his cup of whiskey, belched into his hand, and fished a Kool out of his pocket.

"Now, back then, it took talen to be in a band. You had to look awesome, too. Some guys I knew even got their songs on some radio stations."

Fuckness

"Were you ever on the radio?"

"Yeah, I had me a little song that got played a little bit. It was called, 'Gotta Get God Before I Go to Hell,' when I was with Thunder Hoof. We had those dot things over the 'o's. Never went much farther than that, though."

"Didn't people like your song?"

"Oh, I guess they liked it fine but I couldn't play any live gigs."

"Why not?"

"Ya see, it was always hard for me to play in fronta people, cause when I start playin the guitar, you know, I gotta make my faces. Once all those people got a look at them faces they'd start laughin. It didn't matter where I was, everyone in the club would be laughin. Not even the drunks could take me seriously. Never failed—one person started laughin, ev'ryone else started laughin too cause that shit's contagious ya know. Anyway, I was younger then, keep in mind, I'd get all pissed off and try and beat the hell outta the first person I come to. It wasn't too hard either, since most of them was laughin too hard to fight back. Made me feel kinda bad too, havin to beat someone who's laughin so much."

"That's terrible," I said, but I didn't really mean it. I felt too exhausted to feel any type of emotion at that point. My body had melted into the booth and become just as feeling as the musty cushions. "I'd like to hear you play."

"I'd like to play somethin."

"So why not." I was kind of hoping it would pass the time a little bit. Besides, I'd never seen anyone actually play music before except hideous Ms. Mapes, the music teacher. She'd sit on her knees in front of the class and talk endlessly in a tone of voice that suggested we were all in kindergarten while these hideous spitballs formed on her lips, stretching elastically back and forth. I remember sitting there, paying more attention to the spit strings, waiting anxiously to see when they would break, than anything ol Ms. Mapes happened to be braying.

"I guess I'll swing round here and play somethin but there's one condition. When ev'rybody here starts laughin, and b'lieve you me they will, you just go ahead and stand up and walk out, cause I

105

won't be able to look at ya after that."

I didn't know if I'd really be able to move or not but I nodded my head anyway.

"Get set," he said. He bent down and unlatched the shiny guitar case. "I sure do wish I had my bandanna. Always played better in a bandanna. Plug me in?" He pointed to an outlet at the bottom of the wall. I plugged the amp into it.

I felt incredibly sorry for Johnny Metal. Maybe it was because I knew he wasn't lying. I probably wouldn't get the chance to talk to him after this.

"So why are you here?" I asked.

"Well," he grunted, positioning the guitar on his knee, holding an old chipped pick between his teeth as he did so. He took the pick out and cleared his throat. "I guess I came here to see if I could pawn this guitar. Then I decided I needed some whiskey, so I came here. Maybe I'm just here for you. Maybe you're the only reason I'm here. Sometimes I do things without knowing why. One minute I was sitting in a friend's apartment, the next I was hoppin on a train to come to Milltown. Who the hell knows."

Metal flipped the amp on and lightly strummed the guitar. "I don't sing no more so you're gonna get the instrumental version. The real soul's always been in the guitar anyway."

"It was nice meeting you, Johnny," I said.

"Likewise." He shrugged his head, made a wild chicken motion and laid into the guitar.

The paralysis I felt automatically lifted. It was like he just started playing without really knowing what, without any kind of preparation or any fuckness like that. Chills dripped their way icily down my spine. And then there was the other sound—the rolling, banshee-like shriek of laughter. It was Gout, the man I'd been looking at under the spot of exposed insulation. Looking at him earlier, I wouldn't have thought he was capable of making such sounds. Nevertheless, there he was, bent over, a cup trembling in his hand, a coughing fit the only thing breaking up his laughter.

The other people in the bar were doing the same thing. The bartender pounded his heavy hand on the warped wooden bar. The guy in the opposite corner, Death Swamp, rolled around on the dusty floor. Slow Willy, standing only about five feet away, pointed as he laughed.

I had told myself I wasn't going to look. I looked around the bar at all those fucking blob wastes, laughing away like asses and I told myself I wasn't going to do that. I wanted to listen to the music. And I did, for as long as I could. I sat there looking down at that disgusting table until, finally, the sound of the laughter drowned out the sound of the guitar.

I looked at Metal.

It was one of the most amazing things I ever saw. After the first glance, I couldn't take my eyes off it. The music became like plinking dream notes, coming from somewhere way off in the distance. I was focused in so close to his face that there were moments when I was unaware he was even playing an instrument at all. His tongue lolled out, vast and pink. His lips pursed. His eyebrows went way back. His eyes bugged out. Sometimes he would glance down at the guitar and those eyebrows would go back and his mouth would draw up and he'd raise his shoulders, all at the same time, and he'd look like he was terrified as all hell of that instrument. There were other things. Other things that are truly indescribable. Certain movements, ridiculous affectations, all contributed to some unbelievable show. And I felt the laugh, somewhere deep within me. Whenever you have a laugh buried somewhere deep in your viscera, there's really no way to stop it—and it feels so good to let it come out. It's what I imagined a snake shedding its skin must feel like, to laugh off some outer layer of repression.

Those drunkass blobs were all still laughing away. Meat Sandwich had laughed until throwing up. He now rolled around on the ground beside his vomit. I imagined they had all pissed their pants quite some time ago. I wouldn't let Metal see me laugh at him. That was part of the promise. So I stood up, amazingly easily, with my body hurting like hell, my lungs burning, and took off for the entrance.

Now, apparently, they were finding everything hilarious. As I crossed the bar I noticed Slow Willy, the man who'd been pointing at Metal, was now pointing at me, as if to direct all the blobs' attention in my direction. How long had Metal put up with this? I could feel their malicious stares on my back and I inadvertently started snapping my head to the side and snapping my fingers. Both of those actions hurt worse than all fuck, but I couldn't control myself. I just wanted to be out of that smoky yellow tomb.

Just as I got to the entrance, I heard someone shout, "Horns!"

How observant, I thought.

The more laughter I suppressed, the more I had to look at all those blobbish faces around me, the less I felt like laughing and the angrier I became. The red crawlies were back, scouring the inside of my skin, blurring my vision, lifting me up out of that booth.

I had no control over myself.

I couldn't hear Metal's guitar anymore. The only sounds I heard were the heavy throbbing of my blood and the irritating laugh of all the drunks. My vision turned red. I couldn't see anything.

I could only hear and feel.

I felt skin in the palms of my hands. I felt the skin turn wet. I felt the horns punching into flesh and soft guts. I heard the fine shift of laughter turning to screams.

I don't know if I spun around the room or the room spun around me or how long it went on. Flesh and more flesh in my hands. So much hot wetness covering me. The occasional feel of the horns scraping on bone. The scents of blood and puke and piss and shit all mingling together and cloying at the back of my nose.

Slowly, the screams were eliminated.

I could hear Metal's guitar.

The red faded away, replaced by a different kind of red.

I stood up by the bar, leaning against it, looking out over the room. The room was covered in blood.

The drunks were indiscernible from one another. One of them was propped in a chair, his scalp peeled back from his skull. Another one lay face down on the floor, his back ripped from neck to waist, his spine exposed. Another one lay across a table, nearly ripped in two, his head and torso facing the ceiling, his groin against the table.

Fuckness

I looked at Metal, sitting there in the chair and facing the opposite wall, playing his guitar. His eyes were closed and he was covered in other people's blood. A piece of intestine was draped across his left arm.

I could feel the blood covering me turning sticky. I turned and headed for the front door, leaving Metal to play for an audience that wouldn't laugh. The now deafening refrain of his guitar followed me outside.

Once out there, I thought for sure I was going to throw up. But when I opened my mouth, I started laughing. I leaned up against one of those giant, rusted dumpsters, my whole body shaking. I wasn't just laughing at Metal, I laughed at the absurdity of everything: his faces, the horns atop my head, the drunks who went there every night, who no longer even thought about why they went, who died there, Metal's music taking them to whatever afterlife awaited them.

I tried to stop laughing because I think people usually look pretty stupid when they laugh. The more I tried not to laugh, the harder it came. Just like that, the sadness and its leaden wave had receded and, rather than feeling weightless, I was burdened with laughter. It was an amazing gift Johnny Metal had. However unwanted it was, it was truly amazing.

Chapter Fifteen
The Boy With Horns

Eventually I found my way out of the alley. The laughter had died down and I knew there was a foreboding wave of darkness waiting for me. I wondered why, when I had feelings of intense joy or happiness, I could always sense that black wave, cresting above and threatening to crash down on me at any time but, when I was actually having one of my sad spells, it felt like it was never going to end—like I would never get the happiness back.

I figured it must have been around two or three o'clock in the morning. Most of the businesses looked like they were closing up for the night. A few of the neon signs flickered and then went off. The people in the streets were twice as loud as they were earlier. I'm pretty sure this had something to do with them being twice as drunk as they were earlier. The people in pairs or groups engaged in overly militant babble. They were either going to go somewhere else and, "fuck some shit up," "get into some shit," or, apparently if there was no shit already in existence, they were going to "start some shit." The winos and drunks who were alone wandered along the street, sometimes losing their way and actually curving into the street, mumbling things under their breath, vigorous and confused conversations, imbued with an unusual passion. Or they screamed various names out loud. Sometimes they yelled them at random windows above the bars, "Tina! Tina!!" Sometimes they merely yelled them at the heavens, as though crooning for some lover who was dead and gone or maybe, depending on their blood-alcohol level, never there in the first place.

There weren't many cars in this section of the Tar District. I assumed most of these people were either too poor to own cars or, more probable, had long ago had their licenses revoked for vehicular manslaughter. Whenever a car did come into sight, it traveled at speeds highly inappropriate. A loud roar, a flash of lights, and they were gone.

I tried to stay out of the faint pool of the streetlamps so no one could see me. I secretly willed the horns to go away. Without them, I didn't think anyone would really even notice me. By the standards presented around me, I wasn't even exceptionally ugly. I moved slowly, barely lifting my feet off the cement. My body was essentially numb, but I felt that grinding bonefeel starting up in the joints. If I stopped to rest again, I was sure I wouldn't be able to deal with the pain of moving.

I knew Uncle Skad lived by the river and I figured it was maybe two miles at most in front of me. Slowly, I had wandered out of the lively section of the Tar District and into what the mother and father called the slums. Apparently, even though Walnut was a horrible, hideous place to live, it was still better than the slums of the Tar District. Looking at it now, where the streetlights ended, I could see why the parents made that assertion.

Walnut contained houses in disarray, the ground threatening to consume some of them, but the Tar District contained an area that had *once been* houses. Now, they were entirely dilapidated—a pile of bricks, a heap of wood. To my left, knotted anemic grass covered a vacant lot. If there had once been a house or business there, it had been torn down a long time ago. To my right there were completely demolished houses. They didn't go unused, however. A long tarp was slung over the top of the piles and I could see little fires glowing in there. I imagined seeing the whites of their eyes, peering out into the darkness. Further down the road, in front of me, a group of homeless guys had started a fire in a barrel. I stopped in my tracks because I didn't want to draw their attention. It's not that I was afraid of them hurting me or any fuckness like that. I didn't want to make them feel watched or studied, even though that was exactly what was happening.

I stood there and watched them. They were virtually indistinguishable from one another. Their clothes had all gone indiscernible shades of brown or black. The men, and everyone I saw was a man, had long beards and something on their heads. They held out their hands to the fire, trying to let its pitiful flames spread warmth throughout their bodies. Maybe that's why so many of them drank, I thought. I was sure the alcohol did a much better job of spreading the warmth than that weak little fire did.

Standing there, the sadness came back in full force. The black and yellow wave of soulhurt hit me hard. It started raining again, icy rain. I stood there, letting it beat down on my horns until my head was hot and whumming and my lungs burned. I let the rain peel away the blood and the stink of death. There was something inside of me telling me this was where I belonged. If there was a place where people who didn't belong belonged, this was it. None of these people wore horns, true, but they might as well have. Everything they had had been stripped away and I felt like I didn't have anything either. Whether I had done it to myself or not, I wasn't sure, but something had been stripped away. Being a murderer, a mass murderer now, I guess, I didn't even have my morality to cling to.

I desperately wanted Uncle Skad. He was the reason I came here. He was the only thing, in my mind, keeping me from bottoming out. These people, they were people who had had the nets removed. The reason they ended up here was because there was absolutely no one to help them. I had wondered before how terrifying it would be to look around you and find no one and, if it weren't for the idea of Uncle Skad, I would know. This was where I belonged. In the Tar District. In the land of people who didn't have anybody. They weren't just without a home, they were without anything. Every comfort a home brings with it was denied these poor souls. And that's really all they were. Souls. Maybe they had beautiful thoughts that helped them get through. Maybe their thoughts were genius. Maybe they had firmly planted their existence in their minds. But they didn't exist in the physical world. Not the physical world that anybody sees, anyway. They had been cast out.

I stood there crying. I was stupid for doing everything I'd done. I shouldn't have run away. I shouldn't have killed the parents. I shouldn't have set fire to the parents' house. I shouldn't have stood up to Bucky Swarth. But I did. I did all of those things and I stood there rotting in my decisions, wondering if they *were* my decisions. Maybe that was why I stood there feeling like I belonged in the Tar District, but not feeling like one of them. I doubted their decisions put them here. Did they *deserve* it? Did they feel like they deserved it? That's exactly what I felt like.

What if I *was* what everybody said I was: a molester, a rapist, ugly, a demon, a half-wit, a murderer? If so, then this was certainly where I belonged. But I stood apart because something told me they wouldn't accept me either. Prison would have been a luxury. This was punishment of another kind.

I didn't have nay idea what to do. I just wanted to see Uncle Skad but I didn't remember what he looked like or if he still lived here or not. I stood there and it felt like a billion different things were trying to pull me in all those directions and I couldn't do anything but stand there and cry like a huge baby. A weak demon. The boy with horns.

That's truly what I had become. Everyone I'd been around had found me to be repellent. They could remove my personality if they didn't interact with me. By telling me to shut up, by silencing me every day, they had removed a little bit more of that personality. And the more personality they removed, the more room they created for something more malevolent to fill. Oh sure, sometimes I would find someone else to inflict it upon, but it was never very long before they wised up too. And that was all I was as I stood there in the rain. I wasn't a name or a personality, I was the boy with horns, like the hunchback of Notre Dame, some twisted freak of nature people could no longer even bear to look upon.

I was an embarrassment to the human race. I became a raw soul, unable to exist in the physical world.

No.

The thunder clapped and I took off running toward the Saints thinking maybe I should throw myself in, but that wouldn't happen either. No, I would run until I died. If I died it was going to be in a cathedral or a mansion, any place spectacular, not the Tar District, not where people died every day. Not where death was common. I would die someplace fantastic even if I was only robbing it.

I ran until I got so close to the river I could smell it, my raw lungs sucking that odor in. The Saints' presence was all over me and I collapsed into the mud and the muck, spiraling uncontrollably into some form of exhausted sleep and thinking for some odd reason the strong scent of the mud was what a fish's spine would smell like.

Chapter Sixteen
Dreaming of Hell

It's always the shortest sleeps that breed the longest, most vivid dreams.

The dream I had that night, after passing out under the rain, gave me a desire to go on. I can't explain why. I think it showed me that things had to change. That eventually, something had to give. The fuckness *had* to recede.

When the dream started, it was very dark and I was wrapped up in all these things that felt like spiderwebs. They were very thin and fine but there was also something sort of metallic about them. Slowly, all those cobwebs dropped away and it got a little bit lighter all around me. It's amazing in dreams the amount you can feel. I think that's what really makes them so lifelike—the fact you can *feel*, emotionally as well as physically, everything you can in real life. That weightless feeling I'd had earlier, a feeling I would try never to forget, entered into me and it felt like I was flying, up close to the sun, the air around me thin and blue. I felt the coolness of the clouds on my face, so close I could taste them. They tasted like the purest, coldest water I had ever tasted. Nothing like the orange muck that came from the pipes at home.

And then I saw Bobby DeHaven. He was standing on a cloud further in front of me and I could tell by the way his mouth moved that he was singing but I couldn't make out any words. The wind up there, wherever *there* was, blew his beautiful blond hair off his face. Those feathered sides looked like wings. He wore pants that had the same pattern as the American flag—stars on his crotch and ass and stripes down his legs—and then I was going past him, slowly past him.

I was coming down.

Everything felt so blue and weightless. It ran over my skin, through my veins, like a gentle electric current. I felt like I was in a bubble where no one could hurt me.

And then the bubble broke, the weightlessness sucked away. I found myself in a park. I never saw myself in this dream. I felt everything as though I were inside myself, looking out through my eyes. The parents were there. Off in the distance. They were throwing a bright red Frisbee back and forth. They were my parents but not really. Right away I noticed Racecar had legs. But as I got closer to them, I started noticing other differences. Racecar's legs were prosthetic. He wore a pair of very short running shorts. The shiny plastic of the legs gleamed in the sunlight. They had to have been like twice as long as his real legs had been. He moved deftly around on them, running this way and that to catch the Frisbee and then launching it back at the mother.

The mother looked better, too. She had on a new wig, an auburn one, and it looked like she'd taken the time to put it on straight. A cigarette dangled from the corner of her mouth, comically huge, bellowing a truly abnormal amount of smoke. She still wore a nightgown but it also looked new, bright nearly-fluorescent flowers standing out on a pink background.

Racecar was smoking too. Combined, they looked like a cigarette ad. The smoke from their cigarettes swirled up into the air, darkening it. I realized I could still hear some of the music from Bobby DeHaven's guitar playing except it, like the air around me, also became darker and heavier.

Suddenly, everything became foreboding.

I looked around the park. It was up on a hill. The only thing blotting the surface of its green grass was an orange swing set. The park was surrounded by a huge factory, as though the park itself were little more than a courtyard. Something inside me desperately wanted to be on the swing set, but there was another part of me that knew I had to run, to get the hell out of the park.

The sound of the mother coughing drew my attention back to the parents. She was doubled over, having one of her fits. Racecar wound up with the Frisbee and let it fly. It hit the mother right on the head, knocking her wig askew. She coughed again before retching, unleashing a torrent of bright red onto the grass. The sounds of the factory gained volume, becoming both rhythmic and abrasive, nearly musical, drowning out all the other sounds.

I tried to run, but it felt incredibly hard, like the grass was growing up around my feet. The air felt thicker, also. Not only was it hard to run, it was nearly impossible to breathe. I half-ran until I got to the wall of that factory. I looked back over my shoulder and noticed the parents were following me.

"Come on, Wally," Racecar called. "Come and play Frisbee with us."

I ignored him and pressed on into the factory. Even though there weren't any discernible doors or entrances, I got inside anyway.

"Come on, Wally," Racecar's voice matched the rhythm of the factory sounds.

In front of me, there was nothing but blackness and hell orange. To my sides were walls of dead, charred bodies. Once I realized what they were, the smell nearly made me vomit.

"You come back here, Wallace," the mother strumbled, framed against the comparative brightness of the entrance. "You little fucker. Little shit."

And she let fly with the Frisbee. It approached me in slow motion. I melted down to the floor, pains running all over my body, nearly paralyzing. While the Frisbee came floating toward me, I had the idea that, somehow, Uncle Skad was supposed to save me from all of this.

"Uncle Skad," I called.

Futility, a sinking dread, closed in around me along with the blackness and not the hell orange, but its hot essence.

"Uncle Skad!" I yelled. "Uncle Skad! Uncle Skad!"

I opened my eyes and he was there.

Chapter Seventeen
Uncle Skad

The first thing I saw were his huge, crystal blue eyes surrounded by bloodshot. Those eyes were full of concern. Something in the area around his eyes, in the folds and wrinkles, said he'd done a lot of worrying in his life. Blackish dirt, the dirt of the homeless I'd seen before my collapse, caked his face. A huge steel-gray beard surrounded that face, the same color as his long, dirty gray hair. That strange electric feeling I remembered from my dream was still there, in the room all around me. I realized the energy was coming from Uncle Skad.

"How is it that you know my name?" he asked.

I must have mumbled his name in my sleep. It was a simple question but it caught me completely off guard. There was electricity there, in the air, but it couldn't eclipse that grinding bonefeel. It was back and hurting even worse than it had that morning, after the multiple beatings.

"I'm... I'm..." I stammered.

Skad backed away from me. He was older and a little bit plump, but he moved with amazing fluidity.

"A boy, a peculiar boy, with horns atop his head, staggers and falls. This boy, this stranger, this alien is brought to me, slung across the arms of a stranger. But I'm enjoying a fine sleep. A holy helluva sleep. The door is kicked several times and I lie there, on my soft mat, my makeshift bed, hoping that the kicker, the disturbance, will go away. I lie there, drool trickling down my beard, listening to the kicking and the soft drip drop of rain on the rusted tin roof. I go to the door, look through my viewing slot and see one of my fellow Tar Mates. I open the door and the kicker, the knocker, comes inside with this woesome man-child slung over his arms. He plops him down on the floor and says, 'He was asking for you.' 'Me?' I ask. 'You,' he says."

Skad moved around his dark little space, his arms gesturing in a dramatic fashion.

"And I ask this child, this being that calls for me as he night-mares away a rainy night, I ask him how he knows my name and he stammers, 'I... I...'"

Skad looked at me as though to terrify me and I did feel a great welling of fear from within, those eyes piercing through me. Then he smiled, chuckled, a whole different look, a friendlier one, cover-ing his face. I struggled to sit up.

"Re*lax*," he placed a hand on my chest.

Uncle Skad was the only thing I could focus on. Everything else was completely shrouded in black.

"I'm Wallace Black. Sadie and Carl's kid," I wheezed out. Skad's little place was uncomfortably warm, leaning more toward hot, but whenever I breathed in, it felt more like I was breathing in the icy, rainy air of outside.

"I guess that *would* make me your uncle. I thought we shared some familial resemblance. I knew it was you anyway. I could tell by the freckles and the mouth. Remember? The family reunion about ten years ago. Just you and me stayed out there by the swing set. My arm nearly fell off from pushing you so damn much but I would have done just about anything to stay away from those pota-to salad-sucking fakes that call themselves family. Say, how are your parents anyway?"

I started to answer, to make up something I was supposed to say like, "Oh, they're doing fine," but he put a finger over my lips.

"Wait. You know what? And this is no offense to you, but I don't give a good goddamn how your parents are doing. They stopped believing in me a long time ago. Besides, you know, I didn't really push you on that swing just to stay away from the family, you were pretty interesting. Until you told me about those cloud factories, I didn't have any idea how those things got up there in the sky. If you haven't learned yet, Wally, you might figure out that the truth isn't always what you want to believe. You've grown horns since the last time I saw you. Looks like you've got something stuck on one of those things."

He reached out and poked one of the horns.

"That's an anus," I said.

"So I see." He giggled. "An anus."

"I'm in a great deal of pain."

"Horns aside, you look like complete and total hell. A boy your age shouldn't have those dark circles around his eyes. Anyway, I may be able to construct some form of remedy for that pain. You don't get to be my age without coming up with a few ways of coping with the old pain bug. Can you possibly manage to negotiate the numerous objects on the floor and move over here to the couch?"

I didn't think I'd be able to see my hand if I held it out too far in front of my face. I tried to stand up but my body wouldn't move. Maybe my brain had found a way to wake up, but my body was going to make me hurt if I commanded it to do anything. The mere hint of a movement and a low shriek involuntarily forced itself out of my mouth.

Uncle Skad picked me up like a small child and carried me over to the couch. It felt impossibly comfortable. Like the booth in the bar, my body melted into it. There was even something about the overwhelming smell of ass wafting up around me that seemed comforting.

"There you go," he said. "I guess we have a lot of catching up to do if you don't mind the ramblings of an old man."

Skad walked over to the middle of the room, disappearing into the darkness, and struck a match. He dropped the match and the room burst into a blaze of orange light. A crazy thought sent a sudden shockwave through my body. For a moment, I thought that, either I was still dreaming—all the darkness and hell orange— or I had died out there in the rain and gone to hell. Maybe this was going to be some kind of punishment, like now it was my turn to be burned alive for setting fire to the parents' house. Black smoke shot out of the barrel Uncle Skad had thrown the match into and I realized the fire wasn't going to spread.

I was safe.

The black smoke burned my lungs. On the floor, roaches scattered in all directions. They were some of the biggest roaches I'd ever seen. Most of them were about the size of my thumb. They ran until they hit a pile of papers or furniture. Once they hit the obstruction, they made horrible squeaky scratching sounds as they struggled to crawl over it. Skad must have noticed me looking at the bugs.

"It's alarming at first, I realize, but it's not too hard to grow quite comfortable with them. When I first moved in here, I used any means possible in order to get rid of them, but nothing really worked. Now, I figure, fuck it, let them spy on me. I know they have little camera eyes and microphones on their asses. They'll do anything to know what I'm doing at all times. Besides, a few months ago, they took up religion against me."

Uncle Skad made a broad sweeping motion to the far wall. A mass of roaches had formed a cross on the brown wood slats of the wall. The fire cast an ominous shadow, giving the cross a darkly luminous glow.

"Like their dear Christ, they crawl up there to die. Somehow, they stay. I guess they were trying to prove a point, too. Messianic roaches. Every now and then, all the other roaches will gather under that wall and I can hear them praying with all their little roach voices."

I could tell right away I was going to like Uncle Skad an awful lot. He fell silent. Actually, he went downright limp, and stared at the wall, his eyes a complete blank, the fire dancing across his huge pupils.

I heard coughing come from the back of the house. A hunchback crept out of the shadows and I was somewhat taken aback. I may have even gasped.

"Are you filling the visitor up with your crazy talk already,

Skaddeus?"

"Huh?" the voice brought him back from wherever he was. I wasn't sure, maybe it was just the fire, but I thought I saw something like a *flicker* run through Skad.

"Oh," he said. "Sorry there, didn't mean to wake you."

The man coughed again. "You know, it's not so much the light as it is the smoke. I do enough of that anyway. I don't need to do it when I sleep, too." He pulled out an unfiltered cigarette, put it in his mouth, and leaned his head over the barrel. He brought his head back up and said, "Who needs eyebrows anyway?"

"Introductions are in order, I suppose," Skad said. "Wallace Black, this is Dr. Blast. Dr. Blast, that couch-bound gentleman over there is Wallace Black."

"Nice to meet you," I said.

"Greetings," Dr. Blast said.

I was captivated by this man. He was completely normal looking except for his hunchback ascending to a rounded hump just below the crown of his head.

"You're looking at my hump, aren't you?" he said suddenly. My answer got caught up somewhere in the back of my throat. Of course I was staring at his hump, but I couldn't just tell him that, could I?

"It's a nice one, isn't it?" he asked.

"It is pretty remarkable," I said.

"Remarkable, of course. My only solace comes from the fact that it's not there most of the time."

"Are you having it removed?"

"No, not exactly. You can't just have a hunchback... *lanced* or something. No. This here's a Sad Hump. It comes and it goes. I'll be okay for months, sometimes even a year or more, then the Sad Hump'll come and stick around for a few weeks. That's when I come here and sort of hide out for awhile. I don't know, there's something about this place that makes the hump go away. Have you come here before?"

"Not exactly," I said.

Dr. Blast took a deep drag off his cigarette and threw it into the barrel. "Well, I hope you have a great time." He turned around to Uncle Skad, grabbing some piles up off the floor and feeding them into the barrel. "You coming back to bed sometime soon, old man?"

"I'll be there shortly. You go on ahead."

Dr. Blast bid us both a good night, walked to the back of the smallish space, and collapsed into a heap on the floor.

"Dr. Blast likes his sleep," Skad said.

"I'm sorry," I said.

"No, sleep's good for him. Oh, you mean you're sorry about something else. What is it, Wallace?"

"Just showing up like this."

"Oh, it's better than a stick in the eye. It's so rare that I get company unless, of course, they're sending somebody to spy on me. There's the occasional displaced Tar Mate I extend my hospitality to but they usually end up drinking all of my Scotch and puking everywhere."

"I won't be here long."

"You can stick around me as long as you need to. It has been a very long time since I've chatted with a family member. To be honest, you're probably the only family member I'd want to chat with. On a whole, they're a rather sorry lot, wouldn't you say?"

"Certainly," I said, even though I couldn't really remember any of them.

"I want you to fill me in on what's been happening around the Black family the past ten years or so. It may turn out that you and I have a lot in common. First, though, you mentioned something about being in a great deal of pain, didn't you? And I mentioned something about a remedy?"

I nodded.

"Let me see what I can do about that."

He went off toward the back of the house and I heard some clanking and sloshing and a few surprised exclamations like he'd just found something he didn't know he had. I looked back at him. There was a small counter space he worked on, going back and forth as he went about his concocting, busily stepping over Dr.

Blast, who lay on his stomach, his hump occluding his head. I wished I wasn't in the pain I was. It would have been so nice to join him.

"What, exactly, is the kind of pain you are feeling?" he called to me. "Dull? Achy? Piercing? Thudding? Throbbing? Scraping? Burning? Raw? Stinging?"

"No, it's sort of a grinding bonefeel," I called back, figuring he would know exactly what I was talking about.

"Ah, of course, I should have known. No matter, the secret ingredient's all the same."

He spent a few more minutes of grabbing little jars and holding them up to the firelight. After awhile he brought back a Mason jar full of brownish-red liquid. I noticed he had a glass of what I assumed was whiskey for himself.

"You drink some of that," he said. "Let us toast the absence of pain."

He clicked his glass against mine and lifted it to his lips. Once he got his glass all the way up there, I nearly retched. A roach struggled furiously against the bottom of the glass. He had to know it was there. Had he put it there?

Taking my brief disgust for hesitation, Skad grunted, "Go on... It'll put hair on your chest."

I sipped mine. It didn't taste too bad, but it sent this trail of fire down my throat that landed somewhere in the pit of my stomach and made my anus burn. I didn't even want to think about going to the bathroom in this place. I couldn't even figure out where the bathroom might be. I certainly didn't see how this was going to help the pain.

"So, Wally, why don't you tell me how you got here? People are often drawn here by strange and magical forces. Tell me your story first and then I'll tell you mine." I thoroughly enjoyed listening to Uncle Skad talk. He had a way of placing emphasis on everything and making it seem really dramatic. Except he didn't seem like the type of person I would have pictured being dramatic.

He threw his head back and downed the last of the whiskey. He brought the glass down and looked inside, seemingly noticing the roach for the first time. He poked at it and made a surprised motion with his eyebrows. He grumbled a little bit and directed his attention back to me. "Go on, I know you have something."

Glancing down into his glass again, he gave it a little shake. The roach floated around on the bottom, all bloated up. I took another sip of mine and decided this would be the last time I told the story. No one had seemed the least bit interested in what I had done before. It seemed like they just wanted to know what brought me standing there in front of them. After telling Uncle Skad I would simply tell people I was the devil, sent to the earth to devour souls. Or maybe I would just tell them I was born that way, like I had Johnny Metal. That seemed to be the thing most devoid of any type of philosophy or fuckness like that.

But I started at the beginning for Uncle Skad. I mean, I started with those Clean People who came to our house and I told him about the lawnmower cord and the bad haircut punishment and all the other stupid shit. And I told him about the blobs. I must have went on and on about the blobs. I think I even told him about fantasizing that I was a massive giant and I could piss on all of them, my urine melting them like salt melts a slug.

I drank more and more of that stuff and the pain just melted away and I just kept talking and talking and talking. I don't know how I managed to talk so much. It felt like I could fall over at any moment. And I noticed that, instead of crying like I did when I told Drifter Ken, I laughed. Uncle Skad laughed too, but I could still see that look of concern in his eyes. The entire time I talked it felt like my body was winding up, tighter and tighter. And then I finished, flopping back on the couch—totally relaxed.

Uncle Skad leaned in and said, "Wallace Black, at the tender and transitional age of sixteen, you have already lead a wonderful and most extraordinary immaculate life. I will do my best to aid you in your quest and lend my unflagging sensibility and modest resources."

I don't know if it was that drink Uncle Skad had made for me or if it was just being there, talking to him, but my head was reeling. I felt great. The entire time I told my story to Uncle Skad, he looked completely absorbed in what I was saying. I think it was more his electric stare that made me feel a little better. Looking at Uncle Skad, a strange blue glow emanated from him.

I lay down on the couch, an uncontrollable smile spreading itself across my face. I felt like a dope. I felt like the Cheshire Cat and, what was most amazing, for awhile, I didn't *feel* many feelings at all.

"Perhaps I should wait until tomorrow to tell my tale, Mr. Black."

"No, no, I want to hear it. It'll be a bedtime story."

Uncle Skad's eyes twinkled. "I've never had someone to tell a bedtime story to."

"One night only!" I shouted.

"One night only!" Uncle Skad agreed. "One night only! Ladies and gentlemen, Wallace Black!"

"Pipe down, goddammit!" Dr. Blast hollered from the back.

I laughed. "Begin. Begin already," I pleaded. My head really was spinning.

Uncle Skad stood up from the floor, where he had sat listening so intently to my story.

"First I'm going to freshen up the old glass, friend. Need any more remedy?"

"No thanks." His remedy still felt like it was punching the fuck out of my rectum. Skad walked to the back of the house and I lay there on the couch, listening to the shuffling and clinking. Dr. Blast grunted deeply and muttered, "You're standing... on my *head*, you old troll."

"Sorry," Skad said.

Skad came back with his drink, scooted an old chair closer to the couch, and sat down on the edge. I watched him move, nearly hypnotized, as he dragged that blue light around with him. The light seemed to be gaining some sharpness of color, lingering in the air behind him a little bit longer. He sat down on the edge of the chair and scratched his beard with thick grime-covered fingers. His fingernails were thick and yellow. They reminded me of Fritos. A roach crept out of his beard and scurried up his cheek. He casually flicked it away and began his story.

He rocked constantly as he talked, the speed gaining momentum with his story, and continued making wildly dramatic gestures with his hands, sending that blue all around him. My weightless spirit had returned sometime while I was talking to Skad and I found myself sitting up on the couch and, at times, even whipping my augmented head from shoulder to shoulder. This didn't faze Uncle Skad, though. He knew I was hearing every word he said. At times I would also snap my fingers and I swear Uncle Skad was almost able to time his story to those snaps.

It was then, as Skad told his story, that I suspected him of being much crazier than I was and much crazier than I'd first suspected him of being. Except for his living quarters, he had previously seemed like a sane and rational human being. There was even sort of a determinist sanity to his house.

He began his story with his birth, stating that he was fully conscious and aware from the moment he slid from his mother's womb. He knew this would give him problems later on. From the night he was taken home, his mother (my grandmother, I guess) was wickedly mean to him. She would spend the rest of her life denying she was wickedly mean to him, thinking there was no possible way he could remember any of that fuckness. He had a normal childhood, although he was watched the entire time. Skad said he was well aware of the high volume of airplanes and helicopters that flew overhead, monitoring him while he tried to play outside. When his mother started buying televisions for every room in the house, he realized someone was watching him through those, as well. There were a number of times when he could hear the spies bumbling behind the walls or catch glimpses of them in the mirror.

As Skad grew older, he refused to eat the same food twice, so those people watching him wouldn't pick up his dietary habits and find an easy way to poison him. This had him eating a lot of odd things. You know all those things you see in cans and jars of sickening color at the supermarket—the things that seemed reserved for either the biggest bumpkins or the most pretentious gourmet? Skad had tried them all: from caviar down to pickled pig's feet. He said this strange diet allowed him to keep a totally open mind and avoid any sort of favoritism that would cripple him when he got his first job—the King of Pung.

Apparently, Pung was a very small island nation somewhere in the Pacific Rim and Uncle Skad was able to run this country through the mail. At that point, he launched into a lengthy comparison of political structures. I heard the words, but most of the concepts eluded me. I've never cared much for politics. Eventually, he was dethroned. The airplanes and the television learned he wasn't observing an honored Pung tradition that consisted of shaving off all the body hair, on a daily basis, and saving it in pillowcases.

"I'm just an incredibly hairy motherfucker," Skad said. "I simply found the ritual too exhausting and painful to carry on with."

After this failure, Skad was convinced he spent four years in hell. Until then, he never really believed in the concept of a hell. I interrupted him to ask if he ever got to meet Satan, but Skad said no one ever sees him "down there" because he is on earth doing his work. He was still not fully convinced of hell in the traditional sense of the word. "It's all trickery," he said. "A lot of aluminum foil and high-powered sun lamps is all. The demons are just monkeys in costume."

His sentence served, he came back to the surface and became a photographer. He became quite successful at this before being busted on charges of pornography. Skad said he still isn't sure what was pornographic about his work and, what with the laws and all, it was impossible to find out.

There were a number of other things about Skad's life that he wouldn't tell me, saying they were "Top Secret."

"For instance," he said. "I invented something that has become so commonplace you couldn't imagine that someone had to invent it. Something as seemingly necessary as a pair of pants or a chair. But, when I was bought out, the corporation forbade me to talk about it. Sometime when it's just you and me, Wally boy, I'll tell you all about it but, you know, I'm in a compromising situation here." He gestured to the cockroaches littered around him. And they truly were everywhere.

Fuckness

He pulled out a pack of cigarettes and shook them over his hand. A roach clicked out onto his palm, wet and glistening. He reached his fingers in to pull out a cigarette and got up to light it over the barrel.

The Tar District, in short, was where Skad ended up. He said it made him sad that nobody in the Tar District had anything to their names. How they had all been reduced to nothing. "But these people here aren't the ones who are reduced to nothing," he said. "When people give up their souls for more and more and more, that's when people are reduced to nothing. I *choose* to live in the Tar District. If you ever want to know the true nature of your soul, you'll live in complete and total poverty. Poverty makes people do things that maybe they didn't think were possible. There are a lot of people who are capable of performing great works, either to enrich their lives in the simplest way they know how, or to try and bring themselves up out of poverty. Others find themselves capable of the worst possible deeds when they crack under the pressures of poverty. The people in the Tar District manage to live incredibly full lives. When you find that everything you're doing is done to stay alive it tends to give you a renewed sense of purpose in life."

By the time he was finished, I was very excited and very tired. I shouted, "Hooray, Uncle Skad!" for no reason other than it seemed like a good thing to say. I doubted everything he said was true but, then again, he was glowing and most people would have a hard time believing that. I decided some people live a very real kind of life in their heads. More than anything, I decided I was very tired. I'd done too much of everything that day. I lay down on my back and started spiraling down into sleep.

Skad's voice sounded like it came from very far away. "You sleep tight Wally Black." Then he laughed and said, "May your dreams melt away those awful horns. You sleep tight."

Chapter Eighteen
Skad's Invention

I woke up on the couch and slowly raised my head, expecting the grinding bonefeel to be there. There was no pain at all. All over my body, every trace of stiffness and soreness was gone. Hoping Skad's magic drink had other effects, I raised my hand to feel along the top of my head, but the horns were still there. Happy to be pain free once again, I flung myself off the couch and landed on my feet.

Uncle Skad was already awake.

"You get out of the bed the same way I do," he said.

"Yeah, it really gets me started."

"Come out on the deck with Dr. Blast and I."

I followed Skad through the dim house. He swung the back door open and we went out onto the sagging deck. Standing dangerously close to the far edge of the small deck, I was able to look straight down at the greasy Saints River. Dr. Blast sat in a black soot-covered plastic porch chair, balancing a stained coffee mug on his knee. The Sad Hump was gone. The morning was bright and as clear as Milltown got.

Dr. Blast squinted up at me. "Good morning, Wally," he said.

"Good morning, Dr. Blast. Your hump's gone."

"Strangest thing. I had a wonderful dream last night. It lifted the sadness right away. It's Saturday morning, the sun is out, and I'm going to go home to my wife and kids. We'll take a drive in the country and I'll make them listen to Benny Goodman on the car stereo."

"What time is it, anyway?"

Uncle Skad looked around. "I have no idea of the exact time. Minutes and seconds are so restrictive. I'm guessing it's early."

"Early," I reiterated.

"Are you hungry?"

"Sure."

"Let's me and you fix us something to eat. I've decided that you are on a journey, Wally. If you'll allow me, I'd like to help you. Due to legal restrictions, I can't take you wherever you need to go but I'll take you as far as I can."

"I just want to get out of Milltown."

"Oh, getting out of Milltown's no problem. We can be out of here in no time at all."

"Thanks, Uncle Skad."

"I notice your shoes are looking a little worn."

"Yeah, I've had them for a couple of years."

"Looks like you've grown right out of them. Let me see what I can find."

"That'd be great."

"For now, though, I must find food."

"Well, I better be going," Dr. Blast said and then we were all standing up, our faces grimed with the soot sediment that poured out of the barrel.

Nobody said anything. There were a few moments of uncomfortable shifting and we all went back into the house. Skad and Dr. Blast raced for the front door, both of them slamming out of it and leaving me standing there in the dim house.

I felt good. Yesterday's miseries had faded away. The house was almost dark. Black plastic had been nailed over all the windows but the morning sunlight came in through all the cracks and holes in the ceiling and walls, pressing inward through the wads of paper shoved in there to keep the wind and as much of the rain as possible out.

I sat down and watched the cockroaches. Our house back on Walnut had the occasional roach or two. The mother said that was because we lived by train tracks or the plumbing was old or some fuckness like that. Those cockroaches at home never made themselves visible during the daylight. Sometimes, in the middle of the night, if I went into the kitchen and threw on a light, I'd see one or two of them scurry to some dark area. Apparently, the more roaches there were, the more brazen they became. Uncle Skad's roaches shuffled slowly around on the floor as though they had as much right to this place as Uncle Skad. I got bored, I guess. It never really did take much for me to get bored. I reached down and managed to grab a couple of the roaches. I found a clear spot on the floor, no easy task, and sat them down side by side, hoping they would race. They were slow to move at first and, once they did, my plans were completely foiled. They sprouted off into two opposite directions like the concept of a contest was completely foreign to them. I watched as they each went to join their separate packs.

It wasn't long before Uncle Skad came back. Bundled in his arms were a loaf of bread, a carton of eggs, a few cheese slices and a pair of shoes. He slammed the door behind him and, breathing quickly, made his way to the back of the house where he dumped his finds.

"I still think they might be trying to poison me so now I just borrow food from other people. I went over to see if old Otto had any food and, strangest thing, old Otto's dead."

There was an old, woodburning stove back there. Skad swung the small iron door open, stuffed some newspapers and old boards in there, and lit it up. "Unbelievable, he was just sprawled out there in the middle of the floor." He held a hand over the stove's surface to see if it was getting warm. "That's where I got the shoes. Looked like he was about a size ten, so these might be a little small for you but they have to be better than what you have now." He dug underneath the stove and cracked a couple eggs over it. "See, most of these houses here in the Tar District are actually condemned. No one's really supposed to be living in them. What happens is that, whenever someone dies, we make use of whatever resources we can so no traces are left behind. Old Otto's place didn't look too picked over. I'm guessing he died sometime last night. Possibly the night before. As for the bodies, those usually disappear. It is my assumption that some master chef here in the Tar District can probably cook up a mean leg of human. How do egg sandwiches sound?"

"Anything is fine."

Uncle Skad went about making the food over the small stove. I sat on the couch, the greasy smells flooding my senses. My stomach rumbled. Sitting there, I ran my fingers over my face, feeling its new lumpy form. I was sure my nose was broken. It didn't hurt, but I couldn't really breathe through it very well. Up to that point, I had tried not to be a mouth breather. Mainly so people wouldn't look at me right off the bat and assume I was even dumber than I really was. I mean, I spent a lot of time just fazing out and staring off into space anyway. Now I figured I'd be doing that with my mouth open, also. People would walk by and interrupt my daydreaming to ask if I was trying to catch flies. Fuck them, I thought.

Skad brought me the egg and cheese sandwich on a folded up piece of newspaper. The grease had already soggied the paper. I hungrily went about devouring the sandwich. I had gone all day yesterday without eating a thing and that sandwich tasted like the best thing I'd eaten in I don't know how long. My mouth watered and my stomach made deep gurgling sounds as it disintegrated the food.

We both finished our sandwiches quickly and threw the greasy newspapers in the barrel. A satisfying belch forced its way out of my throat and I retasted breakfast. We sat in silence for a few moments, both of us digesting. Uncle Skad lit another one of his cigarettes. It smelled like a campfire.

Skad finished his cigarette and looked at me contemplatively, cocking his head from one side to the other, studying the horns.

"Those things have been in our family for years. I think they were passed down from our grandfather. No one really knew where they came from, like what kind of horns they are or anything. We used to play with them as kids. I didn't know what had happened to them. I guess Sadie took them, huh?" He quietly studied me again and then said, real out of the blue, "You know, Wally, even though I think they add a good deal of flair and character, I can tell by the look in your eyes that you would sooner live without those egregious horns."

"Yeah," I said. "It's just... well, I have a hard time fitting in anyway."

"I'll see what I can do."

He went into the back of the house. I was beginning to realize anything of importance was located in the back of the house. He returned with a small box.

"Let me see one of those horns," he said.

I proffered my head toward him. He moved my hair around and felt around the base of one of the horns with his fingers.

"What'd she do, super glue the suckers on there?"

"No, they had a strap but it came off when I tried to unbuckle it."

"Like magic."

"I guess."

He gave the horn a little tug, trying to work it back and forth.

"That kind of hurts," I said.

"Yeah, they're in there pretty good. Guess I'll have to try another way."

Skad fished through the little cardboard box and pulled out a piece of sandpaper. He ran a finger along the surface, testing the texture. Holding the square of paper in the palm of his hand, he began rubbing it around in circles on the top of the left horn. There wasn't any feeling in the horn but, I guess with them actually being attached to my head, the scratching sound of that sandpaper sounded like he was scraping at my ear. The dust from the powdering of the horn settled on the back of my neck. I guess I kind of got my hopes up. I imagined the horns would be little more than nubbins in an hour.

But there was no progress to be made.

"My God," Skad said. "This could take days. Those horns are dense little objects. You know what?"

"What?"

"Maybe the horns were just meant to stay on."

Fuckness

"I hope not."

But Skad had echoed my thoughts exactly. Maybe the horns *were* meant to stay on. And what if they were? My life had already been filled with fuckness, the horns could only assure the rest of my life would be filled with the same kind of fuckness and, most probably, even more fuckness than I'd previously ever experienced. If the horns were meant to stay on, then it wouldn't matter how well I could act. If I ever grew out of my awkward stage and learned how to stop twitching and hooting, the horns would ensure that I would always remain an outcast. The horns would become my poverty. What I said before about never being able to get rid of the poor would be the same thing. Like whenever a poor person actually made something of himself, there's always someone standing around and saying, "Can you *imagine*, he used to be so *poor*?" I could be the well-behaved boy with horns. The well- dressed boy with horns. The smart boy with horns. But I would still be the boy with horns.

"Look," Skad said. "I don't think the horns are really going to matter much. You might even find somebody who likes you better *with* the horns."

"Really?" I was hopelessly incredulous about that.

"Sure. There are lots of people who aren't as shallow as the ones you've been around. What did you so adequately refer to them as?"

"Blobs."

"Yes. Blobs. That's perfect. Blobs have no character, do they? They're just shapeless masses of flesh and blood. I've met my share of blobs. I even started drinking with the hopes that I might become a blob, like all of my senses would be dulled and I wouldn't be able to feel anything. Ah, but that didn't work. I simply fell out of society. I couldn't become a blob. I didn't have the instincts."

"I think you have to be born that way."

Uncle Skad laughed and then said, "Wally, I think it would be best if we got on our way before we've wasted the whole damned day. Have you ever flown before?"

"No."

"Well, get ready for the experience of a lifetime. Are you ready?"

"Sure."

I followed Skad outside. This was the first time I got to really get a good look at the Tar District. Unlike the rundown area up by Main Street, where I'd seen the homeless folks the night before, this section, the "riverfront" as Uncle Skad called it, contained actual houses. They could only be called houses in the sense that they had what passed as walls and ceilings and people living in them—they all looked so run down and broken. Standing there and looking around made Walnut seem like a row of palaces. None of these houses were taller than one story. A few of them were up on stilts. I guess that was so they'd be safe when the Saints rose but the stilts looked so decayed it seemed like they would make them fall even quicker.

The sun was huge and warm and threw crazy shadows all over the Tar District. The sun's heat made all of those smells rise up and the whole strip reeked, fishy and oily. There wasn't any grass to be seen. The ground was covered with what looked like roofing shingles. The only signs of life were the anemic wisps of smoke coming from the metal-looking makeshift chimneys.

Black seemed to be the dominant color here. Further up the Saints, on the opposite side, loomed the oldest of those death factories. They were already at work, pumping their black smoke up into that rich blue sky. Uncle Skad's house sat a few yards further back than the rest of the other houses and was about half the size. It was stained a few shades darker than the other houses and the right side of it looked like it was sliding into the Saints. The black plastic covered the outside of the windows, also. In front of the house hung a black flag from a rusted flagpole.

Uncle Skad clapped his thick hands together and my attention snapped back to him. I'd been standing there staring with my mouth wide open.

"I'm so excited you're here, Wally. I've been waiting to show someone my invention."

"Invention?"

Fuckness

"Yes, I've taught my bicycle to fly."

I became incredibly excited at him saying this. Immediately, I began picturing all sorts of things. A flying bike. It sounded magnificent but I figured it was probably about as real as the people who were following him or his visit to hell.

"Let me go get it, Wally."

Uncle Skad disappeared around the far side of the house. I tapped my foot on the ground, looked up at the sun, and threw my head from shoulder to shoulder. Whenever I was able to move around like that, it made all of the other thoughts go away and the time passed twice as quickly.

Skad came around from the other side of the house and I stopped my thrashing. He was pedaling the bike, struggling to keep it balanced. It was a tandem bicycle, one with two seats and two sets of pedals on it. Extending from the sides were two huge white wings. If it did fly, I was sure it would be able to fly higher than any bird I'd ever seen.

Uncle Skad rang a bell on the front of it and motioned for me to hop on. Truthfully, I was almost scared. I wondered what would happen if we got going too high. I didn't see any sort of seatbelts or anything like that on it and I wasn't very coordinated anyway so it seemed like it would be really easy to just sort of fall right off.

"Have you been up in this thing, yet?" I asked him.

"Oh *yeah*... It'll be the experience of a lifetime, Wally. You have my utmost reassurance of that. In no time at all, we will be fully ascended and flying right next to the sun, out of all this blackness."

"What if we fall off?"

"Then it was meant to be!"

Given my theories of the game, what Uncle Skad said kind of disturbed me. I figured if someone were meant to fall off something then that someone was me. So far, I still had not technically left Milltown and I was still waiting for my rotten luck to change. I looked at the bike as though it was the grim reaper, nearly certain it would be the death of me.

"Hop on! Hop on, Wally! You worry too much! We'll be safe as angels in this sad-looking contraption."

Even with my premonitions of death, I was very excited to get on the winged bicycle. I rushed over and hopped on.

"You just have to be very careful not to *lean*. Are you ready?"

"Yes."

"Okay. We have to pedal very, very fast in order to get this thing to take off."

We both hunched our backs and laid into those pedals. The bicycle's tires skidded in the dirt, we started pedaling so hard. I took a look back at Uncle Skad's shack, my eyes fixing on that flagpole. I noticed the flag wasn't entirely black, like I'd thought at first. It was the American flag, covered in dirt and pollution. The flag got smaller and smaller.

And we kept pedaling and pedaling, leaving the Tar District behind and heading for the rolling pale green meadows and sheared down, brown cornfields surrounding Milltown. I kept waiting for us to lift, wanting the closeness of the sun to melt away the chill of the wind.

We were going so fast the wind whistled in our ears. In order to be heard everything had to be shouted.

"Feel that, Wally! We are so high! Like a giant bird! I told you this was amazing!"

One of us was obviously hallucinating. We were still on the ground and, although we were going very fast, we were nowhere near flying. I decided to let Uncle Skad keep his fantasy. I needed it as much as he did. The more I played along with him, the more it felt like we *were* flying.

"This is great! Hooray, Uncle Skad! I can't believe that we're actually flying!"

"We'll be there in no time at all!"

"Where exactly are we going!"

"No idea!"

It sounded like as good a place as any!

"How much longer!"

"Not much! You'll know when we get there!"

Excitement mounted within me. I had no idea where we were going and I didn't care. The momentum, the movement felt good.

Fuckness

It was the first time since starting out that I felt like I was taking more than slowly plodding baby steps. And we pedaled and pedaled and pedaled until we were so close to that fat sun it should have melted the rubber off our tires. I wouldn't have cared if it melted the flesh from my bones.

I've done it, I thought. I've finally left Milltown. And I had no regrets at all.

Chapter Nineteen
The Hilltop Cafe

It was amazing how much ground we covered on the bicycle. It wasn't long before we were away from Milltown completely. It truly was a beautiful day. Out there in the countryside, the sky was a wild vibrant blue. Those fat white clouds hung there, floating slowly along like giant ships. The hillsides around us were nearly artificial-looking green. There had been enough warm days the past week and it felt like spring was here. The heat was palpable in the air. I had worked up a pretty good sweat. Uncle Skad had worked up a completely horrendous stink.

This was probably the most physical effort I had expended in years and it wasn't long before I really started to feel it. I wanted to think my thoughts. I wanted to be able to look around at the beautiful day but I ended up bearing down, concentrating on moving my legs up and down, and focusing on the dead roach caught up in the back of Uncle Skad's hair. Trying not to lean was another issue altogether. My head whummed with exhaustion and strain. It felt like my heart was pumping a bunch of blood into my head and it would only be a matter of time before it exploded like a red balloon. I wondered how many sixteen-year-olds who weren't speed addicts had heart attacks. The only thing I wanted to do was lay my head on Uncle Skad's back and take a snooze. I wondered if he would notice if I stopped pedaling completely.

Uncle Skad rang the bell on the bicycle, something he had done the entire way in order to get my attention. The sound of the wind and the heavy glubbub of the whumming made conversation nearly impossible.

"It won't be long, Wally!"

My mouth was painfully dry. It felt like my tongue was swollen enough to take up my entire mouth so I wasn't able to give him any type of response. My eyes just stayed bulgy and glued to the back of Skad's head, ragged breaths rhythmically ripped out of my mouth, my lungs furiously burning.

"Up there! That's where we'll stop off!"

He nodded his head in front of the bike and I managed to look up. We were about to start up a large hill. We were both still pedaling like mad, those huge white-feathered wings flapping madly up and down.

"Wow!" I think I said. I'm not really sure if anything actually came out or not. It was probably just a dry wheeze.

"Don't worry, Wally! I'm sure this old beast'll be able to clear that mountain!" It wasn't the bike I was worried about.

Skad was truly amazing. When he leaned back to talk to me he didn't even sound like he was out of breath. And then I had a crazy idea. What if I was there, on the ground, pedaling and pedaling and pedaling and Uncle Skad really *was* somewhere way up in the sky, flying toward the sun? Could it be that I was just confused and making the whole thing harder on myself? I looked down at his feet just to make sure that his legs were actually moving. They were, but it didn't look like he was putting nearly the effort into it that I was. Maybe if I hadn't given up to the whumming and the wheezing a long time ago, if I had continued to think we were flying, then maybe I wouldn't be so exhausted now. But it was too late to start flying in my head again. I was down and we were about ready to start the hardest part.

As soon as we hit the base of the hill, the pace automatically slowed. It was a good thing my legs were numb. Whatever movement they generated was of their own free will. The sizable hill I saw became Skad's mountain. I couldn't do anything but look at the top of it and wait. I had faith in our legs. I had faith in the bike.

Uncle Skad rang the bell and called over his shoulder. He was able to speak in a normal voice since we were moving way too slow to create any ear friction, but he still insisted on shouting.

"We should make quite a show, Wally!"

I tried to say something and unleashed a volley of coughs instead.

"You okay back there, Wally!"

"Fine, fine," I managed. "Where are we going?"

"I told you! Anywhere! But first I thought we'd stop and get a bite to eat! I'll buy!"

"Sounds great. Are we almost there?"

"Top of the mountain, Wally! It's called the Hilltop Cafe! A wonderful place! We'll be there in no time! Just enjoy the ride!"

We were going slow enough for me to look around again. It must have been late afternoon sometime. The hill was covered in trees. The air felt cooler since we were in constant shade and everything smelled woody. I always found the woods to be slightly creepy. They seemed completely disorienting, like you'd never be able to remember where you were. And the further you looked into them, the darker it became. I imagined people living in secret houses and doing secret things like making moonshine and fucking relatives. Both of us were up off our seats, putting some weight into the thrusts and taking some of the strain off our legs. The road wound and twisted to the top of the hill. I knew this made it less steep but it seemed to draw the excursion out to a nearly epic proportion.

A huge car headed straight for us before swerving and honking its horn. I realized that cars had been passing us all day. If I'd been more aware, this would have made me kind of nervous but I was too busy with everything, I guess. Uncle Skad had that effect on me. I didn't think it would be possible for me to feel unsafe around him. It had been under twenty-four hours since we met and I already felt comfortable. I hadn't really said much to Skad since telling him my story yesterday, which was another thing. I didn't feel compelled to talk, like I should just say stuff for the hell of it, but I did feel like I could blurt things out. If I had a thought I could go ahead and say it.

Fuckness

My stomach started growling and I wondered where the hell this restaurant Skad was talking about was. The trees gradually thinned and the ground gradually leveled.

"Any minute now!" Uncle Skad shouted. I really hoped he'd stop doing that soon. "We won't take this bird through town!"

We rode it for a few more yards. Once we reached the leveled top of the hill it felt like we were gliding along on ball bearings. We were at the edge of a very small town. Actually, calling it a town was, more or less, hyperbole. It was more like the fractured remains of a town. The top of the hill really wasn't large enough to contain an entire society. To my right I saw the Hilltop Cafe, a small, run-down-looking restaurant. A large red neon sign on its roof flashed "EAT" into the coming dusk. Across the street, to my left, there was a football field, the gruff shouts and plastic clatter of helmets and pads echoing through the quiet. On the far side of the hill were a few houses, built there for the view, no doubt. A gas station sat beside the Hilltop. On the left side of the road, where the football field was, there were a couple of other two-story brick structures. I couldn't tell what they were. I didn't really give a fuck, either. I was ravenous.

We rode the bike over to the side of the road and got off. My legs nearly rubberbanded me to the ground. We pushed the bike over into the edge of the woods.

"How'd you like the trip, Wally?"

"It was all right, I guess."

"It was fantastic!"

"Fantastic!"

"We'll leave this baby right here. Let's go get some food."

"Thanks for being so nice, Uncle Skad."

"Hell. Thank Otto, it's his money. May he rest in peace. Otto was an expert panhandler and he didn't drink so he had a good amount socked away."

Both of us walked very slowly toward the restaurant. It was pretty windy there at the top of the hill and the air was starting to moisten a little. It would probably rain all day tomorrow, I figured. The air smelled much better up here than down in Milltown. I could smell the dirt and the grass—all the smells were good clean smells. And as we got closer to the restaurant, I could smell even better smells, the toasting of bread, the frying of flesh and boiling vats of fat.

Skad took a deep breath. "Ah, the best food this side of the carnival, Wally. You get whatever you want."

The glass door jingled as Skad swung it open. The only people in there were a family sitting over in a corner booth. None of the waitresses were visible. I suddenly had an overwhelming urge to urinate. Apparently Skad also had the urge to urinate. We matched each other step for step, our shoes sticking to the yellow tiled floor, as we retreated for the obscure back location that harbored most bathrooms. In this one, you had to open a door to a small vestibule before the actual bathroom door. I got my hand on the handle first and then Uncle Skad's covered mine. We paused as though both of us were locked in some form of homophobic dilemma. Skad looked me in the eye and issued a challenge: "This is okay. We can have a pee race if you feel up for it."

I didn't grow up with any brothers or any fuckness like that and when Racecar pissed he had to sit down, so I didn't really know what the hell a pee race was.

"What's that?" I asked.

"Oh, it's easy. There's nothing to it. Just do what you normally do."

We crowded into the small bathroom and quickly shut the door. Skad kicked up the toilet seat and had his pants unzipped before I even knew what was going on. He dangled his penis over the bowl and gave it a shake. I unzipped my pants and fished around for my penis. I chuckled with the absurdity of it all. Normally my penis was sucked back into the body cavity. That probably came from being so high- strung. I looked down and saw Skad had already started, his piss pretty much the color of the bathroom. I had trouble starting. I've always been a little bit pee shy. I almost never went at school but if I did I had to use a stall. Skad had a really respectable-looking dick. I was sure he had it named something really masculine like Brock or Rocky or some fuckness like that. Mine looked weak. Long and skinny. A real Mr. Lawrence.

Finally, I started up, the piss screaming out of me. There was nothing like a good piss after a long wait. I was sort of surprised anything came out. Skad's stream was slow and steady, heavy-sounding. Mine was the urinary equivalent of a greyhound. The two streams crossed each other, bubbling in the once clear water. Skad's stream slowly ground to a halt. It looked like he had won. A few seconds later, I finished. Skad's dick suddenly let go with a couple more spurts and he shook it vigorously. He held the entire thing in his hand while he urinated whereas I'd normally only had to use a couple of fingers or perhaps a thumb delicately pressing down on the head. Anyway, now it looked like I had won.

"Damn that prostate," Uncle Skad said. He zippered up and looked at me. "Congratulations, Wally, you're the first person to beat me in a pee race. Maybe I should retire. Wallace Black. The new pee race champion!"

"Hooray!" I said.

"Okay, let me walk out first. When I get to the booth and sit down, you go ahead and come out. Don't want people to think we're weird."

Skad left the dim bathroom vestibule, picked a booth in front of the window and sat down. Once he got a cigarette lit, I went ahead and walked out too. I walked quickly and with my head down. The only time I was really conscious of the horns' weight was when I lowered my head like that. This really felt like the first time I'd been out in public daylight since tooling around Milltown in the wheelchair yesterday morning. Christ, that was only the day before! It felt like a fucking century ago. After I got to the booth and sat down, I felt a little less self-conscious. I mean, I was used to being a freak anyway so you'd think I'd just be able to shut out those voices around me. But it was just the opposite. As soon as I went anywhere in public my body established some form of hyper-awareness to the mocking voices around me.

For instance, when I got to that booth and sat down, I heard a little girl from the family table over in the corner say, "What's wrong with that man?"

The mother whispered something in her ear, I couldn't quite make out everything she said, but I'm pretty sure I heard the word "dangerous" in there. That made me want to laugh. I found the notion absurd. Maybe someone who knew about the murders would think I was dangerous but I didn't think the horns made me look dangerous. I figured it probably had more of the effect of watching a prepubescent boy struggle with his first set of weights. Nevertheless, after hearing that, after knowing I'd been noticed, I sat there in dread. I sat there in dread because I kept waiting for some sort of macho instinct to kick in with the father of the family, like he'd have to come over to our table and kick the shit out of me and Uncle Skad to show his family how protective he was. But he made no attempt to stand up. He just kept glancing back over his shoulder to make sure we weren't moving in to rape, rob, and loot his family.

"Hungry, Wally?" Skad asked.

"Starved."

"Make up your mind quick. Here comes the waitress."

"Oh, I know what I want."

The young waitress sauntered up to the table wearing a one piece skirt the same color as the toilet bowl once it was filled with mine and Skad's piss. She couldn't have been much older than me and she already looked totally beaten down by the world. Snapping her gum between her teeth, she lackadaisically ran her eyes up my horns. She wiped her greasy brown bangs off her greasier forehead and slapped her order pad down on the table, leaning over it. She wore her hair pulled back into a sloppy ponytail, dandruff flaking rampantly around the canyon of her part.

"What can I getcha?" She refused to make eye contact.

Skad ordered a cheeseburger, fries, and coffee. I ordered country fried steak. This place seemed like the type of place that would have especially good country fried steak. Country fried steak was the wonderful invention seemingly designed with the express purpose of creating a heart attack. You start with a cut of the poorest quality beef. The beef is then covered in breading and deep fried. Once fried, it is coated in a thick white gravy. I also ordered a

Fuckness

Coke.

The waitress schlepped back to the unseemly looking kitchen. I hadn't eaten in a lot of restaurants so it must have been something instinctual telling me we probably wouldn't be seeing the food for quite a while. She did, however, return immediately with our beverages. She lingered at the table for a few uncomfortable moments before going back to the kitchen.

I looked out the window, across the street to where the high schoolers were playing football. I realized Skad was staring at me.

"You don't say a whole lot, do you, Wally?"

"I guess, no, not much."

"I think talking is something you have to practice, anyway. Sometimes, if there's no one around to talk to, you just kind of get out of practice."

I nodded my head. I just assumed I didn't talk because I didn't really have anything to say.

"Myself, I don't normally talk too much, either. But when I saw you, I had the overwhelming urge to talk. I don't know why." He took a sip of his coffee and flicked his ashes onto the floor, neglecting the ashtray sitting right there on the table. "You know all that stuff I told you about at the house last night?"

I nodded my head.

"Lies. There wasn't any truth to that at all. It was a story. Actually a series of stories. You're the first person to hear them though. Well, that's not true, either. The stories aren't entirely my own. Dr. Blast and I cooked them up. That's what we do when we get together. We drink, we smoke, we tell stories... We *build* stories. My life has not been that eventful at all. If only it was, Wallace, if only it was. I'm surprised Sadie never told you the truth of it.

"They wanted me to go to war. Only they didn't call it a war. They called it a conflict. I almost went to Vietnam, Wally boy. Fortunately, I was completely fucking nuts. At first, I was only a little bit crazy. But then, all of that stuff started happening and I started imagining myself thousands of miles from home. I'd heard about what it was like. Something snapped, Wally. Something just snapped. You've felt the snap, haven't you, Wally?"

147

I nodded again.

"Do you know what happened when I snapped, Wally? Do you know that what I did was of catastrophic proportions and it directly involves you? Do you know what I did when I snapped?"

I shook my head, whispering, "No," because there was something about Uncle Skad that had made me completely captivated. He no longer moved his hands in the dramatic fashion. He stared straight into me, his eyes reaching in and wringing the soulhurt I suddenly felt.

"I imagine it. There's a metallic kind of feel in your body. This feeling, it has a way of completely and totally overwhelming you, driving you to your knees. It feels like a lifesize railroad car is roaring through your head. Sometimes, when this feeling comes over you, you are not you anymore. You have no control over yourself and you'll do anything, anything to make that bending, warping feeling go away. It's so consuming that it blocks your vision, blinds you. The logic it imposes is its own fever logic. The ends to the means are completely ridiculous because the means themselves are ridiculous. One time I woke up while pulling out one of my teeth because, according to this dream logic, I had to excise the tooth so the car would start when I woke up in the morning. I didn't even have a car. Do you know how numbing it is to wake up to something like that? To 'come to' and realize that, for however brief a period of time, you were not able to exercise any self-control whatsoever? Of course you do.

"So one morning I wake up, I come to, because I was never really asleep, you see. I come to and, in my hands I'm holding a sledgehammer. And I'm standing in a bed soaked red with blood. My parents are below me. Smashed. Pulp. I threw the hammer down and rolled out of bed and lay on the floor and cried and cried and cried. Do you know why I cried, Wally?"

"I think... maybe."

"Not so much because I had killed my parents. Anybody could have killed them. Part of the crying, of course, was the sadness of their death. But what made me really break down was that brief period where the dream logic overlapped reality and what I was

doing made perfect sense. The fact that I remembered, quite clearly, bringing the hammer down onto their heads, that was what
made me break down. The fact that I was capable of doing something like that. That I could have, at any time, found that behavior
rational. But the act was done. And I had to go away for awhile. It
was a departure that I welcomed, that I deserved. It was there, in
the hospital, that I discovered myself.

"I spent most of my time there wondering this: is a man who he
is, should he be *judged* by his actions of the past and maybe even
the present, or should he be judged by who he wants to become,
what he is *trying* to be? Should a man be judged at all? And who is
he judged by? Look out there." Skad motioned out the window, at
the high school kids practicing football. I turned my head to watch
them.

"You see those people out there? I'm afraid they may be the
judges of people like us. Oh, that's not to say all of them are like
that or, for that matter, that you and I are exactly alike. But their
mentality, think about it. They want glory, they want recognition.
So once a week, they have a heap of lights pouring down onto
them and, for a couple of hours anyway, they have everyone's attention. Most of them even have their names across their back so
they can be identified. The strongest, the most cunning, the one
who can *smash* the most people down—that's the one that gets the
most recognition. And look where they play, a field covered in
lines. Cross some of the lines and you're out of bounds—the game
stops. The entire game is about getting to the end zone—the final
prize. Sometimes I think that's what's missing, the final prize. But
it's not their fault, of course. That's just a metaphor. Sometimes I
feel like I'm only living to die."

The waitress came over and sat the plates of food down on the
table.

"Can I get you anything else?" she asked.

"We're fine. Thanks," Skad said. Then, to me, "Dig in."

We devoured our food, our mouths making sounds like rabid
animals. Skad alternated between taking bites of his food, sips of
his coffee, and drags off his cigarette. The rapidity with which he

performed each of these actions looked like an amazing task. Comical and demonic looking smoke rolled out of his mouth as he chewed the food. While I ate, I couldn't stop thinking about Uncle Skad. I found myself periodically glancing at him, trying to find the murderer somewhere within. I couldn't do it. His eyes were too gentle. There was an overall deliberate delicacy in his movements that rendered him incapable of taking anyone's life. Something about the way he held his head suggested he was the type of man who was perfectly content with food, drink, and smoke. He'd probably forgotten about women a long time ago.

There was that other stuff he said, too. The fuckness about only living to die. Sometimes I felt exactly like that. Sometimes I waited to die. I thought that him telling me all about that stuff would make the wave of soulhurt come back over me. But it made me feel better. Knowing he felt like that too somehow made me feel like I didn't have to feel bad. He stated it as though it was a fact of life.

We pushed our plates aside once we finished and the waitress came over to refill my Coke and Skad's coffee. She laid the check down on the table, a waitress' subtle hint to settle up and get the hell out.

"You can pay that at the register," she said. She turned to walk away and then, pausing, turned back around and looked at me. "Why the hell are you wearin them stupid horns?"

I was expecting someone here to point that out. I don't exactly know why. Nevertheless, I think I fielded it a little bit better. I reached up and felt them, stroking their grandeur, feeling the confidence from Skad across the table.

"My mother, uh, fucked a bull," I said.

The waitress's mouth dropped open, but she was clearly angered by the comment.

"Well, them's the most retarded things I ever seen. Nobody from my school would date a boy with horns."

"Thank you," I said.

"I think you better pay that and get out. Boss told me to tell you we don't need no freaks and bums in here. This ain't that kind of place."

Fuckness

Then Skad asked, "Just what kind of place *is* this, ma'am?"

The waitress, looking about ready to cry, clenched her teeth and said, "This here's a decent place."

Then she turned to walk back to the kitchen. I felt and heard my bowels shift. I had religiously had a bowel movement a day ever since I turned twelve. I managed to hold it in yesterday but this was the big one.

I stood up and leaned over the table. "Excuse me," I winced to Uncle Skad and hurriedly walked toward the bathroom. I undid my pants as I opened the door. I turned, facing the inside of the door, angling my ass toward the toilet and pulling down my pants in one swift motion. My bowels released with an explosion of sound and stink. It was a succinct shit, however. One heave and it was over.

Finished, I wiped and stood up to wash my hands in the sink. I don't really know why I bothered. It's not like it really mattered, the rest of my body was so filthy. I caught a glimpse of myself in the mirror. I'd felt the horns, but this was the first time I really saw them. And it was the first time I'd really seen myself. I looked truly hideous. My face was lumpy and swollen. My nose was crooked. One of my eyes wouldn't quite open all the way. The horns rose up from my scalp, monstrously large. It made me sad to look at myself. The wave of soulhurt quickly washed over me. Was it panic? Maybe it was panic. Every time the soulhurt would infest me, I had the overwhelming urge to sabotage everything I had. To escape from wherever I was. And it was with that feeling I had another terrible idea. Another terrible idea I knew I would follow through on. Not as terrible as my ideas of the day before, but terrible nonetheless.

I was going to leave Uncle Skad's side. It had nothing to do with Uncle Skad, there was just something inside of me screaming that I deserved to be alone. I knew the voice was right. No, I knew it was true. It may not have been right. I would undoubtedly be happier if Uncle Skad were to accompany me wherever I went but I started alone and I felt like I had to end up some place alone and I didn't want to drag Uncle Skad into anything else I might do. Knowing that I was going to follow through on it gave me the most soulhurt of all.

I shook my hands out over the sink and finished drying them on my pants. How was I going to tell him? I briefly thought about just running out but I didn't really think my legs would work very well and that just didn't feel like the right thing to do.

I walked out into the restaurant and was surprised to see that Skad wasn't sitting in the booth. Maybe he'd left without me. That would have certainly been a relief. I didn't think that seemed like Uncle Skad but, then again, how much did I really know about him? I didn't think he seemed like a murderer either. It seemed more likely he led a country called Pung and spent time in hell than murder someone. Was it the brutal reality of murder that should have made it seem more likely to believe? Did I seem like a murderer to him? Because, most definitely, that's what I was.

Lowering my head, I quickly walked out of the restaurant. When the door shut behind me, I was sure I heard the waitress shout something at me, but I couldn't make out what it was. Outside, the sun was well on its way out of sight and the air felt chillier, the wind having a slicing quality on the top of the hill. Skad was out there, smoking a cigarette and turning in circles. He saw me coming and stopped his rotations.

"You don't look so good," he said. "I hope I didn't scare you with that stuff back there."

"No," I said.

"Because, you know, when it's all said and done, we are really living to live. Happiness can be easily obtained. All I need to do is wake up to a cigarette and a cup of coffee. Maybe have some whiskey before I go to bed at night. A roof over my head. A warm fire. Those are the essentials. Where we off to next?"

I gritted my teeth and mumbled, "Gonna go."

"Eh, Wally?"

"I think I'm just gonna go."

"By yourself?" I could tell by the gleam in his eye that he was disappointed. Not angry, just sad.

"I think it's just something I need to do alone." I moved closer to him and hugged him. "I've enjoyed being around you."

Fuckness

"You're a good kid, Wally." Then he grabbed me by the upper arms and thrust me away to arm's length. That electric feeling shot through me and I could see that bluish glow glittering around in his eyes. "You can do anything you want to do! Just *find* something! Go wandering and it will come to you. Anything you do, do it with *passion*! That's the problem with the world today, there's no passion. Walk like God, Wally! Walk like fucking God! What do you think of when you think of... *God*?"

Truthfully, I didn't really think about God too much, unless I was feeling especially pitiful. "I don't know... creation?" It was the first thing that popped into my head.

"Then create. No one creates anything anymore. Now we want machines to do everything for us. Create a fantastic life, Wallace. Start now and spend the rest of your days creating the perfect life so you'll die a happy man."

Then he let go, but I still felt that electricity sizzling through my marrow, through my head.

"Go, Wallace! And don't ever look back!"

I turned away from him, that electricity crackling all through me, and took off running.

Chapter Twenty
You Are

The best thing about pollution is the brilliant sunset it creates. Behind Uncle Skad, the entire time he was talking, I kept looking at that violent red sunset smeared across the sky. Now, as I ran down the other side of the hill, the sun had completely disappeared beneath the horizon. The whole sky glowed an amazing pink color. I was glad I had Skad's blessing. I mean, I'm glad he didn't seem to mind me going. I knew he was probably just a lonely old guy, as eager for friends and company as I should have been. But I wasn't. I meant what I had said to Uncle Skad. I didn't know where the hell I was going, I just felt like it had to be done alone.

I did feel kind of bad, but it wasn't anything Skad made me feel. It was something from inside. It was like, no matter how much I liked a person when I first met them, it was only a matter of time before that feeling turned into one of bitter hatred. I didn't want to have to end up hating Uncle Skad. It was like that with the parents. After sixteen years with the parents, even if they *had've* been decent human beings, I still couldn't have stood them any longer. It was the same at school. Like old blob Pearlbottom. I just hated her more and more every year. I didn't like feeling that way at all. And I didn't want to let myself feel like that about Uncle Skad.

At that moment I didn't hate anybody, I simply ran the pink twilight into night. I ran until I couldn't run anymore which, I guess, really wasn't for that long. My lungs itched. My legs shook. Even when I slowed down and started walking, my legs wobbled each time my feet hit the ground. I didn't know where the hell I was. I couldn't even see the smokestacks from Milltown. At least I was away from *that* godforsaken place.

It smelled good out there in the countryside. Everything was coming alive, clawing its way out of the ground, breathing color into the world. It wouldn't be long before everything was in bloom. I looked up at the moon, nearly full but not quite. Black clouds wrapped themselves around it only to be quickly yanked away. And somewhere, under that good night smell was another scent, more familiar to spring, the smell of a storm coming up from behind me. Thunder rumbled. It was going to come up quick.

My circumstances weren't as good as they were last time. Although I didn't have the handicap of two merciless beatings, I also no longer had the comfort of walking along the smooth asphalt and unflinching direction of the state route either. I'd started out going west, into the sun, but had no real idea of which direction I now traveled. Where was I? It really seemed to be the middle of nowhere. There were no lights. That meant there weren't any houses, either. No roads. I couldn't hear any cars. How far away from people was I? It didn't seem like it could be very far. Ohio may not be the most populous state, but it was difficult to drive more than twenty minutes without seeing *some* sign of civilization.

I tried to gather up the energy to skip, hearing a Bobby DeHaven tune in my head. That made me feel not so alone for awhile. Only it wasn't really the feeling of being alone that bothered me. How could it when I had brought the loneliness upon myself? It seemed like sticking your head in the oven and complaining about the heat. What really bothered me was the fear of being devoured. I mean there was a moment there when I thought the earth was just going to open up and swallow me whole. A shiver ran through my body. I stopped skipping, put my head down and walked as briskly as possible.

Lightning shot across the sky. Thunder roared. The rain came down in huge fat splashes. I was thoroughly soaked in under a minute. It wasn't like the rain just hit me and rolled off. It was more like the rain penetrated me, tearing its way through my skin and soaking my flimsy soul. I dragged along. And what was it for? What the hell was any of it for? And how could I go from feeling so great one minute and then, a half an hour later, become nearly suicidal?

Except I didn't really know if I actually wanted to kill myself or if there was some masochistic instinct inside me enjoying it. There was some feeling, some belief I was raised with that made it seem like the more a person suffered, the more rewards they reaped. That belief, like many others I'd been raised with, was a huge blobby lie. Did I really think I was going to get any type of reward from suffering? It seemed like almost everyone I'd known had suffered a lot and they didn't seem to get any rewards. Racecar's legs fell off, the mother had a stroke, and they almost lost their child and what were they rewarded with? Assassination? Death? It seemed like Uncle Skad had suffered and he was a lonely old bum. Where were his rewards? And when does the suffering end? Wasn't that what suicide was? The school slogans and ad campaigns and all that fuckness always said suicide wasn't a way out but it really was. It was an end to all the suffering. Only, the idea of it seemed absurd. It seemed particularly absurd at the moment because, not only could I never imagine actually killing myself, I didn't know how I would feasibly go about doing it.

I don't think suicide is something you plan for. I think one day you just have to say to yourself, "This is it, I can't take it anymore." No, in the end, suicide is something performed with a great amount of haphazard willy-nilliness. So, if at that moment, I really did want to kill myself, what was I going to do it with? I had the lighter Drifter Ken had given me but I didn't reckon it would do a lot of good in the present deluge. I briefly considered grabbing hunks of soggy grass and shoving them down my throat. How many people killed themselves by intentionally choking to death? There had to be a puddle big enough to drown myself in somewhere. But I knew that wouldn't happen. Maybe I would just flop down and die of exposure. That was more my style—to just lie back and let God, nature, and man gang fuck the holy hell out of me. With the grimmest of fate, I saw myself eventually dying out

Fuckness

there in the middle of that neverending field, vultures descending down to consume me, only to later shit my remains out somewhere over Milltown. Maybe if I were really lucky, nature would invent some way to shove me back up the Wig's rotten birth hole.

There was something pulling me along. I could hate everything as much as I wanted but something told me that, somehow, I was going to get wherever it was I was going. My shoes were untied. I had always worn Velcro shoes and had no idea how to retie them. But even as I felt the pitiful dead man's shoes dangling at the ends of my feet, I didn't think that would be my fate. No, if it was suffering I was after, I was suddenly, hopelessly aware that I would have a full life of it heaped upon me.

Not only would I get to go through life as a freakishly ugly social half-wit, I would get to go through life as a freakishly ugly social half-wit with horns. With *horns*? The ridiculousness of it all was astounding, overwhelming. I would be forced to live up in the mountains somewhere. Or maybe to wander around with a pillowcase tied over my head like the fucking Elephant Man. Then I thought of the opposite. What if I were successful? A big house, a beautiful wife, smart children, and a great job. How old would that get? The people at the office would undoubtedly start calling me something like "Coat Rack" or some fuckness like that. And they would say it completely harmless like, but every time they said it I'd want to burn the fucking place down. At home, I'd be completely unable to play Santa Claus because I would be, so obviously, a reindeer. And the neighborhood kids would make me crawl around on all fours while they mounted me with their piss-stained bottoms. The wife would constantly hound me to get cosmetic surgery. That's when I would kill myself. When people ceased to be openly aware of my obvious faults. If people weren't going to openly display their derision and hostility, then I was certain they would be doing it behind my back. That would give me overwhelming feelings of anxiety which would probably be a lot worse than the overwhelming feelings of anger.

That force kept pulling me through the raining dark. My skin was completely numbed. What was it for? Shouldn't I be defining myself instead of this battery of ignorant questions? I had been a child. Wasn't it time for me to choose what kind of *man* I wanted to become? That rope kept pulling me. I was violently exhausted. Fuck it, I thought, let the rope decide.

In front of me, I saw a soft yellow light. Where there was light, there were people. I took off my shirt and wrapped it around the horns. The only thing I could ask for would be to find a nice dry place to refuel in and then pass through the town as unnoticed as possible. If that had to be my life, wandering from place to place, then so be it. But if I had to do it, it wasn't going to be with those fucking horns on my head. At least let me slip by unnoticed, I thought. If it meant living like a wild man in the woods, that was fine. I didn't want any more fights. I didn't want to struggle with people anymore. Hell, at that point, I didn't know what the fuck I wanted.

I wanted to get to the light. That's all I *really* wanted and the rope pulled me faster and I sped up into a trot, the light getting closer and closer and, around the original light, other lights. I became aware of nothing else but that light—I focused on it and sped up more and more, running faster than I ever had.

The air was cold. My breath plumed out around me as I ran. Fog rolled around its gray self, spreading the yellow light out. One of those other lights approached quickly from my left. I strained to stop running and my knees buckled, weak legs tossing me to the soaked ground. Beside me I heard the quick sluicing slap of tires and felt the cold grimy spray coat my face.

I stood up, my legs shaking. My whole body was shaking, the light convulsions rattling the burning sensation around in my lungs. The yellow sign was right across the street. It was one of those cheap yellow advertising billboards. The kind rolled out on wheels for special occasions announced in blocky black letters. The sign read, at the top:

FARMERTOWN COMMUNITY CHURCH

And below that:

CH_ _CH
WHATS MISSING?

Fuckness

I wanted to laugh with the ridiculousness of it all. This is what I had run and run for?

The church loomed behind the sign. It seemed too grand for such a low budget sign. The steeple looked like it was stabbing the moon, jaggedly erect atop the bell tower. Houses sat on either side of the church and, looking around, it was surrounded by a whole tiny town. Farmertown. This was as close to my birth I could get without an uncomfortable proximity to the mother's vagina. Farmertown was where I was brought home. Standing there, I couldn't really remember much of my childhood here. Had it been happier than Milltown? I didn't know. Whenever the memories did come back, they seemed like bright and sunny things—yellow-filtered visions of a time maybe only made happier through my innocence. This was kind of where I wanted to go, really my last stop before moving on to the rest of the sad and lonely world, and something had brought me here. That rope had dragged me at breakneck speed and then stopped me so I wouldn't be devoured by the road.

Cautiously, I crossed the road. The rain still beat down. A certain warmth emanated from the sign. Shivering there in the rain, I wanted to crawl inside that sign. I put my hand on the top of it, taking note that it didn't have a large blinking arrow, braced myself, and vomited. The vomit splashed steaming on the asphalt. A wave of dizziness hit me and I joined the vomit. I looked up at the moon and the fat drops of glistening rain dropping down onto my face. I felt intensely comfortable. I had a million thoughts in a second and was completely incapable of seizing upon a single one of them. And then I was gone.

Chapter Twenty-one
Maria Thiklet

I lay there for a long time, without opening my eyes, feeling good and warm. I kept smelling the comforting smell of food but couldn't figure out where it was coming from. Then a sinking feeling overwhelmed me. I thought I was back home. The rain became the blue light that sometimes filled my room. I scraped around on my asphalt cot. Somewhere, off in the distance, I couldn't tell if the sounds were screeching car wheels or blaring railroad horns or the high-pitched strumbling of the mother, come to wake me up and pull me through another day of hell. Then I flinched because I could have sworn Racecar was parked right up next to the bed and sticking that cigarette filter into my cheek. This made me awake with a violent start.

I brushed the filter away and sat up, trying to focus my eyes and stop the spinning. Being awake didn't help lessen the confusion.

I sat on a couch. Sitting across from me in a rocking chair was a honey-haired woman. I could tell by the way she kept her hands drawn up to her chest she had been poking me in the face. They were somehow drawn up *guiltily*. A thick blanket covered my legs. I felt sweltering and my eyes must have burned into the woman across from me. Not out of any type of hatred, just an intense effort to try and make some sense out of what was happening or what had happened. Studying her, I decided she was remarkably pretty. Her hair hung down past her shoulders, straight and shiny. The light wrinkles around her eyes and mouth, although she tried to hide them, put her age somewhere in her thirties. Her eyes were a wonderful blue.

"How are you feeling?" she asked.

A dry croak was the only thing I could get to come out and I had to cough it away. "Good, I guess."

She reached out toward me and placed the back of her hand against my forehead. I flinched.

"You were burning up earlier. Feel a little cooler now."

I reached my hands up to my head. The horns were unsheathed. She didn't look up at them. She just kept staring into my eyes like, instead of asking me any questions, she was just going to stare into my brain and get the answers out that way.

"What's your name?" she asked.

"Wallace Black."

"I'm Maria Thiklet. It's nice to meet you. I hope you don't mind. I threw that old shirt out and put one of my husband's shirts on you."

"Thank you."

"You feel good enough to eat?"

That was the smell. It smelled great. That would be like the third time I had eaten that day. I was beginning to learn, even though I'd never regarded food with any importance other than survival, most people planned their days around it. Like the electricity that came from Skad, that drew me to Skad, there was something I was picking up from this woman that said I really shouldn't be there, succulent scent of the food or not.

"You really don't have to. Thanks, but I'll just get my shirt and go." I had a hard time standing up from the couch. Two or three times I got almost up to my feet before collapsing backward.

"You still don't look too good," she said. "You should stay here tonight. We have plenty of room. Come on into the kitchen and eat something. One of us can drive you wherever you need to go tomorrow."

Drive, the word sounded like time travel. How much ground could I cover if I had a car? The promise of this advanced transportation kind of canceled out my previous feelings. After all, if I left in the morning, it couldn't really be considered *staying*. Besides, this woman seemed hellbent on nurturing *something*. I was probably just another wounded dog found by the side of the road.

I followed Maria, watching her long skirt flap around her ankles.

I admired the interior of the house as we crossed from the living room into the kitchen. It was impossible for their house to be any cleaner than the parents' but there was something about it that seemed nicer, homier, more decorated. There was something about the soft yellowish lighting that seemed a little bit depressing but that was only because the parents' house was usually as brightly lit as the set of a porno. I tried not to look around too much so she didn't think I was some sort of criminal, casing the joint. The kitchen was much brighter and less depressing. She motioned toward the huge table and said, "Take a seat."

I sat down. I wondered why she was being so incredibly nice since she looked like she had the potential to be a huge blob. She put the plate of food in front of me and I was beginning to think that, since I'd never been good at just walking up to people and introducing myself to them, I should pass out somewhere within close proximity to them. Apparently she had assumed I must be incredibly hungry. The entire plate was covered; half with some sort of thick beef stew, the other half with warm cornbread.

"I hope you like it," she said. There were six chairs at the table. She sat me at one end and pulled back the chair on my right and closest to me, sitting down and crossing her legs.

I felt kind of uncomfortable. The family hadn't eaten together since I was like maybe eight. The burden of small talk nagged at the back of my mind. She just sat there staring at me. By glancing at her in brief snippets, I couldn't really tell if she was more concerned or more afraid. I suddenly panicked, thinking she had maybe called the police on me. My hands trembled as I brought a forkful of food to my mouth.

"You're shaking," she said.

"I'm okay," I said, then, "Slight palsy."

"I'm so sorry."

Fuckness

Then I took a deep breath and asked, "Did you call the police?"

She giggled, "Why would I do that?" And then, maybe because for a brief moment she felt unprotected, like maybe I had just given her a reason to think she *should* have called the police, she said, "Besides, Boo's gonna be home any minute."

"Thank goodness," I said.

"Boo's my husband. His name's Robert Thiklet but everybody calls him Boo." A strange look came over her face. Then she said, "I don't know why."

She got up and went over to the counter, grabbed a coffee mug from the cabinet and poured herself a cup of coffee.

"You want some coffee, Wallace?"

"No, thanks."

"Are you thirsty? You want some Coke?"

"Sure. Thanks."

She opened the refrigerator and grabbed a can of Coke, sitting it down in front of me. I pulled the tab and drank down half the can. Maria came back over to the table and sat down. She slowly sipped her coffee, staring out into space with those calm blue eyes.

"Are you a runaway?" she asked.

"I think I'm too old to be a runaway."

"How old are you?"

"Sixteen."

"A sixteen-year-old should still be at home with their parents. That's what I think. Are you running away from *them*?"

"I guess I'm running away from everything."

She paused, taking another sip from her mug, looking as though she was trying to find an answer to that.

"Me and Boo can't have any kids. That's why there aren't any running around. If I could have kids we'd have a whole bunch of them. I guess your parents aren't very nice to you, huh?"

"It's not just about them."

"When I was your age, I think I wanted to run away, too. That's probably why I got married so early. Boo and me got married when I was seventeen. He was twenty-two. My parents had to give permission for us to get married. They were probably glad to get me out of the house. We had to go to Tennessee to do it."

I briefly thought about this sober-looking woman giving anyone a hard time.

"What about you? You gotta girlfriend?"

"Good Lord, no." Look at me, I thought.

Then Maria fell silent again, staring at me.

"Dinner's really good. Thanks."

"You're very welcome. I guess I found you about the right time. I have dinner waiting every night for Boo. I don't mind being the one who cooks and cleans, though. All I do is some work at the church. He should be home by now but sometimes he goes out with the boys. He's gotta unwind, you know. Boo works for Korl out in Milltown. He works an awful lot. You work?"

Not a day in my life, I thought. "No," I said.

"Boo works real hard. He's already paid for this house."

I was glad to be eating so I had something to do. Otherwise I would have been thrashing all around with boredom, the patented vapidity threatening to suck me in. It sounded like Maria was talking from a script, saying all the things she knew she was supposed to be saying. Except, when I looked up and glimpsed into her eyes, there was something there that said maybe she knew this life was a joke. I'd been awake and conscious in the house for under an hour and I already had the feeling the only thing this house had to offer was comfort. The stagnancy clung to my skin with sticky little teeth. I had an impulse to reach out and shake Maria. Where was the passion here? I scraped up the last remnants from my plate and fatigue overwhelmed me. I could have dropped right out of the chair and went to sleep right there on the floor.

"You look tired," Maria said.

"A little, yeah," I said, my eyes drooping with drowsiness.

"You're more than welcome to stay here tonight. Like I said. We have a guest bedroom. Keep waiting for the day we can turn it into a nursery."

"Can I really?" I asked. I was genuinely surprised. It seemed unusual to drag me in from outside and feed me dinner but it was completely unexpected that she invited me to stay for the night.

Fuckness

"Sure. You look like you've been through a lot. We humans hafta help each other out. Besides, you don't look like you'd hurt a flea. Follow me."

I stood up, sluggish, and followed her back through the vaguely depressing and dimly lit family room all the way to the far end where brown carpeted steps led to the upstairs. Maria turned a light switch and I followed her up the steps, my legs straining. Sleep will do me good, I thought. A night of genuine rest. It occurred to me that I hadn't slept on an actual bed for years.

I followed Maria down the hall. She pushed a door to her right open and said, "That's the bathroom up here. If you wake up in the middle of the night you don't have to go all the way downstairs." She took a couple more steps and opened a door. She stepped across the threshold and turned on a light. "This is the guest bedroom. Just make yourself at home. Me and Boo'll be right across the hall if you need anything. We'll probably just eat dinner when he gets home and then we'll probably go to bed."

"Thank you."

I walked into the bedroom and kind of stood there. She took a step toward me and looked at me with that curious stare. She put her hand on my forehead and said, "Still kind of warm."

"I feel fine. Really. I'm sure sleep'll do me a lot of good. Thanks."

"I guess I'll just leave you alone, then."

She shut the door behind her when she left. I wandered around the room, kind of pacing, feeling the plush carpet mush beneath my feet, looking around the room. A small lamp with what I figured must have been a 40-watt bulb illuminated the room. The walls were primarily yellow, light pink flowers spaced throughout at wide intervals.

The dresser shoved against the wall had a large sparkly mirror on top of it. I avoided looking at myself. I dragged the dark green comforter off the bed and threw it over the dresser. The one window in the room looked over the churchyard. The church itself was a huge brick thing. I noticed the graveyard behind it. It was one of the old graveyards with the gargantuan tombstones sprinkled with a few heavy square mausoleums. I waited for the melancholy feelings to hit me, that giant wave of sadness. But standing there I didn't feel much of anything at all. Like my emotions had just run up on a brick wall. I seized the opportunity. I pulled back the skin-colored blanket and climbed into bed. Maybe I would let this feeling give me a good night's sleep but I sure as hell wasn't going to let it lull me into a sense of complacency. Some moments I might be exuberant and other moments I might be melancholic but complacency—the complacency would allow the fuckness to trample all over me. And I knew the fuckness wasn't gone. It was simply poised in some dark corner like a snake.

It took me longer to fall asleep than I thought it would. The house was entirely quiet. Like an intimidating void. I couldn't hear the wind or the big machines wrestling with sheets of steel, or the dark railroad speeding through the night. Lying there wide awake, I thought to myself, this *is* sleep. Being awake in that house was as good as being asleep. Maybe I was just being cynical. I didn't know these people, these Thiklets, but I imagined them. Tomorrow was Sunday. They would undoubtedly rise and go to church. They'd get all dressed up too, a brimstone-threatening end to their complacent week. A few hours of being bombarded with fiery hells and mortal sins and morals, morals, morals. Then the week would begin anew. Maria Thiklet would run around town, rushing to pay bills, buy groceries, running home and hurriedly preparing dinner for Boo. I was sure Boo was a real cockwrinkle. Gotta work to pay the bills. Gotta pay the bills to live. There may have been fun in Boo's world but it was probably the kind of fun you had to buy. I was sure he came home and sat down in that big recliner I'd seen downstairs, pressing his tainted ass-reek into the buttocks- indented cushion. I imagined him sitting there, maybe drinking some beer and watching auto racing on TV. Maybe he just sat there and made Maria give him head, the crumbs from his sandwich dropping onto the top of her head. He probably asked her to hop off so he could shoot his wad into her face. "But it gets in my *eyelashes*," she'd complain. And I was sure he didn't just blow farts but was also the type of person to comment on the flatulence. "*Whoo hoo*," he'd say, waving his hand in the air and wrinkling his nose, "'bout ripped the seat of my pants out on that one." A real cockwrinkle.

And what would I be when I was that age? Would I be *anything*? If this is what I became by going and getting a good job as a steel-worker, how would I tolerate it. I would have to find some illicit habit to throw my money toward. Some type of heavy narcotic that would sugarcoat the daily death march to work every day. Every fucking day. How could anybody do anything every fucking day of his life. That certainly wasn't what I wanted. I just wanted the fuckness to go away. Maybe the parents weren't too bad. Maybe the fighting made me happy. Maybe being someplace where my bitterness and anger was completely understood was just what I needed. I decided I'd start back home the next day. I was tired. The burning in my lungs and the nearly constant whumming in my head told me that I was probably sick. I didn't think I'd be able to spend the rest of my life running. I would go home and pretend nothing happened. I could probably do that. It's what I did most days any-way. It's what I had to do because *most* days, something did hap-pen. Maybe somehow, I kidded myself, the parents were still alive. I could only hope the parents would be more enthralled by having me back safe and sound than the fact that I'd put them through a couple days of hell. Maybe I could tell them I was abducted. Maybe as I rubbed some sort of burn salve on them I'd ask, "How did this happen? *Me*? Oh, no, I was out in Farmertown finding myself."

And that was what scared me the most, wasn't it? The fact that, maybe there wasn't a self to find.

The thought of that overwhelmed me to sleep.

Another short sleep, another vivid dream.

Some dreams are seen from my eyes. Some dreams are seen from some place far above. This was one of those dreams. Below me was a dark forest but the trees were jaggedly cut sheets of metal with corrugated iron trunks. The trees were tall, huge, the forest floor littered with cans and bolts and shredded tarpaper. The par-ents were down there. Not the vibrant parents of the last dream. These parents were the rundown gutter version of those people. The father wore a stained white t-shirt stretched over an enormous gut. Blackened jeans truncated at the tops of his thighs. His shiny new legs were now thickly rusted iron springs. He bounced heavily around the forest floor. The mother drank her gin out of a pitcher, sloshing the brownish-tinged liquid down her chin. Even from my vantage point, I could tell she had had another stroke, something in the way she carried herself. She wore no wig at all, strands of gray-black hair pasted down to her filthy scalp. They both scurried around, kicking the stuff on the ground away, occasionally bending down to move something with their hands. They were looking for something.

"Wallace," the Racecar called.

"Wallace," the mother strumbled. "Where's Wallace?"

"Wally!"

They got moving faster and faster. I felt dizzy and sick, saddened at their downtrodden appearance and hopeless search. A terrible screeching filled the dream, the sound of one of those giant iron trees slowly loosing itself, pulling its bolts up out of the forest floor, and heading straight for the parents. I looked away, up at the moon, filled with Maria Thiklet's face.

"Wallace!"

Then I woke up. The room was dark and at first I didn't know where I was. Once I remembered, I figured Maria must have slipped in and turned off the light.

The room was dark but the house wasn't still and whatever complacency I'd felt before was gone. I heard Maria sobbing. Then I heard Boo, the beloved husband.

"What the hell you doin bringin a fuckin freak in mah house?"

I was immediately gripped by fear. It was like hearing him talk, from the accent to the tone of the things that actually came out of his mouth, proved my assumptions true. Here was a grownup Bucky Swarth, swelled up to hideous adult proportions. A giant cockwrinkle.

"What was I supposed to do, just *leave* him laying there?"

"Somebody woulda come and picked eem up. Why'd you gotta go and make it our problem?"

"He's not a problem. It's good to do things like this."

Fuckness

"You think you know what's good? He's in there layin in his own stink. You know what he smells like? Smells like *death*. What he done to get himself here? You ever thoughta that? You don't know what's good. Whatcha oughta do is be waitin here for me with yer legs open when I get home. That's what'd be good."

"You'd be so drunk you couldn't get it up." The hatred in her voice surprised even me and I didn't even know her.

There was a struggle after that. I heard thumping. And then silence.

The rest of the night I lay there, hating God, hating the parents and myself and everything. Of all the places for that rope, that force to bring me, why did it have to be here? I'd get out. I'd wait until the Thiklets were asleep. I'd find my shoes and I'd get the hell out. Probably go back home. Maybe I would go ahead and turn myself in. I'd only been away two nights and I already had the feeling there wasn't going to be anything better further down the line. I'd just get more and more beaten down as the world clawed at my soul.

I just kept thinking thoughts like that, lying there stiff as a board as my fever or whatever the fuck it was broke me into a cold sweat. The thoughts went around and around, creating that other emotion besides the exuberance and the melancholy sadness, the red panic. I'd felt the red panic at school a few times, had out and out fled on one of those occasions, but never like this. The worst thing about the red panic was that it only created the feelings and no solutions, no way out. The only way out, I figured, was the red crawlies. My body was so rigid I felt like it was cutting into the bed. Before I knew it, it was dawn and then, I don't know how, but I drifted back to sleep. A cool, calm, dreamless sleep.

Chapter Twenty-two
Building a Secret Place

I woke up to a knocking on the door. It was Maria.

"Wallace. I cooked us breakfast."

"Thanks," I called.

I jumped out of bed and something pinched my hipbone. I reached into my pocket and pulled out the lighter Drifter Ken had given me. I yanked the comforter off the dresser and threw it on the bed. I put the lighter on the dresser. Turning around, I set about making up the bed. I'd never done this before. Of course, ever since I'd been of bed making age I hadn't really had a bed to make. I'm sure I did a horrible job, but I tried. It didn't look nearly as good as it had before I'd slept on it. The comforter was all wrinkled- looking, sad and pathetic, the Mr. Lawrence of comforters. It didn't seem nearly large enough to fit the bed. I gave it a quick smoothing with my hand and went downstairs.

Sunlight filled the entire house and I felt good. I'd tell Maria I was leaving after breakfast and then I'd do it. Maybe I'd wander around Farmertown a little and look at all of the old buildings. Then I guessed I'd go back home to Walnut and see if the house was still there. I still didn't know if I'd go in or not, but I'd at least go by.

Maria had cooked bacon and eggs and toast for breakfast. That food mingled with the smell of coffee and all of it seemed really comforting. Maria was already sitting down. She looked up at me. "Help yourself," she said.

Fuckness

If she looked tired yesterday, she looked outright beaten down today. As we ate, there was none of the chatter that accompanied the dinner last night. When we were finished she asked, "How are you feeling?"

"Good. Actually, really good."

"Good." She smiled.

I thought it would be easy to tell her I wanted to leave. I thought it would be even easier to do the actual leaving but as I looked at her, sadly smiling over her half-eaten breakfast and mug of coffee, something inside of me didn't really want to go. Rather, there was something inside of me that told me I should stay.

"Where did you put my shoes?" I asked, staring down at my plate.

"They're in the living room. Are you leaving?"

"I think so."

"You should stick around. Boo said he really wanted to meet you."

"I think I'm gonna go back home."

"Look, stick around for dinner and one of us'll drive you home tonight. Where are you from?"

"Milltown."

"That's not an easy walk."

"It's not that bad."

"I'm making roast beef. It'll be really good. Besides, I could kind of use the company."

"Okay," I mumbled. Maybe I was just flattered that someone wanted *my* company.

"Staying?" she asked.

I nodded my head.

"Great," she said.

Her beaten down quality lifted and there now seemed something more genuine about her. She might be more entertaining today.

We got up from the table and scraped our plates over the trash. I helped her with the dishes. After the dishes, I followed her around the house, listening to her talk about just about everything as I stood by, completely useless. Once the living room was completely restored to a condition very similar to what it was already in, she flopped down on the couch.

"The best thing about cleaning the house is sitting down afterwards," she said with an exasperated sigh.

"I guess," I said. But I didn't sit down. I think I was still waiting to leave. I never really liked sitting down on couches anyway. I would gladly sleep, but it was rare for me to just sit down on a couch and not do anything at all.

"You like music?"

"Some of it, I guess."

Maria got back up off the couch and went over by the television, where the stereo system was. She bent down and flipped through a small record collection. The afternoon sunlight came in through the glass sliding door at the back of the house. Last night it hadn't seemed like the house was capable of being this bright. I watched Maria put the record on the player and drop the needle down.

A familiar music filled the room.

"Bobby DeHaven," she said.

"I know. He's my favorite."

"It's pretty good stuff. You like to dance?"

This was an interesting question. I didn't really know if I liked to dance or if, upon hearing Bobby DeHaven, I was simply filled with an overwhelming urge to dance. Nevertheless, dancing made me happy, so I said, "Yes." I knew my particular style of dancing was somewhat embarrassing and probably painful to watch, but I figured I'd be gone soon anyway, so what did it matter?

Fuck it. Right? And to think, it wasn't that long ago I'd actually entertained thoughts about being a backup dancer for Bobby DeHaven. Why had that not seemed insane at the time? It certainly struck me as ludicrous now.

She started dancing first, swishing her hips around, her long khaki skirt billowing out from her legs. She opened her arms, beckoning for me to join her. I moved in, tentatively at first, not sure how to really dance while conjoined with someone else. Her

arms encircled me and she dragged me into her laughing warmth.
How could I not feel happy? Pressed up against her body, I felt
ecstatic. The firmness of her breasts sunk into my stomach. We
turned around and around in circles, feverishly matching the music.
She kept pulling me into her as we drifted toward the couch. I
think she meant to pull me down with her, but I stayed upright,
letting her crash there on the couch by herself. I burst into my one-
man routine—the one I worked on in my room by myself. I hadn't
danced like that in some time and figured I might be rusty. But it
was just the opposite, as though the break had done me some
good. My movements were quick and precise. The weight of the
horns on my head added some excitement, as though they threatened to throw me off balance. I must have gone like that for some
time, throwing myself all around the living room, Maria unabashed-
ly laughing. Before I knew it, the side was over and I was standing
over by the sliding doors.

"Why don't you turn the side over and come take a rest."

I flipped the record over. The second side contained DeHaven's slow, syrupy love ballads and fuckness like that. The kind of
shit people write to get girls to think they're sensitive types. I went
and sat down on the couch, way over on the other side.

Maria turned sideways on the couch, so that she was facing me,
tucking her feet up under her legs.

"That certainly was unique," she said. "Where'd you learn to
dance like that?"

"On my own."

Looking at Maria, curled up there on the couch, made me think
of her completely differently than I had the night before. Maybe it
was just the dancing, but it kind of felt like we'd created some secret world between just the two of us. She had danced with me,
something I didn't think anybody else would ever do. And I had
helped her with the dishes and cleaning the house, which I would
say nobody else ever helped her do. And I also thought I knew
something else that I doubted anyone else did.

Suddenly, I realized what that peculiar look on her face was last
night. She hated Boo Thiklet. Probably with a great unabiding pas-

sion. I'd only heard him talk for a few minutes and I hated him.

"Nobody ever dances with me," she said.

"Me either," I said right back.

"It felt kind of good."

"It sure did."

"It's nice to have company. Someone to talk to. Boo won't even let me keep a pet so I just wander around here most days talking to myself like a crazy woman." She laughed, a light breathy thing. "I guess we're all a little crazy sometimes, huh?"

"I guess."

A sudden wave of self-consciousness swept over me. It coincided directly with the fact that, at that moment, I found Maria Thiklet incredibly attractive. And it wasn't a trashy kind of attractiveness that blobby Mary Lou Dover exuded at school. It wasn't even the attractiveness I'd found in her when I first came to on the couch. It was something else. It was the way she did things. Or maybe it was the way she acted. She seemed innocently imprisoned in her house with her husband as the captor and yet she brought me in from outside and hadn't even mentioned my goddamn horns. And my self-consciousness didn't have anything to do with the way I looked. I just started thinking about how I should act and, top priority, how I smelled. I remembered Boo Thiklet saying I smelled like death last night. That was probably while I was in there wrestling with my fever. Sometimes, if you just let it go, stink will die down a little. But when you sweat, like after dancing for a half an hour, it'll break that stink open so it's a degree worse than it was before. Sitting on the couch, I was incredibly aware of my stink.

"I stink," I told Maria. "Can I go take a shower?"

"You're more than welcome. I have to go out and pick up sticks. That storm yesterday really did it. Blew all kinds of branches from the tree. Boo'll complain if he comes home and finds a bunch of sticks laying all over his yard. Especially when it's something he specifically asked me to do. Were you out in that storm yesterday?"

"Only a little."

"Go ahead and shower up."

Fuckness

I crept upstairs to the bathroom and stripped down. I ran the shower nearly scalding hot. The fuckness is melting away, I told myself. It was like removing a layer of soulgrime I'd accumulated over the past few days. Why was I interested in that? It wasn't just my stink, which had never bothered me before, it was everything else I'd done, too. And I was doing it because, for that moment when I looked at Maria and felt that sense of creating a secret place I'd wanted to forget every bad thing I'd ever done, every bad impulse I'd ever had. But then again there was something else in Maria's eyes that worried me a little bit. There was the honesty, yes, but there was something about that honesty that made me think maybe the secret place was only going to be her place. Fuck it, I thought. I was sixteen. I'd pretty much go any place she wanted me to.

The water steamed all over my body, reddening my skin, and I really did have a feeling the major fuckness was almost over. The fuckness would never leave completely, I knew, but it would be entirely possible to put off the next bout of major fuckness for a number of years. Spending the day with Maria would be nice. Then I'd go home. Then I'd go home. Then I'd go home, I kept telling myself.

I grabbed a fluffy, deep blue towel and dried off. I put my dirty clothes back on. Well, I guess they were Boo's clothes with my dirt. They only slightly smelled like death. When I got downstairs, Maria still hadn't come back inside. I opened the sliding doors and stepped outside. Maria was bent over, hurriedly snapping up small twigs and placing them in the growing bundle supported by her left arm. I watched her move with industrious speed and put the bundle of twigs into a black trashbag. She was so immersed in her work she didn't even notice me. She went back around to the front of the house. I went back inside and stood absently in the middle of the living room, only vaguely aware of pulling my right ear with my hand.

When Maria came in she looked upset, like she'd been crying.

"Are you okay?" I asked.

"I'm just fine. Just a lot of stuff I gotta do before Boo gets home. I tell you, he doesn't have to lift a finger around here, that's for sure. Not a goddamn finger. Did you make your bed this morning?"

"I tried. But I don't think I did a very good job."

"Hey," she said, "why don't you give that ear a rest and come upstairs with me."

I followed her up the stairs much closer than I had last night. I got close enough to smell her natural shampoo and soap smell, the airy breath of outside clinging to her.

Without thinking, when we reached the top of the stairs, I blurted, "You smell nice."

"Thanks," she said. "It's White Rain and Dove."

"Nice," I said.

I followed her into the guestroom and watched as she, with a few tugs and jerks, made the bed look better than I could have given an hour. I found myself staring at her and I felt kind of guilty because I could feel Mr. Lawrence hardening. Her skirt clung to her buttocks and I noticed the blue veins running through her feet. When she finished, she gave a cursory but expert glance around the room. She spotted the green lighter on the dresser, picked it up and asked, "This yours?"

"Yeah," I said.

"You smoke?"

"No."

"You're not a pothead are you?"

"No."

"Good. That stuff'll make you stupid."

Birth had already done a good job of that, I thought. She put the lighter back down on the dresser.

"I'm gonna go straighten up the bedroom."

She crossed the hall, leaving me standing there in the guestroom. I looked at the church through the window. The house was too close to see the entire thing. I felt the minutes drip slowly by.

"Come here, Wallace," Maria called.

I crossed the hall and went to her bedroom. She was lying down on the bed, her legs over the foot with her feet on the floor. Her hands rested on her lower stomach and she looked at me, right into my eyes.

"Boo makes me wear dresses every day." She looked up at the ceiling. Her hands unbuttoned the top button on her dress. Then the next one. "Nobody wants to be told what to wear." She went all the way down with the buttons and opened her dress. Her underwear were white. The whumming picked up in my head. I wasn't really sure what was happening. I just knew I didn't want to look away.

"How old are you, Wallace?"

"Sixteen."

"Sixteen," she said wistfully. "Have you ever made love to a woman?"

Her question kind of put me on the spot and the whumming built and built up. It seemed like it should have been a relatively easy question to answer. Perhaps if she had been younger I would have lied right away. Like when I told Mary Lou Dover that I kissed girls all the time. But Maria was older and, some of the older people I'd met treated sex as though it were something akin to sticking a gun to your temple and pulling the trigger.

I shook my head.

"Of course you haven't, you're only sixteen." She lifted the bottom of her shirt up, exposing her creamy white stomach. "Sixteen-year-olds don't make love, they *fuck*. I thought I knew what love was when I was sixteen, but I was wrong. Have you ever fucked a woman, Wallace?"

I shook my head again. I liked the way she said my name. She drew it out real slow and put most of the emphasis on the "S"-sound.

"Do you know why people fuck?" She sat up a little, her belly wrinkling into small folds, and pulled off her shirt. The realities of her body and flesh sent the whumming slamming around inside my skull.

I shook my head. I'd never really thought about why people did that other than I assumed it felt good.

"People fuck so they can come. You've come haven't you?"

I nodded.

"Did you like the way it felt?"

I nodded again.

"It's been two years since I've come, Wallace. That's a long time. It's been longer than two years since Boo's fucked me. I mean really fucked me. And I never, you know, because I thought that would be like being unfaithful to him or something. He gets so drunk he can't get it up, Wallace. It just lays there like a big worm. And I'm pretty sure he fucks other people. I want you to fuck me, Wallace. Don't feel like you have to make love to me. Just fuck me. Make me come."

She undid her bra. The whumming was at an all time furious pace. She slid off her underwear. The hair at the "V" of her legs was much darker than the blond hair on her head.

"Take off your clothes. Take your time. I'll wait." And she rolled over onto her front. I was frozen between removing my clothes and trying to take in the sight of her. I didn't want to look away and I didn't know how any of this had happened. I got my clothes off and then everything blurred, like walking through a soft dream.

I moved over to the bed and put my hands on her, her skin and body growing rigid. But it was a rigidity she responded to, pressed up against, and she touched me back. The dry, silky touch of her fingertips seemed to be everywhere at once—the dampness of her mouth. And I did the same. I touched her every place she touched me, caught my hands up in her hair, ran my fingertips over her eyelashes, her nipples. It shocked me but I found myself running my lips and tongue all over her body, her hands guiding my head, her mouth whispering my name. I enjoyed the taste of her skin, the light dusting of sweat, and how her taste intensified closer to those areas she found most pleasurable.

Our secret place swelled. A sense of timelessness born from our act. I realized it wasn't about trying to kill the other person. It wasn't about killing or destruction at all. It was about making. A substantial construction of the secret place. Secrets are always made more meaningful when they're between two people. The twoness of the act was what I found to be the most overwhelming aspect. I couldn't stand most people for more than an hour and here I was completely naked with another person and letting her guide me wherever she wanted to.

"Fuck me," she whispered. "It's time."

Suddenly she was beneath me, her legs on either side, my penis against the warmth of her sex and the dream was pulled up into quivering reality. Mr. Lawrence was soft as gelatin, hanging there like a "worm." I'd never even thought of that happening until she'd mentioned it. I guess it had been in the back of my mind the entire time. Except it hadn't been soft. From the second I saw Maria spread out there on the bed, Mr. Lawrence had been properly engorged and happy as can be.

"Relax," she said and moved it up against herself.

I willed it into erection again and she guided me inside. It was a glimpse of heaven, the heat sinking through my entire body, but Mr. Lawrence wilted again, tumbling out of her. She sat up, one leg pulled in close to her. She was on the verge of tears.

"I'm just a big frump," she said.

I didn't really know what to say. Mr. Lawrence's behavior certainly didn't have anything to do with the way Maria looked.

"I'm sorry," I said. "I really want to. I just don't know what's wrong. Maybe I should go."

She grabbed my arm. "You're not leaving this house until I've come. You can fuck me in front of Boo and God himself but, so help me, it's happening."

Awkwardly, we sat on the bed. At that point, I really didn't know what to do aside from like attaching a penis splint or something. Then Maria had a notion.

"Of course," she said.

She lay back and put a hand between her legs, massaging the area. With her other hand, she guided my head down. I figured she wanted me to kiss her there. I'd heard of women coming that way, but she kept pushing my head down. She moved my head to the side until the left horn, the dull one Uncle Skad had tried to sand away pressed against the opening. She reached into a drawer by the bed and pulled out a bottle of lubricant, slathering it all over the horn. She slid herself down onto it, moaning lowly. I couldn't really see anything. I could hear the sounds of her sex opening and her rapid, ragged moans as she worked against the horn, using the other one as a lever, her legs wrapped around my chest and clasped at the ankles. She shuddered to a climax. The sound of her moaning stood Mr. Lawrence back up again. I pulled the horn out and moved up between her legs again.

"Please," she said. She put her hand around it to guide me in and I went off. She giggled. "You don't know how happy you've just made me."

We lay in the bed for awhile and I enjoyed the secret place as much as I did when we were coupling a few moments earlier. I guess we dozed off for a few minutes. I woke up to Maria shaking me.

"Wallace! Wake up!"

The world was out of focus and far away. Her words were jumbled and, slowly, they started making sense.

"Wake up! You gotta get dressed so I can take you home before Boo gets back. Hurry!"

I threw myself out of bed. She was already dressed. I hurriedly put my clothes on and chased her downstairs.

"Your shoes are over there," she said.

My shoes were over there! I was confused as all hell.

"Hurry!"

Since it only required slipping them over my feet. I got them on pretty quickly. She was already hurrying for the front door and I followed her. The keys jingled as she lifted them from a hook by the table. She wrapped the ring around a finger, said, "Come on," turned, and saw the same thing I did—Boo's silhouette as he twisted the doorknob to come in the house.

Chapter Twenty-three
Boo!

Maria quickly plunged the keys into her dress pocket just before Boo swung the door open. What he saw when he opened the door, the look on mine and Maria's faces, it must have been like, well, the look of a cheating wife and the man who fucked her. I wondered if he could smell her vagina on my horn. What I saw was, strangely enough, exactly what I expected to see. Boo Thiklet was a strapping man. Taller than me and quite a bit bulkier, which wasn't hard, so maybe that's an understatement. I knew he was a steelworker and I imagined he could carry one of those giant steel I-beams, the kind that weigh like 1500 pounds, all by himself. He wore his hair in an ostentatiously-styled mullet—short, spikey and heavily gelled on the top and sides, curly in the back. It hung down well past his collar. A skintight Steeltown Beer t-shirt adorned his barrel chest and was tucked staunchly into his navy blue jeans. So the strange thing about seeing Boo Thiklet was not the way he looked, but the way I saw him. The moments were slow and crystalline and for a few heart-jumping seconds, it felt like we looked right into each other's soul.

He raked his mustache with the back of his thumb, his other four fingers jutting out oddly in front of his face.

"Honey, you're home!" Maria said. It turned my stomach. Did she greet him this way every day or was she just as nervous as me?

"You two looked like you was goin somewheres." Boo fully entered the house, haphazardly tossing his lunchbox in the corner of the kitchen.

"Well, I was just gonna run Wallace home."

"You live round here?" He talked slowly and loudly. Like he put all of his bulk into his speech.

"Milltown," I said. I was surprised I could speak with any clarity whatsoever. When I first saw him at the door, all of the saliva had left my mouth.

"Milltown, huh? Why dontcha stay for dinner. What're we havin, babe?" He looped an arm around Maria and gave her an inappropriately long kiss. No one should really have to watch people kiss like that. Maria broke the kiss and Boo thrust a cold stare at her.

"Well, it's not made yet."

"You ain't even started it?"

"You're home a little earlier than usual."

"Didn't you say you was makin roast beef? Seems like it should be started."

"I was gonna start just as soon as I got back."

"Seems like yer a little behind today. Didn't the boy help ya clean up none? Why dontcha go ahead and get that started. You ain't gotta go nowheres now, do ya? Boy said he's stayin for dinner."

"I'm sorry, it's just we had that storm the other day and I picked up all those sticks..."

"You didn't get all of em. There's a biggun out there by the road. The enduh the driveway. Like you just left it there ta make me mad."

"I'm sorry. I always forget about that spot."

"At's partuh mah yard too. First thing people see."

"Did you want me to get it now?"

"It can wait. You make that hair appointment fer me?"

"Not yet."

He grabbed her again, roping her in for another kiss. Boo was randy tonight, I thought. This time he put his hand against her back and lifted up her shirt. She pried his hand off and broke the kiss again. He gently pushed the side of her head and thumbed his mustache again. "She's a fuckin ice woman, boy. So what's yer name?"

He pulled the chair closest to the door out and sat down.

"Wallace Black," I said.

"My name's Robert Thiklet. Friends call me Boo. While yer here I want you to call me Mr. Thiklet. Or Sir. All right?"

I nodded my head.

"Don't think I'm a dick or nothin, it's just that, well, we already been pretty nice to you. Ain't we?"

I nodded my head.

"In this house, in mah house, we talk. If yer a fuckin deaf mute, you nod yer head. We gotta fuckin mute nigger up at the plant, that's all he does all day." At his point, Sir Boo hideously panto-mimed the head bobbing motion of someone who had to be not only mute, but deep in the throes of multiple sclerosis, as well.

"Yes, sir," I said.

"That's good. Hey, babe, why dontcha bring me a beer?"

Maria, who upon Sir Boo's insistence had automatically begun dragging out the ingredients and equipment necessary for making dinner, ceased what she was doing and crossed over to the refrige-rator. She put the bottle in front of him and went back to dinner. He raised the bottle, clinking the metal cap to his teeth. Maria again stopped what she was doing, grabbed a towel and twisted the top off the bottle. Shooting a stare at Boo she went back to preparing dinner. Boo sprang up out of his chair and grabbed her around the arm.

"I don't think you need to act this way in front of company."

She lowered her head and said, "I'm sorry. You're right."

Sir Boo went back to his chair and sat down heavily.

"Sit down, boy."

I pulled out the chair Maria had sat on last night and stiffly sat, trying not to look at Maria so Sir Boo couldn't automatically bring my lust into focus. He downed half the bottle of beer and belched, a sickeningly wet sound.

"So what'd you guys do here all day?"

I waited for Maria to answer, but she was busy pounding the hell out of the roast. My head involuntarily flicked to the left.

"I *said,* 'What'd you guys do here all day?' Besides lose yer god-damn hearing?" This time, he specifically addressed me.

"Oh, uh, well... I slept in. Then I helped with the dishes and helped pick up the house."

"What about them sticks? You help with them sticks?"

"Yeah, uh, I helped pick up the sticks."

Sir Boo took another healthy slug of beer.

"Did ya take a shower?"

"Yes, sir."

"That's good, cause last night you kind of..."

"I know, sir, I smelled like death."

"Yeah, that's exactly what you smelled like. You know, when Maria stopped the car for you, when she saw you layin there in the church parkin lot, she thought you mighta *been* dead."

"No, sir. I just smelled like it."

He enjoyed a laugh at that, his cheeks flushing. He polished off the beer and thumbed his mustache.

"How bout another beer, babe?"

Maria retrieved it and opened it for him. Again, he swallowed roughly the first half in a single gulp.

"You wanna beer, boy?"

"No thank you."

"Prob'ly just think I'm a big drunk, huh?"

"Not at all."

"You know, when Maria first saw ya with that thing on yer head, she thought you was one of them ragheads."

"Oh, the shirt."

"Is that what that was? You know what else we call ragheads? Sand niggers. That's pretty funny, ain't it? Of course, you was just wearin that to hide the..." And he waved the beer bottle around the top of his head.

"Horns, sir."

"Yeah, *horns.* Why you wearin them crazy ass things?"

"I was born with them."

"Kinda like in *Ripley's Believe It or Not,* huh?"

"A little, I guess."

Fuckness

"You ever been in one uh them books?"

"No, sir."

"Might be able to pick up a little money that way."

"Maybe."

"You got a job?"

"No, sir."

"See, then ya ain't got no money. You a runaway?"

"I guess I am. But I'm going back later."

"Cause ya ain't got no money. Ya gonna do a stupid thing like run away, you need some money. Why, if we was some *mo*tel, you'da had to pay forty or fifty bucks just for last night."

"I know, sir. I'm very thankful."

"I bet you are. It was nasty last night. Real pretty today, though. You been outside yet?"

"A little bit."

"Oh, right. When you's helpin Maria pick up em sticks. Warm."

"It certainly is."

"How bout another beer?"

Maria grabbed another one out of the refrigerator, opened it, and sat it down in front of him. Behind Boo, the evening darkened. I wanted so desperately to be out there. I was hating every second of the conversation. Periodically, I noticed my foot was bumping up and down and I knew if I had to sit through much more of this I'd be going crazy.

"I'm glad you weren't one uh them sand niggers cause if you was, I'd uh made Maria throw ya back out. We don't need them people here, ya know what I'm sayin? They just here to make our money."

"Of course." I hated myself for saying it. It's amazing what I'd say for survival.

"So, you still in high school?"

"Middle school," I said, without even thinking.

"Middle school? Ain't you sixteen?"

"Yes, sir. I've been held back." This time my head flicked to my right and I could feel my lips draw back from my teeth.

"Mustuh been held back a *coupla* times. You a dummy?"

"I guess so. I'm not very good at school."

"I went to school with a halfwit nameuh Roger Willem. He was a real candyass, too. Now, he never got outta the seventh grade, so far as I know. You know him?"

"No, sir."

"I thought maybe he's your dad or somethin but, that's right, yer name's Black, ain't it?"

"Yes, sir."

"That kinda makes you a nigger, don't it?"

"I guess so."

"You like niggers?"

"I've never known any, sir."

"That's good. I ain't never known me none, neither. Course, if I did, I guess he'd be a dead nigger."

He chugged down another beer and fished around in his jeans pockets, coming up with a flattened pack of Marlboro Lights. He pulled one out and lit up, casting a glance at Maria.

"She don't like for me to smoke in the house. Says it smells. But we know whose house it is, don't we, babe?"

"Sure do," she said without much conviction.

She put the roast beef in the oven and stormed out of the kitchen. Sir Boo turned around to me, thumbed his mustache and said, "We don't need no bitches in here anyway. She's just a dried up old cunt. I need summa that fresh pussy."

His voice became gruffer and noticeably slurred. His cigarette ash was incredibly long. He knocked it off in one of the empty beer bottles in front of him, half of it scattering around the bottle.

"If you ain't got much brains, what do ya plan on doin for the rest of yer life."

"I don't know."

"Dontcha think ya better get somethin figgered out?"

"I guess."

He gulped down the rest of his beer and barked, "Beer!"

Maria stormed back into the kitchen, opened the bottle and sat it roughly down in front of him, rushing back out. Sir Boo balled his right hand up into a fist and slammed it into the palm of his left.

"Now me," he said. "I ain't exactly a whiz or nothin. But I'm smart when it comes to money. I started workin down at the Korl mill when I turned eighteen. You ever thought about doin steel work?"

"Not really."

"Now, my job was pretty tough at first, loadin them sheets of metal onto the lifts but now, shit, I ain't gotta do shit. Them supervisors up air, they saw that I had a real knack for takin control. At's all they want, someone at can do their job so they can take some time off. At's why I work a lot, cause it ain't really work at all. Someone wants to pay me for doin more sittin around, who'm I to say no. That extra time done bought me this here house and here I am only thirty-two. My folks's still rentin. Yer folks rent?"

"I think so."

"Them some good ol boys they got up at Korl. Lot've em come right from the hollers of Kentucky. Them boys know what a dollar means. Most of em raised up dirt poor. Yer folks from Kentucky?"

"West Virginia."

Boo Thiklet lit up another cigarette. He put a considerable amount of pause in between his questions. Now he paused a little bit longer, taking slow drags off the cigarette, his head kind of leaned back, studying me through partially slit eyes. I looked nervously at the table, conscious of his eyes burning into me.

He finished his beer, ashed his cigarette on the floor, thumbed his mustache and said, "Them horns make me mad."

"I'm sorry."

"Bring me a beer, bitch!"

"Get it yourself!" she called back. That kind of surprised me. Up to that point, however, I found it impossible how she could see Sir Boo with anything but contempt.

He teeteringly got up and stumbled the two steps to the refrigerator door. He swung it open much harder than necessary, all the condiment bottles tinkling in the door. He belched and reached in for another beer.

The smell of roast beef filled the kitchen. Night had come outside the kitchen door window, turning it into six black squares. He twisted the cap off and tossed it into the kitchen sink. He stumbled back over and plopped down in his chair, almost turning it over.

"I don't know why I keep her around. It's the pussy I guess. She had a real sweet pussy. She was a virgin when I met her." He leered at me. "That didn't last long, though." He poked a finger on the inside of his cheek and hooked it out so it made a popping noise. "She's all used up now, though. Barren as a rock. I'm gonna have to find me someone else gonna make em sheets all bloody."

I couldn't help it anymore. I'd been sitting there all rigid, managing to keep my feet tapping and not much else. I let out a hoot before restraining myself, before launching into the whole routine.

"You act like a boy who ain't never had any pussy. You ever had any pussy?"

That did it. I snapped. I beat my fingers on the edge of the table, letting out a whole slew of "Do, do, do"s, snapping my head back and forth.

"What is this shit?" Boo said. It sounded like he was filled with anger but I couldn't be sure without looking at him. Whenever I had an outburst, I had a tendency to either close my eyes or stare straight ahead. I managed to bring it under control. Sir Boo was the only thing standing between me and the outside.

Sitting there and listening to him talk made me think maybe I'd been had. Had Maria lead me into her bedroom simply because she was mad or had Boo really not touched her in the last two years?

"You know what I think?" Sir Boo thumbed his mustache. I ticked and thrashed. "I think you know exactly what Maria's pussy's like. Joo fuck Maria?"

I never really thought he'd ask that. My lips drew back, tenuous against my gumline. I tried to say no but my tongue wouldn't get out of the way and I could only make a kind of gurgling sound.

"Hey, you stupid bitch!" Sir Boo called. "Come in here and get the roast outta the oven!"

Maria came back in the kitchen and turned off the oven. "This is nowhere *near* finished," she hissed.

"Hey, you fuckin whore, you fuck ol freak boy over there? You let him slip his horns in you?"

I almost laughed. I was sure Sir Boo thought he was being ridiculously absurd when he said that but it was the exact truth.

"You're an ass," Maria said. She pulled the roast out of the oven and threw it into the sink, cracking the thick glass dish. "I'm leaving."

"Like hell you are." Boo grabbed one of the multitude of beer bottles in front of him and threw it at Maria. It shattered on the cabinets behind her, the acrid smell of beer filling the kitchen.

"Fuck you," she said, practically running out of the kitchen. This time Boo followed her.

That's it, I thought. Now's the chance. I could have easily run for the door, out into the night. I could have left the Thiklet house behind me as only a grim memento of why I should probably not get married. I could be home by tomorrow. I could. I could. I could. But I didn't.

It wouldn't let me. Whatever had guided me here. That rope. That force. It wouldn't let me leave. Not before getting the lighter that Drifter Ken had given me. The lighter had become like a talisman. It was presented to me at the beginning of my journey, my stumbling, whatever the great white fuckness it was, and it now seemed vital that it remain with me all the way through to the bitter end. I stood up to go get the lighter.

Hearing their yelling, I wondered where they were. A thumping or shattering immediately followed a shout. I wondered how many times this happened. They seemed to strive for a perfect house, keeping everything in order. I imagined Sir Boo coming home every night, slowly undoing what Maria did through the day. I pictured him walking down the halls, crooking straight pictures, tilting lampshades, wiping his feet on the floor, his ass on the shower curtain.

I stood on the landing, knowing all I had to do was dart into the guest bedroom, pocket the lighter and dart out of the house. Slowly, I took the few steps to the bedroom, trying to glean some sense out of what they were saying. They were in their bedroom, the door shut, probably locked. I went into the guest bedroom, crossing over to the dresser where the lighter lay on its side. I reached down, took it into my hand and stood there, numbly frozen, staring out the window at the illuminated side of the church. Somewhere unseen, a tree wavered in the soft breeze, producing a dancing shadow on the side of the church. An exceptionally loud crashing, like the ceiling falling down or some fuckness like that, raised me from my stupor.

The fuckness. Yeah, the fuckness was going to pour.

My body's rigidity turned into near palsy, my nerves jumping around inside me, that jittery motion carrying me to the Thiklets' bedroom door. In a way, I thought, as inevitable as their conflict may have been, I contributed to this. I got to the door.

"Please, please, please," I heard Maria say.

"Joo fuckem!" Boo savagely grunted.

"Just let me leave. I swear I'll never come back. I don't want *anything*."

I opened the bedroom door and almost vomited. It was like all that shaking, all that jittering, zoomed straight into the pit of my stomach. The whumming started up good and strong.

A burning smell singed my nostrils. I quickly scanned the room for the source of it and took in the devastation. All the pictures were gone from the wall. They lay in a shattered heap in the far right corner. One half of the curtains and blinds had been ripped down so they hung there with a psychotic cant. The bed was disheveled and, in the center of it, lay a rifle, the barrel pointed sinisterly at me. The room seemed brighter and harsher than it had earlier and in this was the source of the smell. A lamp lay on its side in the corner to my left, the bulb melting into the plastic lining of the shade that directed all of its light upwards. Then I saw the sickening thing.

Their room also had a dresser, pushed up against the wall to my left. Boo had Maria bent over the far side of the dresser, his right hand tangled in the hair on the back of her head, his left hand clasped around her left arm, cinching it up tight to the middle of her shoulder blades. Her skirt was gone, her underwear tangled and stained. She saw me first but her eyes seemed unable to really focus. Bloody strands of hair clung to her cheek. Her nose was fat and swollen, blood running out, combining with the blood and spit from her mouth and waterfalling lugubriously down the front of the dresser. Sir Boo lifted up the back of her head and slammed it back down into the dresser's unforgiving wood with each word as he said, "Did. You. Fuck. Him."

Then I said, "Yes," mainly to get his attention. The word sounded muffled among the whumming in my head.

Sir Boo snapped his head back at me. Maria had managed to claw deep red streaks into his face. His eyes were huge and all pupil. He was so mad they jumped around. I closed my hand around the lighter, drew it back and threw it at Sir Boo. Amazingly, it smacked him right in the middle of the forehead. However weakly, it made him let go of Maria. He looked at me and thumbed his mustache. Maria slid off the dresser and hit the floor with a thump. Boo moved toward the bed. I took off running, hearing his footsteps behind me.

I got to the top of the stairs and heard the gun go off. The bullet hit me in the back, to the right of my spine, the impact catapulting me down the stairs. Immediately, with the slightest exertion, both of my lungs started burning. There wasn't a lot of pain, but the pressure made it hard to breathe. I scrambled through the living room, managing to stand by the time I got to the kitchen. My breathing raggedly mixed with the whirring iron whumming and I slammed into the front door, fitfully trying to grab onto the handle. My body shook violently. I felt like I had to run to make that shaking go away. If I were to just stand, I'd have the overwhelming desire to rip my skin off.

I got the door open and ran out into the night.

The church was the only thing really lit up so I ran for that, some hopeless feeling telling me the doors would be locked. Where was he? Was he behind me? I couldn't hear anything over the breathing and the whumming. The church seemed a mile away. My body had shook itself into exhaustion. I felt like a gelatinous slab but, nevertheless, my legs carried me. Everything spun around me. One of my shoes flew off. I was dimly aware of the blood trickling down the crack of my ass.

I reached the door, the iron handle feeling like a rare treasure in my hand. I put all my weight against the door and pushed the handle. It collapsed inward. I collapsed with it into the dimly lit interior.

At the far end, the baptismal pool cast a rippling white reflection against the wall. I lay in the deep red carpet of the aisle. I couldn't stand up. For a panicked minute I thought it was blood all around me, extending up to the pulpit area. I crawled up the middle of the aisle, those big heavy pews on either side of me. Then I had a thought.

I'm dying.

The fuckness had caught up with me, striking a final deadly blow. I rolled over, collapsing onto my back and staring up at the rafters of the church. Fuck it, I thought. Fuck it. Fuck it. Fuck it.

Everything melted away. The whumming, the ragged breathing, all of it melted away. If I was still breathing, and I couldn't tell if I was, it had to be through my skin. My chest wasn't moving.

Everything was quiet. I stared up at the rafters. The soft light. A flash of blue. Blue. White. A jagged razor of death. Boo Thiklet positioned over me. He lowered the barrel of the rifle down to my forehead. Still there was silence. It felt like everything happened through a thick plate of glass. I looked at his hand as he pulled the trigger, awaiting the explosion, the inevitable end.

Nothing.

Again he depressed his finger.

Nothing.

Again and again and again. Nothing. Nothing. Nothing. For a second, I thought it had happened and I just didn't hear it. I thought maybe I was watching everything from someplace above.

My body was numb. He grabbed me up, wrapped his arms around me and tossed me onto the edge of a pew. I landed on the floor and flung myself back into the aisle. Finish me off, I thought. Now Boo held the gun by the barrel and swung the stock at my head. It connected with a hollow- sounding impact. Every sound I heard came from inside my head. I lay on my side, my back resting against the row of pews. He grabbed my feet and pulled me up to the pulpit. I noticed my other shoe had come off in the meantime. I didn't see how anyone could brutalize someone whose shoes had fallen off.

A long wooden altar sat squatly in front of the pulpit. The scripture, "For he so loved the world..." was stenciled in blood red letters on the front of the altar. What was the rest of the scripture, I wondered? Why didn't they put it on there too? Boo turned me around, grabbed both of my horns and thrust my face into the floor. He rolled me over onto my back. Figuring out what he meant to do released some feeling into my body. Like I was cast suddenly and coldly back into life and reality. A wave of sickness burned in my stomach, turning my bowels and throat to acid.

He placed one of his brown construction boots on my left horn. Holding the rifle by the barrel and aiming it downward like a jackhammer, he brought the stock down at the base of my right horn. I didn't know how they were connected so I had no real idea of how he was going to go about the excision. Each impact of the rifle butt sent a sickening bone impact through my body. I figured Maria had confessed our indiscretions to Boo. I wandered if she had confessed the small details of the fling also. He came down on it with increasing ferocity. I heard the horn first separate from my head with a sick wet peeling sound. My skin ripped as Boo bent down and yanked the horn to fully remove it. My head felt wet. More and more of my senses were coming back. It was like the more he tortured me, the more alive I became. He had the horn in his right hand, a giant hideous thing. The anger was still there, hopping around behind his eyes but it was a focused anger like he had some sort of renewed purpose, fulfilling a job he desperately wanted done. He slid the horn under the base of the still attached left horn, creating a fulcrum. This caused my head to turn to the right and I stared at his boot and the tip of the gun.

A violent force yanked my head to the left. I felt the horn give. He had brought his boot down on the tip of it. The whole thing made me think about trying to remove a tooth. Sir Boo brought his foot down again and this one went with a pop. I rolled to my right and vomited. The horn was still attached to my head by a thin string of skin, hanging with a sickening weight. In a smooth, continuous motion, I reached back, grabbed the tip of the horn, yanked it free from the skin, and swung it into Boo's knee. I didn't feel any pain with this one. Just the tearing tug. I got up on all fours, feeling the blood running down both of my cheeks. Boo raised a foot to stomp on me and I launched myself at his supporting knee. It went from being very rigid to oddly jointed. I spun off to the side. He tried to follow but his knee no longer pivoted that way. He went down, smacking his head on the pew and lying kind of dormant in the middle of the aisle. The gun was right beside me. I grabbed it by the barrel, the metal cold in my hot hand. I wrapped the other hand around it and used it like a cane to stand up.

Something surged over me, totally overwhelming and empowering. I stood over Boo, wielding the gun like an ax. I brought the stock down onto Sir Boo's head, the connection rattling through the gun and twinging my hands. A hungry rage swirled through me. I brought the gun down for Racecar, for the mother, for Mary Lou Dover and Bucky Swarth and Pearlbottom. I did it again and again, watching as Sir Boo's skin reddened, thinned, and then split. His eyes rolled around in his head. Exhausted and sickened, I couldn't do it anymore.

I turned the gun around and aimed the barrel at his head. I looked around the church. Most of the blood, mine and Boo's, had sunk into the carpet and it didn't really look like anything out of place had happened here. The baptismal pool continued making its slow magical ripples on the wall. I suddenly thought of Uncle Skad, standing in a bed filled with his parents' blood, unaware of what he'd just done. I thought of myself back at Toady's, surveying the carnage I'd created. This time, I'd been conscious all the while and felt as alive as I ever had at that moment, the barrel of the gun resting against the rubbery weight of Boo's face. I had hit him for all those other people and now I saw myself. I saw myself after I did this. Who would I be? If I pulled the trigger, would I even get the chance to try and define myself? Or would I be put into a system where society defined me?

Fuckness

I wasn't the boy with horns anymore. And I was tired as hell of being Wallace Black.

I turned the gun toward the carpet beside his head and pulled the trigger. It went off with a thunderous explosion, tearing up the red carpet to expose the raw wood underneath. I dropped the gun on Sir Boo's bloody face.

Every bit of aliveness I felt drained out of me. Raced out of me. My body felt like a used condom. I had to get out of the church. I was suddenly overcome by the smells around me—the musty wooden odor of the church, the sour age of the hymnals, the smell of steel, cheap cologne, and beer clinging to Boo, and everywhere, everywhere hung the iron stench of blood. And beneath that. Yes, somewhere just below the scent of coagulating blood, was the scent of death. It wasn't Boo's death that I smelled. His chest heaved as he lay there on the floor, merely passed out.

I turned toward the half-open door, the purplish blue light glowing outside. I dragged my feet along the carpet, feeling its damp squishiness, the door approaching me more than the other way around. My hands touched the door and I pushed it open and I was outside. Outside in a dense fog, the clear night sky above me.

I felt like I was floating away from everything around me, that power still pulling me along. I was sure I was dying. If not from blood loss, then from shock. The fuckness had got me, sneaked up on me and crushed me out. If I died, the fuckness would be over. Slowly, I made my way to the graveyards behind the church. The obelisks and headstones were stubby shadows in the fog. The night air felt warm on my skin, but I shivered uncontrollably.

The whumming screeched like a stopping train in my head. A red vision splashed all over my mind's eye. The fog out there was a prison. A glaucoma blanket over my physical eyes. I could feel myself falling. No, it was more like that grinding red feeling drove me to the ground, flattening me and rolling over me, a dark and violent fever dream. All of the faces, the hateful fuckness faces of the past came blaring through the red fog, angry and accusatory. All mingling in a huge screech. I collapsed onto the fiery ground, those people enveloping me, wheedling beneath my skin and along my nerves. They yelled incoherence in unison, a tattoo that beat out my last remaining breaths. I had the feeling death was right there next to me and these people were going into some new hell with me. Like I was going to have to spend all of eternity hating them. They were inside of me, ripping at my viscera, tearing my brain to pieces, and vomiting on my soul.

I tried to fight them. There had to be some way to get them out of me. I tried to scream, tried to force them out through my mouth. There was nothing left inside. Inside, there was no me, only them. I didn't have the strength in my legs or lungs to run or scream.

I was on the ground but I still felt myself falling. It felt like I was falling from some place that was very very high, falling through the sky and the clouds and the dense powdery fog. There was nothing to catch myself on and I couldn't think of any reason for wanting to catch myself because the more I fell, the greater distance I went, the higher I got, so that when I landed I was right there with the stars, close enough to reach out and palm them with my hands. Then the stars came down on me like a net, coolly roping my body, and the people were gone.

I lay there on the cemetery ground waiting for death. Was I already dead? If I breathed, I was completely unaware of it. Not even like the skin breathing thing I did back in the church. I didn't breathe, I didn't need to breathe. I lay there and felt the dew on my back, watched the fog swirl around me, staring up at the few stars littering the sky, listening to the endless quiet surrounding me. The quiet, boundless silence. Maybe the soft rustle of a tree, maybe the low hum of a car somewhere in the distance but, there beneath it all was the quiet—no blood thumping behind my ears. No whumming in my brain. No screaming.

That's when I heard the scuffling shapes come out of the fog. They were spirits, I had no doubt, risen from the graves around me, ectoplasmic green against the gray of the fog. And they shambled toward me, a whole army of them, coming right up out of the ground, through the grave markers, all of them formless. They got to me and I felt their hands on me, the energy radiating from them

Fuckness

and into me, strengthening me. They moved into me, through me, rebuilding me from the inside. The dead come to replace what the living stole. The nothing I felt was replaced with something other. Something completely indescribable because it was so all encompassing. They were healing me. They took away the fuckness. They gave me new skin, swelled my soul to the point of bursting and, as quietly as they had come, they disappeared.

I felt weightless and alive and real. Everything that had happened to me, every person who had conspired to hold me down, now surged through me and lifted me up. I took off running into the dawn, barefoot and stark raving mad with joy.

Conclusion:
Happiness In Exile

So that's my story. Only it's not really my story at all. It was only a period of my life. The period of heavy fuckness. Sometime later that morning I was whisked away to the hospital where I was put into the care of a bunch of nurses. They were like a flock of angels, moving around the white hospital rooms in their starched white uniforms. It occurred to me the hospital society might've been the lifestyle I'd been striving for all along. No one ever got mad. I could have flung my excrement at those nurses and they would have just smiled, casually wiped it off, and suggested I use a bed-pan. I never had to leave the bed. I just lay there and they brought me things. I had to stay there longer than I normally would have because the doctors were convinced, from what I told them while ranting in my sleep, that I had suffered some sort of trauma, even though they couldn't find any type of physical evidence to substantiate that claim.

But they were all just tending to a moribund body that had seen better days. I guess it was my last hurrah.

Officially, I died of natural causes. I was a John Doe.

Wallace Black had died three days earlier in an arson.

Mainly what I thought as I watched myself all laid up in the hospital was that question Uncle Skad had posed: Are we who we really are, with all the ugly layers peeled away, or are we who we are trying to become? The more I thought about it, the more the question terrifed me. It seemed like if you took people and stripped away all their layers, you ended up with Boo Thiklet. If you meas-

Fuckness

ured most people by what they were trying to become, it seemed like you'd just end up with a lot of rich, self-absorbed fucks. I don't really have any idea of what I'm trying to become or if it's possible to become anything in death, but I know there's always a small part of me that is going to remain the boy with horns.

As for God and divine punishment, I'm still really not sure. I know I was punished, though I question the divinity of it. There were feelings I had—the force, the rope, the inner pulling. If that was God, then I'd have to say he has a really sick and sort of mean sense of humor. And he has, quite clearly, exiled me from the kingdom of heaven.

The fuckness seemed to lessen when I left my body. It wasn't that the world seemed any less absurd. If anything, with a little bit of maturity and a little bit of death, things only seemed more absurd. I still don't understand why people do the things they do. I don't think I want to understand. Sometimes the reasons are far more ridiculous than the acts themselves. A man wears a tie because he has to. Why not wear two ties, or three or four, an insanely wide array of ties, just because he wants to?

So, somehow, I've blended in with this absurdity by not blending in at all. I stay on the outside, invisible. Once I stopped being Wallace Black, no one noticed me at all. There was the occasional person, usually a child, who could look at me and I could tell they understood everything. In life, there were a few adults, the people like Uncle Skad and maybe even Maria, but those were rare. With this invisibility I've been able to think about my philosophy of fuckness, structuring it into a politics of poverty.

I've tried to go back and find the people who helped me along the way, but they've all disappeared. Drifter Ken has drifted on. Johnny Metal said he came to me, so I didn't even know where to begin looking for him. Uncle Skad must have exploded into some blue electrical oblivion. The Thiklets' house had a sign that said "SOLD" out in the front yard. It may seem self-centered, but it felt like all of them only existed for a short period of time, there to help me through the heavy fuckness.

I don't know what happened to the horns. I have no signs suggesting they were ever there. Just like the doctors and nurses couldn't find any bullet holes or internal damage from the shooting before pronouncing me dead. Nobody at the hospital ever said anything about them. Maybe the church found them lying somewhere and took them. I hope they exorcised them first. I was kind of glad I couldn't find them. I never really want to see them again.

Just a few days ago I went back to Walnut. I finally had to know if the parents were really and truly dead. I think it took me a few years to do that because I had to punish myself. It was like, if I knew they were okay, then I couldn't feel the proper amount of guilt. And if I knew they were dead, then I could just stop thinking about them. I walked by their house, keeping to the opposite side of the street. It was a warm summer day and I stood there staring at the house. I knew I could never go back in there. That was one of the worst things, feeling like there was never really a place to go.

They had really fixed it up a lot. A fresh coat of white paint gleamed in the sunlight. Vibrantly colored flowers lined the ground. It was like an oasis there on Walnut. The mother and father were out in the front yard. The father had a shiny new wheelchair. The mother wandered around in an honest-to-God practical outfit, watering the lawn. A boy of about four or five stomped around the front yard, hurling a red Frisbee at Racecar. They must have adopted, I thought. Probably took on a foster kid for the extra income. Maybe they were just babysitting. The boy spotted me, creepily standing there, out of place in a world that wasn't really mine anymore.

"What's that man doing?" he said.

The mother and Racecar both looked across the street.

And that image dropped away. Three black kids stood in front of a low-income apartment building.

"There's nobody there," the oldest said.

"Yes huh. He's right there." The child pointed again.

"You're full of shit."

I waved at the little boy, did a little dance for him, and skipped off down the street.

CPSIA information can be obtained at www.ICGtesting.com
Printed in the USA
BVOW02s1503101013

333302BV00012B/32/P